To Brian

G000130594

Follow the Money

With Best Wishes !

Clifton Hughes

Follow the Money

CLIFTON HUGHES

authorHOUSE®

AuthorHouse™ UK Ltd.
1663 Liberty Drive
Bloomington, IN 47403   USA
www.authorhouse.co.uk
Phone: 0800.197.4150

© 2014 Clifton Hughes. All rights reserved.

No part of this book may be reproduced, stored in a retrieval system, or
transmitted by any means without the written permission of the author.

Published by AuthorHouse   02/07/2014

ISBN: 978-1-4918-9146-9 (sc)
ISBN: 978-1-4918-8709-7 (hc)
ISBN: 978-1-4918-9147-6 (e)

Any people depicted in stock imagery provided by Thinkstock are models,
and such images are being used for illustrative purposes only.
Certain stock imagery © Thinkstock.

This book is printed on acid-free paper.

Because of the dynamic nature of the Internet, any web addresses or links contained in
this book may have changed since publication and may no longer be valid. The views
expressed in this work are solely those of the author and do not necessarily reflect the views
of the publisher, and the publisher hereby disclaims any responsibility for them.

To: My father Trevor, for all his help and encouragement throughout the entire process of writing this book. I'd like to thank Isa for reading the initial manuscript and providing important positive feedback.

I would also like to extend my sincere thanks to my many friends who have been an important source of inspiration and motivation in helping to bring this book to fruition.

PROLOGUE

"Idiot! Imbecile! Lunatic!" Oscar just couldn't contain himself. It had all started out as a bet. A really stupid bet, the sort where no one ever pledges any money. The Fatman had said it would work! He'd said no one would even suspect. Who would think of a skip lorry?

"A skip lorry!" he shouted aloud. "I told him it wouldn't work, but he wouldn't listen, he never listens to me!"

Incensed, he punched the kitchen door of his apartment. The pine panelling cracked loudly splitting under the heavy blow, as his fist perforated the timber amidst a shower of splinters.

Oscar cursed loudly. Quite apart from the fact that the door was now ruined, he had hurt his hand. He sensed the pain only peripherally. His mind was totally elsewhere as he plunged his bleeding knuckles into the kitchen sink. The cold water would help the bruising but not his temper.

"Then he has the cheek to blame me!" he yelled. "As if it was my bloody fault!"

Oscar grabbed a bottle of Bushmills single malt and a glass from the shelf. Opening the fridge door, he quickly dropped a single ice cube clinking into the glass. Uncorking the bottle he sloshed out a large measure.

He sat his burly frame down heavily at the table, cursing quietly. Briefly, he held his head in his hands. He wasn't thinking straight at all. He wanted to kill the Fatman. He was still beside himself with rage as he nursed the whisky glass in his hands rolling it gently to and fro between his fingers. It was then that he became aware of something. Without even realizing it, somehow he had lit a cigarette and taken a deep draw of smoke into his lungs.

"Dam-bloody-nation!" he cursed, instantly stubbing it out. He'd quit three months ago. "If that doesn't just top it all off!"

He took a great gulp of the whisky. He still couldn't quite take it all in. How could the Fatman be so unbelievably stupid as to think that it would have worked?

Taking another great slug of the whisky, he sat there mulling it over. They'd been aware that the police were watching them, but why the skip lorry? What a stupendously stupid idea! Not only that, but now Leslie was gone too. That had been the Fatman's fault also. It occurred to him that now they might never know what had happened. The thought grew leaden within him as his rage descended into a dark depressive gloom.

"Aye." he said in a resigned tone, sighing to himself.

"Now we may never find out where it went."

1.

Earlier that day . . . .

Standing at some six feet two inches, the Fatman was huge. His burly shoulders would not have disgraced an international front row forward. For all that though, it was his sheer mass that was most impressive. He must have weighed in at well over three hundred pounds.

Leslie, the little man he was clutching by the throat wore an expression of sheer terror.

"Where is it Leslie?" The Fatman's query was guttural, threatening.

"Where's what?" The little man looked puzzled.

"You know bloody well what!" growled the Fatman. "Don't mess with me. Do you think I'm some sort of stupid fool you can just fob off?"

"No."

"Then tell me where it is!"

"Look, I don't know what you're talking about, I really don't."

The Fatman thrust his particularly ugly face close in front of Leslie's. His bulbous nose was rife with spidery, purple blood vessels, doubtless the result of dissipation. His eyes seemed to bulge out of his skull indignantly. The breath of the man was simply vile and would rival any emanation from an open stagnant sewer.

"You're sure about that are you?"

"Yes."

"Quite sure?"

"Yes I am."

The Fatman released his grip momentarily and instead firmly propelled his victim in the direction of the kitchen table.

"Let's be civilized about this then," he said quietly. "Let's just have a wee seat at the table and we'll all talk about it like friends." He smiled.

Leslie sat down warily. The Fatman's sinister undertone betrayed an underlying maliciousness.

"Now, I'm going to ask you again Leslie, where is it? Just tell me and all of this will soon be over." The Fatman's voice was suddenly all soothing and comforting.

Leslie looked up at him hopefully. The Fatman nodded a tacit reassurance.

"It will soon be over and then you can just go home. All I want to know is what you did with it?"

"What I did with what?" Leslie still looked confused.

The Fatman's expression was starting to darken. His voice was again deep and menacing as he slowly enunciated.

"What . . . . You . . . . Did . . . . with . . . . it!"

"I don't know . . . ."

That's all Leslie managed. The Fatman simply lost it. With astonishing speed he grabbed Leslie by his hair and violently rammed his face into the table in front of him.

"Where the hell is it you stupid little bastard?"

Again he slammed Leslie's head onto the table. "Where is it?"

The third impact was perhaps the most brutal. There was a horrible sickening thud. Bone was breaking somewhere. Blood came streaking out of Leslie's mouth. The nose was at a crooked angle. It was also profusely weeping blood. The little man grabbed it shrieking with pain.

"You've broken my nose! You've broken my nose!" he howled.

The Fatman threw him a large wad of kitchen roll.

"Here, use that. Stop bleeding all over the bloody place will you."

Oscar sniggered. He'd been standing with his arms folded in front of him like some ominous bruiser of a bouncer on a watching brief. The remark had amused him.

Leslie was coughing and spluttering. He spat a tooth out onto the tabletop. It sat there, point up, a small ivory iceberg amidst a salivary sea of crimson.

"Are you going to tell me now?"

"I don't know what the hell you want," Leslie sobbed.

The Fatman threw his arms in the air in exasperation. He looked in the direction of Oscar.

"Over to you mate. Your turn."

Oscar grabbed Leslie from behind. He curled his arm anaconda like around his neck and started to crush the breath from him.

"Where is it Leslie," he roared. "Mr. Cartwright has been far too gentle with you. I really couldn't be arsed with all this, so just tell me where it is or I'll choke you."

The Fatman watched as Oscar applied progressively more and more pressure. Before long, Leslie's face went first white and then a strange bluish colour. His eyeballs looked ready to pop out and his tongue was lolling.

"For frig's sake stop or you'll choke him to death!" he yelled.

Oscar instantly released his grip. The little man was gasping for breath. He was choking and coughing desperately attempting to recover.

The Fatman took Leslies head in his meaty hands and gently rolled it to and fro in a motion calculated to restore some sort of rudimentary circulation.

"Do you have anything you want to tell me old son?"

Beyond a spluttering gasp, there was no intelligible reply.

The Fatman waddled ponderously away towards the kitchen window. Looking outside he thoughtfully rubbed his face. In stark contrast to his bitter mood, the sun was cheerily shining. He cast a long glance in the direction of the bottom of the garden.

"O.K." he said at last, wearily. "This obviously isn't working so we'll have to go to plan B. Bring yer man here," he instructed Oscar.

As the Fatman opened the kitchen door, Oscar grabbed Leslie and got him unsteadily to his feet. The two thugs frog marched him down the garden path. Leslie was vaguely aware of the sunshine. He felt its welcoming warmth against his face. The lawn had been freshly mown and bees were buzzing about in the flowerbed.

He was now in front of some sort of outhouse. The ancient building might once have been an air raid shelter and had grass growing all over it.

"Last chance now Leslie. Tell me where it is?"

"I don't know what you're raving about."

The Fatman was once again incensed with rage. He slapped Leslie hard in the face. The little man clutched his face nursing his previous injuries and howling out.

"You bastard! What the hell do you want you fat bastard?"

"Alright, that's it. I've had enough of this. Throw him inside." He motioned to Oscar as he opened the outhouse door.

Leslie was thrown into the small room and heard the door being bolted from outside. Although it was pretty much pitch black, he could just about make out some rough, wooden bench seats built into the wall of the small room. Gratefully he sat down on one.

He soon became aware of an ominous hum emanating from somewhere inside the room. The only light came from a small circular hole high up in the door. Suddenly a stout cane came through the hole and began to savagely prod a dark mass hanging from the ceiling. With abject horror, Leslie realized it was a wasps' nest. The paper sides of the nest perforated as the hum increased in pitch and volume. Soon he was engulfed in a cloud of enraged wasps.

"Help! Let me out. Help!" he screamed.

"Where is it Leslie?" came the flat reply from outside.

"I don't know! Help!" he yelled, panic-stricken. "There's wasps everywhere! Let me out!"

The wasps were stinging him now. They stung his arms, his legs, his face and even his eyes. There were hundreds and hundreds of them. Stinging and stinging! The more he flailed and yelled the worse it got! The stinging had become a seemingly endless torment. The pain was unbearable.

"Very last chance Leslie. What did you do with it?" the Fatman yelled from outside.

But there was no reply. Sobbing, Leslie had fallen to his knees. Soon he was writhing about helplessly on the ground. The wasps were in his mouth now. As they stung him, he started to go into anaphylactic shock. His airway was closing up. He couldn't breath. His struggling heart was beating irregularly. It would soon be all over.

"Leslie! Leslie! Can you hear me?" The Fatman shouted.

But all he could hear now was a terrible wheezing amidst the swarming buzz of the wasps. Soon even the wheezing had stopped. They knew then that Leslie was dead.

The Fatman walked slowly over to a garden table and lifted a spray can.

"Wasp killer!" he grinned towards Oscar. He held the can up to the hole in the door and depressed the plunger. After about a minute, he threw the can away into the bushes.

"Let's go and get a cup of tea whilst this bloody lot dies off."

He looked over at Oscar and started to chuckle. The big man was white.

"For frig's sake, you should see yourself!"

"That was awful boss, just terrible. Even for you that was bad!"

The Fatman cackled softly to himself.

"Do you see Boss if you ever get really upset with me, will you give me a head start to get away first?"

"Don't worry Oscar, if I ever get angry with you, I'd never do anything like that to you. It would be far worse than that!"

Oscar looked at him in horror. The Fatman's shoulders rocked with mirth as he started to laugh.

"I'm only joking, you big rascal you!"

They both started back towards the house. As they reached the kitchen door the Fatman abruptly paused and turned to face Oscar.

"I don't get it. Something just doesn't add up here. Why wouldn't he tell us? Why would he want to die like that?"

"Beats me boss." Oscar shrugged.

"You know what?" continued the Fatman, "I'm not sure the bum knew anything about it. What do you think?"

2.

Two days earlier . . . .

The sky above had grown darker. Just to the north of Belfast, huge ominous grey clouds had gathered over the Cavehill mountain. You can't ever trust the weather in this country, thought William as he pedalled along the cycle track. You start out in bright sunshine thinking all is well, and then, before you know it, it clouds over. He knew he was probably due for a drenching before he got home.

It wasn't just the weather dampening his spirits today though; they were already at a particularly low ebb. He reflected that everything in his life was gradually changing and none of it for the better.

"Everyday, in everyway, things are getting worse and worse!" He shouted out loud, purposely misquoting Emile Coue as he rode along. It seemed appropriate and he chuckled at the irony. He'd bought this German made, electrically assisted bicycle some six months ago. That had been back in early spring. The idea had been to lose some weight, but that hadn't happened. At least, though, he felt fitter for the exercise.

Somehow, the action of pedalling along the cycle track was strangely therapeutic. It helped him to forget things. A year ago all had been well with the world, or at least as well as a suburban married man could reasonably hope for. Back then he had a good job selling medical supplies, a nice Company car to drive and a wife that loved him. Now, it seemed that some cruel and wicked force had been employed to gradually strip all these things away from him.

He'd had a sales job with English Company Reddington Medical. Based in the midlands, Reddingtons manufactured all types of surgical tubing, catheters and cannulae in addition to a large range of urinary drainage bags. The latter had been the mainstay of the Company and they had enjoyed many profitable years in the business. They had become so successful that they had contemplated floating the Company on the stock exchange. The elderly founder and sole owner of the Company had thought this a most attractive idea when his financial director had first postulated it. He would retire soon and a successful flotation would greatly bolster his fortune and he believed, ensure the continuing healthy future existence of the Company he had spent a lifetime building up.

As part of the preparation process for the flotation, Ian Head, a new red-hot accountant had been drafted in to serve on the board of directors. He'd quickly gained the nickname 'Hatchet Head' as he had a habit of cutting everything that came into his sights! The managing director had endowed him with awesome powers to the extent that everyone became subservient to this accountant.

That had been the start of their downfall. The new accountant started influencing all parts of the business. He was only interested in profit and had scant regard for the long-term future of the Company. This myopia had initially promised much success when, after the first six months of his reign, the figures showed a great improvement on the bottom line. There was no doubt much whooping and back slapping in the boardroom. Unfortunately though, for all involved, the euphoria would be short lived. The Company began a gradual downward spiral. The interfering cost-cutting accountant was damaging the very core of the business. He had started sourcing cheaper materials for the urine drainage bags in particular. This led to failures and problems with the medical staff in the hospitals.

William replayed in his mind the comments of a consultant Urologist in a leading Belfast teaching hospital.

"We've been using Reddington bags for many years Mr Forsythe. They've always been of a good usable quality and given us no real problems. Recently we've been experiencing difficulties with them. The bags leak at the seams. The tap valves leak. Mr. Forsythe, the one thing a urine drainage bag must not do is LEAK!" He bellowed, outraged.

"These recent bags are just rubbish! There is urine all over the floors of our wards! I don't know what you people are doing, but if you don't fix this problem soon, I personally will make sure you don't get the new contract which, as you very well know, is due to start in three months' time!"

His words had proved to be most prophetic and the vital, very profitable contract had been lost. It had been the core of the business in Northern Ireland. Reddington's were also losing contract business right, left and centre on the mainland.

There had been no dissenters at an extraordinary meeting of the board of directors. It was unanimously decided to sack the accountant. In an unprecedented action, in all the forty odd years of the Company's history, Head was frog marched out of the building, holding a cardboard box full of his personal belongings, and put into a taxi. He was further instructed never ever to return!

Joe Baxter, the Northern regional sales manager, had phoned William to give him the good news. Hatchet Head was gone! Both men had laughed and indeed guffawed with mirth! There was vast relief at the departure of this odious little man.

Unfortunately, though, the damage had already been done. It wasn't very long before Joe was back on the phone again.

"William, I'm really sorry but I'm afraid I have some very bad news for you. The Company has been hit so badly by the loss of the urine drainage bag business, that the Board of Directors have had to make some very difficult decisions. In particular, they've decided to reduce the sales force by about fifty per cent. Unfortunately, reluctantly, we are going to have to let you go."

"You are joking aren't you?" he'd replied in utter disbelief. "My sales figures have always been really good. You know I'm a top performer!"

"Sorry William. Due to the cutbacks, Jason Saunders, who does the North of England, will also be covering your patch in the future. It was decided that it would be easier for Jason to look after your area than it would be for you to do the North of England. Sorry mate. I've been dreading having to call you. It's taken me all morning to summon up the courage. I really feel terrible about this. It isn't your fault at all. It was that effing accountant that did all this!"

That had been about three months ago. His job and the company car were now all just ancient history. In the midst of the recession there had not been any decent sales jobs going. Not jobs for medical reps anyway. Now, the money from his redundancy was fast running out. He had credit card bills to pay, but the mortgage payment was the big killer. Things were getting bad. He worried about it constantly. He had developed nervous tingling in his legs and couldn't sleep at night. The fear of financial catastrophe hung over his head like some malevolent ogre. It never went away.

To aggravate matters even more, Julia had begun acting strangely the last couple of months. His wife had always been a little highly strung, but recently she was worse than ever. If truth be told, it had never really been a bed of roses marriage anyway. The impending financial doom that now lurked ahead was opening a chasm between them. The marriage was starting to come apart at the seams.

In a state of grim contemplation William rode slowly on along the dimly lit cycle path. The route followed close to a motorway at this point and he could hear the persistent roar and drone of the traffic. The bicycle rode roughly over some ruts in the tarmac where tree roots had damaged the surface. It shook him out of his reverie and he noticed that he was close to the underpass. Here, a tunnel led beneath a minor road, conducting the cycle path safely below it. The road above had a sharp turn in it, just at this point, and William had often heard motorists braking heavily above as he whizzed into the tunnel. Tonight was different.

A heavy diesel vehicle of some kind was approaching the corner above. William would not have given it a second thought except that all of a sudden, it gave a terrific screeching sound as its brakes locked up. There was a deep thud followed by a metallic clanging noise.

Anxiously William looked above him. He was alarmed to see what looked like a skip lorry up on two wheels teetering perilously close to the Armco. The barrier was all that now prevented it from falling over onto the cycle path beneath. William locked up the bicycle brakes in a panic! It squealed to a halt. Petrified, he was frozen on the spot like a rabbit in car headlamps! Above, it seemed for a terrible moment that the skip lorry was going to come down right on top of him! For what seemed an eternity, it careered along precariously on just two wheels, rasping the Armco and issuing showers of sparks.

Then, suddenly, with an enormous banging and clunking sound, amidst a gigantic cloud of dust, it settled back onto all its wheels and roared off.

"Wow!" exclaimed William. "Gee that was close!" His heart was fairly thumping.

For a brief moment he considered that that had very nearly been it. He could very easily have been crushed to death under a bloody skip lorry! What a rubbish way to go! Still, that would have solved all my problems he mused to himself.

"Bet you need a change of underpants too mate!" he shouted up at the overpass even though the lorry had now gone.

He gathered himself and was just about to ride off when he noticed a dark shape on the path ahead of him. It was a large black bin bag. It was sitting in a huge puddle of water in the middle of the cycle path. Water had splashed out in all directions across the otherwise dry tarmac. Must have come off the back of the skip lorry, he thought to himself. Gosh, if there had been something heavy in it and it had hit me, that alone would have caused serious injury.

He was about to ride on when he noticed it. There was something very red lying on the ground beside the bin liner. It was close to where the bag had burst open upon impact. It was a colour he had seen before. The oblong shape was familiar also.

Catching his breath, and hardly daring to believe what he saw, he dismounted the bicycle. He leant down and picked it up. The piece of paper he now held in his hand was about six inches long and perhaps three inches wide. The Queen's portrait on the right hand side had that Mona Lisa smile. The pink colour told him before he saw the numerals on the paper that it was indeed a fifty-pound note!

"Fantastic!" he said to himself. "Wow! This is great! Who the hell would throw away a fifty pound note?" He leaned closer to the bin bag examining it in the growing gloom. Good grief! There was a whole bundle of fifty-pound notes poking out the side of the split bin bag! He lifted the bundle and flicked the notes between his fingers. They were all fifties! There must have been several thousand pounds in this bundle!

Suddenly, he became aware that this was all rather odd. It felt surreal and eerie. A shiver of excitement coursed throughout his entire body.

He glanced right and left along the cycle path. There was nobody there. He looked inside the bin bag. A very old faded and fraying rucksack with straps was inside. Hardly daring to breathe, he undid the straps at the top and opened the bag.

"Good God! It's absolutely full of money!" he whispered to himself. The inside of the bag was a veritable Aladdin's cave!

The hairs stood up on the back of his neck. His heart was thumping now. What should he do about this? He closed the top of the bag up. Quickly, he ripped the rucksack out of the black bin liner and rapidly adjusting the straps, he was able to put the bag on his back. As he looked around, there still was no sign of anyone. He climbed back onto his bicycle and carefully began to pedal away. The bag on his back was very heavy. "There must be thousands in that bag! Hundreds of thousands even!" he whispered to himself, unable to contain his excitement!

As he cycled along the path his mind was racing. What was he to do now? Should he hand the bag into the police? That was surely the right thing to do. He remembered he had his mobile phone with him. He could stop and phone them and they would soon be here.

He was only a few hundred yards from where he'd found themoney. He stopped the bicycle and got off. Two brightly coloured cyclists passed him going the other way, but they barely noticed him.

He got the mobile phone out of his cycle jacket pocket and pressed 9-9-9. He was just about to hit the call button and then he hesitated. No! He wasn't going to do this. He'd ride home with the money and give this some thought. Better not do anything rash here he thought.

Just at that, the rain started. It was just a few spots, but the dark sky promised much more soon. Clouds had been gradually gathering the whole time he'd been preoccupied with the skip lorry and the bin bag's contents. William cycled now for all he was worth. He wanted to put as much distance as possible between himself and where that bag of money had landed on the cycle track. He pedalled like fury!

3.

"Boss." said Oscar. "Now I don't want you to get annoyed about this, but do you really think the wasps were a good idea as a means of interrogation?"

The Fatman leaned back in his executive desk chair. Beneath him the soft bottle green coloured leather creaked quietly as it absorbed the strain. The large desk in front of him was covered in papers and files. The office was dimly lit, which somehow contributed to the inimitable menace that perpetually surrounded him

After a long thoughtful silence he replied.

"Well Oscar, maybe with hindsight it wasn't one of my better ideas. I mean, the bastard was unlikely to tell us much when his mouth was full of wasps and him chokin' on them." He chuckled dryly.

"However, it does have one advantage. The story will spread throughout the under world. Whoever took my money will eventually hear about this and will know that I mean business!"

"Suppose that's true enough!" Oscar shivered as he remembered hearing Leslie's dying sobs and wails.

The Fatman was amused at how his very hard, toughened number one could possibly be so upset about the method of Leslie's demise. "That really got to you Oscar. Didn't it?"

"I hate bloody wasps!" growled Oscar.

"Leslie didn't like them much either!" grinned the Fatman.

Then, gradually, his expression darkened. It was as if a thundercloud was gathering within him.

"I want that money found!" he bellowed. "I didn't spend all that time distributing drugs to those bloody morons for nothing. It was a lot of hard work and you know that Oscar."

Oscar nodded. "Only thing is boss, where do we start?"

"We follow the money!"

"What do you mean?" Oscar looked at him blankly.

"We follow the money. Look, we decided to move the money because we think the drug squad are closing in on us. I had what I thought was a foolproof plan. We have a scrap yard. We regularly dump rubbish like old rubber tyres, broken glass and all the other tripe we can't sell on for parts or scrap value. So, as you know, we moved the money out of here in a skip lorry."

"Yes boss. I know that. But the skip lorry was only going a short distance and then Leslie, the driver, was supposed to stop the lorry and throw the bag of money over the wall of the disused house. I was waiting in the yard for the bag and it never came. We know all that!"

"What I don't understand is why Leslie wouldn't talk about it." said the Fatman. "Why would he even think about betrayal? He knew enough about me to know he'd be a dead man if he stole from me!"

The Fatman abruptly got up out of his chair. Oscar was often surprised at just how quickly he could move for a man who must weigh well over twenty stones.

He waddled over to the window of his office and surveyed the scene below. A forklift was running across the yard carrying a pallet of old batteries. Scrap cars, neatly stacked on racks, awaited stripping for parts. In a shed, men in oily red boiler suits were working dismantling old cars. A shower of sparks from a grinder splashed out into the yard. At the far end of the premises, an ever-growing pile of scrap iron awaited shipping to China.

"I spent years building all this up." He gestured out the window. "Nobody would ever suspect a scrap metal dealer as a drug importer or so I thought. I wonder how the hell they got onto me? If I ever find the wee rat who grassed on me, his life will be very short and extremely painful I can assure you!"

Oscar did not require any such assurance. He was already convinced. He'd worked for the Fatman for many years now and was thoroughly conversant with his methods. People who messed with the Fatman suffered either terrible pain or death, often both!

No mercy was shown or indeed expected. Often, it was Oscar who carried out the prescribed sentence of the Fatman. He had, over time, learned to carry out his work with a mechanical, emotionless precision. He rarely thought much about it and dwelt not on morals or grieving over consequences. He just did it. Sometimes, he even derived a quiet satisfaction believing he was in fact a master of his dark art.

"Where's wee Geordie Taylor?" the Fatman suddenly enquired.

"I haven't seen him the last couple of days." said Oscar. "Hey! Maybe he knows something about all this. After all, he was supposed to be with Leslie in the skip lorry that night."

"I actually told Geordie to drive the skip lorry." corrected the Fatman. "I couldn't do it as the police would probably be watching me. I didn't get you to do it Oscar for exactly the same reason. I asked wee Geordie as he's low profile and nobody would give a damn about him."

The Fatman turned away from the window and faced Oscar.

"Go you and find wee Geordie Taylor and bring him here to me. I want a word with him!" he said ominously.

Oscar nodded and got up to leave.

"By the way, what did you do with the body?"

"Dumped it up amongst some gorse bushes on the Cavehill Mountain." replied Oscar.

"Good. They'll think it was a natural death then."

4.

A day earlier . . . .

William was still in a state of disbelief. The ride home on the bicycle, the night before, had really taken it out of him. The skies had opened when he had got about half way home. The rain had pelted down with tropical ferocity. At one point, he'd had to stop and hide under a tree. Even then large drops of rain were landing on him. Despite the rain, he'd never ridden as hard in all his life. He'd pedalled as if the hounds of hell were after him!

Upon arrival home, he'd put the bicycle away in the garage and hidden the bag of money under a pile of old newspapers at the back of his garage. A warm shower was most necessary to revive him before a further quick excursion to the garage was made. He had to check the moneybag before bed to make sure it was still there! He also checked he'd locked the garage at least three times.

That night was largely a sleepless one. He'd seen every hour pass on his illuminated bedside clock. It was as well he and his wife now slept in separate bedrooms. He'd slept so restlessly she'd have been bound to guess something was up.

Next morning, as soon as his wife had gone out to work, he'd rushed into the garage and carefully locked the door behind him.

Using sticky tape, he'd then stuck up some old newspaper to cover the window at the side of the garage. Once he was convinced that no unexpected visitor could see in, he opened the top of the old rucksack. Hurriedly, he cleared the top of his small workbench of tools, oils, polishes and all the usual paraphernalia that all such surfaces attract.

Reaching inside the bag, he started to set out piles of notes onto the bench so that he could do a count. He lifted one of the bundles of fifty-pound notes. It was bound with an inch and a half wide purple wrapper, which had obviously been hand cut and stuck around it by somebody. It wasn't a proper bank wrapper. William excitedly counted the notes. There were one hundred notes in the stack. That meant there were five thousand pounds in that bundle alone! Some of the bundles were made up of hundred pound notes. There were ten thousand pounds in those bundles!

Most of the notes were in hundreds and fifties. Many were nice new bank of England notes although there were also Bank of Ireland, Dansk Bank and Ulster Bank notes. All of the latter bore the all-important legend "Sterling" upon them. The last bundle he found was made up of Bank of Ireland tens and twenties.

Over the next couple of hours, William counted and recounted the bundles of notes. On a scrap of newspaper he added up a total. It worked out at One million and ninety three thousand; two hundred and thirty pounds! That was almost one point one million pounds!

Holy Moses! William thought to himself. Stunned, he sat down on an old stool that had been relegated from the kitchen at some stage. He stared in disbelief at the pile of money on top of his workbench. This was absolutely incredible!

"Only problem is, I dare not tell a single soul." he said quietly to himself. That would be very difficult. He was so excited about what had happened! At the same time, he remembered something he'd recently seen on television. It was a program about the secret service in which one agent said to another.

"One fundamental rule within the service is that you never divulge any information to anyone who absolutely doesn't need to know it."

William had thought that a very wise statement when he'd heard it. It most definitely applied in spades to this situation.

"Firstly", he said to himself quietly. "My darling wife is never going to know anything about this! She has made it quite clear that she doesn't love me anymore. She's not going to see any of this money!" he chuckled gleefully to himself.

Suddenly, for the first time, he felt an immense wave of energy pulse through him. This money would empower him. He could now do all sorts of things he'd formerly only ever dreamt of!

"Jeez! This is like winning the Lottery!" he mused to himself. His whole life would now change dramatically. He was no longer an impoverished little man with no job, no money and no prospects. No, he was now a Millionaire!

5.

"Forty seven to control. Forty seven to control."

"Control, forty seven. Go ahead." The radio reception was very crackly.

"Forty seven, we need the next shift to bring up a new memory chip for the camera. This one is nearly full. Over."

"Control, forty seven. Understood. We will organise that for you."

Detective Sergeant Henderson set the radio down. He opened the dirty, dust-covered venetian blinds a crack more and for the umpteenth time stared out at the buildings and yard across the street. A small crane was unloading old scrap cars off a low loader and setting them down onto the yard. A young lad was dragging a pallet load of alloy wheels across the yard. He unloaded the wheels onto a rack inside a shed. A forklift truck driver was dumping old rubber tyres into a skip at one side of the yard.

"Same old same old." said Henderson sipping cold coffee.

"We're wasting our flippin' time here." replied D.C. Butler. "We're not going to see anything. Old Fatman Cartwright is much too clever to show anything out front. If he does anything at all, it will happen under the cover of darkness I can assure you."

"You're probably right, but it's not down to us to make that call. Let's consider what we do know. We have it on good authority that Cartwright here, alias "The Fatman," is importing and distributing drugs to dealers all round the Province. He operates this scrap car business as a front to cover up his illicit dealings. He is a real cunning operator as he's never been caught, never been behind bars. He's one of the very few who actually does prove that crime pays if you're intelligent enough and well organised. We don't ever want anyone to televise this sort of criminal behaviour. That would be a nightmare!"

"Oscar Jamison." Butler was reading from a file. "Cartwright's right-hand man. Two short stretches inside. Both for grievous bodily harm. Says here, he once beat the hell out of three other hardened criminals who attacked him for reasons unknown. He put one of them clean through a plate glass window. One of the others was hospitalised for nearly six months for reconstructive surgery so that he could eat again without the use of a drinking straw!" He paused for a moment reading the final part of this litany.

"Seems Oscar stamped hard using all his body weight on the third guy's foot. The hood had so many broken bones in his foot that they couldn't fix it. He now walks with a permanent limp!"

"What a lovely man. You meet the nicest people in this business." quipped Henderson. "I mean, can you just imagine him playing Santa Claus at a Christmas party or something? He'd have a six year old boy on his lap and ask him what he'd like for Christmas. A flick knife? A pistol? Or a sawn off shot gun?" he chuckled.

"Then there's Cartwright's other boys." continued Butler.

"George Steven Taylor, otherwise known as Geordie. He's been inside since birth practically. Spent much of his childhood in borstals and did several stretches in prison. Burglary, possession of drugs, stealing cars, G.B.H. the list goes on . . . ."

"John Philip Thompson." Henderson now had the file. "Otherwise known as 'Shorty,' obvious enough as he's only about five feet five inches tall. Other nicknames used in the under world include "The Mouse" and "Taxi"

'Why Taxi?" Enquired Butler.

"Because his ears stick out like the open doors of a taxi!" laughed Henderson. "He's a fairly recent addition to the gang. We know very little about him except he's been caught many times for minor burglaries. He's usually the get away driver. Unfortunately for him, he's useless at it." He paused whilst reading the next bit. "Says here, he was once caught by a W.P.C. who had only passed her driving test the week before!"

Both men laughed loudly at this.

"Leslie Brown." continued Butler. "He's a recent addition also and we don't know much about him. Haven't seen him the last few days...."

"Shhhhhush!" said Henderson holding his finger up to his mouth. "I forgot the windows open. After all we are on surveillance duty!"

Butler peered out from between the venetian blinds.

"The Fatman's just arrived." he said.

Henderson got the camera out. It was fixed to a tripod for easier use. He only needed to part the blinds slightly to push its telescopic proboscis through and operate the motor drive on the shutter. It clicked away as he photographed the Fatman's arrival. He was driving a Mercedes car. It was a dark ruby red colour and definitely not a new model. Unusually, for such a hardened criminal, it had a soft convertible top on it.

"Aye." said Henderson. "Apparently Cartwright is a real petrolhead. It's rumoured he has quite a collection of interesting cars hidden away out at his farm."

"What type of cars?'

"Oh the usual for drug dealers. 911 Porsche Turbo, Ferrari, Mercedes SL AMG. All that sort of stuff."

"The dirty bastard!" said Butler. "I'm a petrolhead myself and I'll never be able to own any of those. Who says crime doesn't pay?"

"It doesn't pay!" Interjected Henderson suddenly. He was angry now. His face a little redder than usual "We're going to get this bastard. We'll have him behind bars. His fancy cars won't be much use to him then! I have a nephew who died from a drug overdose. I swore to my brother that, one day, I'd catch some of the evil bastards that exploit kids like that. I don't know if it was the Fatman here that sold the drugs to a dealer, but I don't care. He's one of them. I'm going to have him Butler! Just you see if I don't!"

They both watched as the Fatman said something to Oscar and they both disappeared into his office.

6.

"I really can't do this any more!" William's wife, Julia was on the warpath again.

"You sit here all day long doing nothing." She was vigorously scrubbing some pot in the sink. Her long dark hair was quivering with the effort. After only the slightest of pauses she continued.

"You make no effort whatsoever to find a job. I'm out working my butt off down at the Supermarket just to try to make ends meet. Meanwhile you're here doing bugger all to help!"

William was eating his breakfast of tea, toast and marmalade.

"It's not really fair you saying that. It's only been three months love."

"Three months! Three bloody months!" she yelled. "It might as well be three years for all you care! And don't you 'love' me! I'm not you're love. Love has gone out the window in this house!"

She was getting very upset now. Ever since he'd lost his job, things had been going steadily downhill with their relationship. He now realised, with sober reflection, that the marriage had not been built on a very solid foundation. The first time a real problem hit them, the weaknesses had become abundantly clear. Things were not good.

"There aren't a lot of sales jobs going at the moment. We are in a recession! Don't you ever watch the news!" He gesticulated at the small flat-screen television set which stood on the kitchen counter."

"What do you think I am? Bloody stupid?" She was ranting and raving now but William's attention was drawn to the local news on the television.

". . . . The body of a man has been found on Belfast's Cavehill Mountain. The man's body was covered in wasp stings. Early indications are that this was indeed the cause of death. The police are not treating the death as suspicious . . . ."

That's rather odd William thought to himself.

"You aren't listening to a bloody word I say are you?" He was vaguely aware of her nagging voice in the background.

"Never heard of anyone being stung to death by wasps before!"

William had said it out loud without thinking. He was briefly aware that something had passed over his head at high speed. It had just ruffled his hair and no more. There was an enormous crashing thud as the pot of raspberry jam exploded all over the white paintwork of the kitchen wall behind him.

He turned around to look. It was like a meteorite impact zone. The wall was now covered in red jam with radiating streaks and splinters of glass were strewn all over the tiles of the kitchen floor. Suddenly he felt euphoric and remembered something Winston Churchill had once said.

'There is nothing more exhilarating than to be fired upon without result!'

"Ha ha, you missed!" Once again, he'd said it without thinking. Instantly, as it left his lips, he knew his comment was ill-advised.

There was another ferocious tirade of verbal assault. He'd never before heard or indeed seen his wife in such a bad mood. She was totally out of control. She slammed an iron pot into the sink with a tremendous clang. He decided that the best course of action was to say nothing and hope that she would cool off a little.

After several more minutes of vitriol, at last Julia's rocket motors were beginning to run out of fuel. Eventually she started to become just slightly calmer. Her parting comment was:

"I'm off to work now. You'd better have this bloody mess cleared up by the time I get home. And go and look for a job while you're at it. If you don't, there will be hell to pay when I get back!"

Pulling her coat on, she went out slamming the door with a terrific bang for an encore. The glass panes in the door rattled fit to shatter.

After she was gone, William rose to his feet and looked after her. Rhett Butler came to mind.

'Frankly my dear, I don't give a damn!'"

7.

Wee Geordie Taylor was sitting on a nice comfortable chair in the Fatman's office. He didn't feel one bit comfortable though. Beneath him, the soft green leather creaked quietly as he shifted nervously. He was absolutely shit scared. Geordie wasn't exactly Einstein, but he had figured out that the next few minutes would decide whether or not his wife would collect his life insurance policy or not!

Across the desk from him, the Fatman was staring intently at him. Slowly, his eyes never once blinking, he tilted his head slightly to one side increasing the intensity of the stare. Geordie felt like some insignificant little insect about to be swallowed by a monitor lizard.

"Where is it Geordie?" the Fatman asked slowly and very quietly.

"Boss, I swear to God, I don't know!"

"Why don't you know? You were driving the skip lorry. You had Leslie with you. You may recall we had a rather large bag of money in the back of it? There was nearly one point one million pounds in that bag Geordie!" The Fatman's voice had become louder by a few decibels, but he wasn't shouting. Not yet.

"Boss, I wasn't driving the skip lorry."

"What the hell do you mean? I told you to drive it! It was a very important job. We had to move the money because, as we all know, the police are watching us. I gave you the job because I trusted you to do it correctly. You only had to drive about two miles, check no one had followed you and then get out and throw the bag of money over the wall of the old house."

Oscar took up the running. He thrust his face close in front of Geordie.

"I was standing on the other side of the wall. I was up to the waist in bloody stinging nettles, standing there ball-froze for nearly two hours waiting for you! Where the hell did you go?"

Wee Geordie was a pathetic looking sight. He was shivering with fear by now. He'd heard what had happened to the unfortunate Leslie!

"Look, I know about what happened to Leslie. Leslie knew bugger all about it!"

"Tell us something we don't know for a change." The Fatman scowled. His face was starting to redden. "Where is the money?"

"Leslie didn't know anything about it." stammered Geordie again. "He didn't want to go that night, because it was his wee nieces' wedding earlier that day. He had been to the wedding and had got totally pissed. He'd asked me to look after the job that night. I took Shorty with me. It was Shorty who was driving the skip lorry!

"Shorty!" yelled the Fatman. "You let Shorty drive the skip lorry?" He paused incredulous. "Everyone knows Shorty couldn't drive a nail into a turnip!"

Geordie hung his head in shame. "I know." he almost sobbed. "He is without a doubt the most useless bloody driver I've ever seen."

"Then why the heck did you let him drive?" Oscar wanted to know. "We all know he's a crap driver! I mean, how many times has he got caught when he was doing getaway driver? It's three times now?"

"Four!" corrected the Fatman.

"Four times Geordie!" Oscar shouted. "And you let him drive the skip lorry on a job that was of crucial importance! Over a million pound in the back and you let Shorty drive." Oscar had his hands on his hips exasperated.

The Fatman stood up now. He rested both his hands on the desk in front of him and glared at Geordie. His eyes were like lasers boring savagely into the little man. Geordie could barely make eye contact.

"Why?" yelled the Fatman, banging his fist on the desk with a great thud. He was gradually getting more and more irritated. Spittle was starting to fly out of his mouth now like the ejecta from a volcano that was threatening to erupt violently!

"Why did you let Shorty drive?"

Geordie was silent for a moment, looking intently at a small chip in the woodwork at the front of the Fatman's desk. Somehow focusing on something totally irrelevant calmed him sufficiently to finally own up.

"I've lost my friggin driving licence."

"What?" The Fatman looked puzzled.

"I was totally blocked one night coming out of the pub. It was wee Willy Wyllie's birthday. It was back about October last year. I crashed my car into a bloody bus. The peelers were just across the street. They caught me and it only came to court about two weeks ago. I've lost my books for eighteen months."

His two interrogators were temporarily so astonished they were stunned into silence by this admission. Eventually, it was Oscar who shattered the stillness.

"I take it you were going to tell us sometime?"

"I was trying to find the right moment." sighed Geordie.

"Well fuck me pink!" exhaled the Fatman. "So you let Shorty drive the skip lorry because you couldn't."

"That's right boss."

"So what exactly happened? Where the blazes is my money?"

He stared at Geordie enquiringly.

"Well, you know, Shorty drove the skip lorry out of the yard here and up over the bridge. You know, the bridge at the cycle track crossover on the Mahon road?"

The Fatman nodded in acknowledgment.

"Well. You know, there's a very bad tight corner there, right at that bridge. Just as we were approaching it, you know, a badger ran across the road in front of the lorry. As you all know, Shorty is a real softy for wee furry animals."

"What happened?" Oscar asked looking bored.

"Well, you know, Shorty swerved to avoid the badger. Then, you know, he hit a massive big pothole, so he did. Then, you know...."

Suddenly, the Fatman brought both fists down hard upon the desk in front of him with a tremendous bang. A small paperweight became briefly airborne and then rolled off the desk and scuttled away like some small-terrified rodent into a corner of the office.

"I do not bloody well know!!!!" he yelled at full volume.

Wee Geordie nearly jumped out of his skin. Even Oscar looked startled.

"Stop telling me I know! I do not bloody well know! That's why I'm asking you. Now will you get on with it!"

Geordie looked very shaken. Ashen faced he continued.

"Well, as I was saying, Shorty swerved to miss the badger. He hit this massive bloody pothole and the whole lorry went up onto two wheels! I thought she was going over, I swear before God I thought we were dead. It yammered along the guardrail for a moment or two and then, bang!" Geordie hammered his fist on the Fatman's desk.

"It came back down onto all four wheels again."

"And?" The Fatman glared.

"Well, you know...."

The expression on the Fatmans face darkened.

"Sorry boss. Well, the lorry righted herself and then gave a wiggle and ran straight over the badger and fuckin' flattened it."

The Fatman put his hand up to his face and tried in vain to suppress and conceal his amusement. He cocked a quick look at Oscar who was about to crease with laughter. That did it! They both burst out laughing!

"Well bugger me senseless!" laughed the Fatman. Briefly he was absolutely helpless with mirth. "That's the only time I've laughed in days!"

Oscar did a mock impression of the flattened badger rolling his eyes to one side, sticking his tongue out at an angle and stretching his arms out wide. The Fatman laughed even more!

Briefly, wee Geordie looked relieved . . . .but it was short lived.

"So, what happened to the bag of money?" Oscar was suddenly serious again his voice full of menace.

"I'm honestly not sure."

"What do you mean you're not sure?" growled the Fatman. "You either are sure or you're not. Now. No more pissing about. Where is the fucking bastardin' money?"

"Well, after the lorry righted itself, Shorty drove a couple of hundred yards more and then he stopped, so he did. He crossed himself about six times."

"I always knew he was a wee fenian bastard." said Oscar.

"No, Shorty is alright you know. Anytime we go into a pub, he's always the first to put his hand in his pocket and buy a drink."

"And that qualifies him as alright!" The Fatman's eyes were out on stalks, their grey blue centres surrounded by a sea of indignant white.

"For the last time Geordie, and I really am just about to let Oscar throttle you. Where is the money?"

"I don't know." Geordie replied anxiously.

Just at that, there was a barely audible knock at the door.

"Come in." the Fatman said.

Geordie turned round to see who it was. It was the last person on earth he expected to see!

8.

William had had a very busy day. As soon as his wife left for work, he had started work on his own project. He had cleared away a space at the back of the old garage behind their house. The original owner must have been a car enthusiast as he had built a very long two-car garage. It had room for two cars parked one in front of the other. Behind that, there was even more room as a small workshop with built in workbenches had been added to the rear of the building.

During the time that the Forsythes had lived at 32 King's Wood Park, neither of them had ever bothered clearing out the back of the old workshop. There were still some ancient gardening tools, now well in the death throes of terminal rust. Several very old tea chests full of metal gearwheels and assorted ancient corroding car parts languished in the shadows. William had often considered clearing it all out into a skip, but for some reason had never quite got around to it. There had always been something of higher priority to attend to.

Now, this neglected old workshop behind the garage was literally a godsend to William. Once a space had been cleared underneath one of the old workbenches, William had put his very best D.I.Y. skills to good use. He'd visited a large local D.I.Y. store and purchased a fireproof safe which he had then installed, bolting it to the concrete floor for extra security. Inside it, he had carefully stacked nearly all of the money. The safe was then locked by its combination lock. He had fastidiously painted the exterior of the safe with a matt black paint. A final mixture of cement dust, sand and old cobwebs were added to age and help conceal it.

The safe had then been covered up with a very old tarpaulin that had been lying about for years. The cobwebs and mouse droppings on it would not encourage its removal by the casually curious. He dragged two of the old tea chests in front of the tarpaulin. He had weighted them with sand and stones. This would ensure that, even if his wife ever became overly inquisitive, she could not move them. Julia had never shown the least interest in the garage, nor the old workshop at the back. But William wasn't taking any chances.

"What are you doing out here?" It was Julia. She'd suddenly arrived at the garage door. He hadn't heard her coming.

"I've been doing a little bit of maintenance work on my bike love. The chain needed oiling. That sort of stuff."

"Oh." she said unimpressed. "What about the job centre? Did you go down there?"

"No. Not to-day." He had absolutely no interest in going to the job centre. Not with all that money hidden away in the safe!

"That's just typical! I'm out knocking my pan in, down at that supermarket. Working for hours, trying to be nice, smiling at people at the damn till, meanwhile you're out here oiling your bloody chain!"

"Well it needed to be done." William defended himself.

"Its all a question of priorities isn't it? If you were a responsible person you'd be out looking for a job."

"O.K. I hear you." It was best to concede a slight apology to get her to stop moaning.

"Anyway, I'm making tea early tonight as I'm going to the gym later."

"You never mentioned that."

"Didn't I? I'm sure I did. At breakfast to-day but you seemed preoccupied with your own thoughts. Anyway, it will be ready in ten minutes." She began walking back in the direction of the house and then stopped and turned again.

"Can I smell paint?" She looked puzzled.

"Maybe." William remembered the freshly painted safe. He'd have to think fast! "I upset a tin of paint at the back of the garage when I was looking for the oil."

"Hope you cleaned it up!" she retorted and paused looking thoughtful. "Wonder if there's anything amongst all that old junk back there that we could sell?"

She had started towards the back of the garage to look. William was really alarmed now. If she somehow twigged on to what he'd been up to, all his cunning plans would be in tatters!

"I really doubt it love. Its just a load of old rubbish."

"What would you know anyhow? I'll bet there is something among that old rubbish we could sell. They're always finding stuff and bringing it onto Antiques Roadshow!" Excited now, she was walking towards the back of the garage in determined fashion. She was looking into the attached workshop in the direction of the workbench. She was on a mission!

William was inwardly panic-stricken. This was a disaster. He'd worked so cleverly to hide the safe and now the old witch was going to find it! She had a nose like a bloodhound! Then, instantly he had the answer. Very casually he said in as disinterested a tone as he could possibly muster.

"Watch out back there, love. Quite a few mouse droppings around. Some of them are quite big actually. Wouldn't be surprised if there was a rat or two about."

"A rat!" She froze in her tracks horrified. A hasty retreat began, mission aborted.

She hurried off in the direction of the kitchen. Her parting comment was to make sure and get some rat poison as a matter of great urgency.

William breathed a sigh of relief. "Phew. That was close!" he said to himself.

As he locked up the garage he was wondering about the money. What if it was marked? What if it was counterfeit? Then he couldn't spend it! He'd have to figure out a way of testing it. A way that would not put him at risk of getting caught!

9.

Geordie Taylor looked like he'd seen a ghost. Oscar was wide eyed with disbelief. Even the Fatman looked surprised!

"Well, well, well." said the Fatman. "Shorty Thompson! Come on, on in!" The invitation was far from being a friendly one.

"Hello boss." Shorty looked fearfully at the Fatman. He nodded respectfully at Oscar who was eying him with a look of some bewilderment.

As Shorty entered, Oscar closed the door behind him with a great thud. He then dramatically turned the key in the lock and pocketed the key.

"Good idea Oscar." approved the Fatman. "Now, nobody goes back out that door alive until I find out where my bleedin' money is!"

"I must say," Oscar pulled up a chair for Shorty and encouraged him to occupy it with a firm shove. "I must say I'm really surprised to see you."

"Frig!" said Geordie. "I thought you were dead!"

"He very soon will be if someone doesn't tell me what happened to my money!" snarled the Fatman maliciously. "And you with him too!" he glared at Geordie.

"Now wee Shorty." Oscar had grabbed Shorty by his large taxi door like ears. He spoke softly, even smiling as he did so. "Time to spill the beans or I'll spill you all over the bloody floor." He flapped Shorty's ears playfully up and down and then twisted them evoking a slight squeal from the little man.

Shorty glanced sideways at Geordie. "Did you tell them about me driving the skip lorry?"

"Uh huh." Geordie confirmed. "And about the pothole and the badger."

"Fuck the bleedin' badger! Get on with it Big Ears!" The Fatman was now sitting leaning on the front of his desk so that he came threateningly close to Shorty's face. Shorty could smell the awful breath the Fatman was notorious for. It really was absolutely horrendous.

Shorty writhed attempting to back away from the foul odour but Oscar's firm hold on his ears prevented his escape.

"O.K." said Shorty. "Here's what happened."

"At long last!" the Fatman assumed a mock attentive stance, his arms folded, looking straight at Shorty. "I'm all ears!"

"O.K. I hit this pothole. It was like the Grand Canyon! The lorry went up onto two wheels. It near went over, so it did. It landed with a big bang like bloody thunder. It scared the shit out of me so I stopped down the road a bit. I got out and Geordie and I had a wee smoke to steady our nerves."

"So what happened next?" Oscar pulled Shorty's ears again to spur him on.

"Well. Geordie decided to check the money was alright. He climbed up into the skip and started to look for it, but he couldn't fuckin' find it."

Geordie took up the story. "It was gone boss. I'd put it at the nearside rear corner of the skip, so I could easily find it when we got to the old house where Oscar was waiting. But when I looked for it, it was gone."

"So it had obviously fallen out hadn't it?" Oscar continued the interrogation.

"That's right." Shorty nodded. "We went back to where the pothole was and looked around. No sign of it."

"Then I looked over the edge of the bridge." Geordie added. "It was just starting to get dark, but in the gloom, I could just make out a black bin bag on the ground below."

"So we climbed down the bank onto the cycle track below." Shorty continued. "Sure enough, there was a black bin bag lying on the ground, but it was empty. There was a big puddle. It must have landed in the puddle as water was splattered all over the place around the puddle. But the rucksack that had been in the bin bag was gone!"

"How do you know it was the same bin bag?" the Fatman wanted to know.

"Because we had wrapped a bit of silver tank tape round the top of the bag when we put it in the skip. There were lots of bin bags in there going to the dump. We didn't want to lose it . . . ." Geordie suddenly realised how stupid he sounded and dried up.

"Only thing is boss, we saw a bloke on a bicycle pedalling away in the distance," added Shorty. "Now we are not sure, but it looked like he had a big bag on his back."

"Do you think it was the money?' asked Oscar.

"You can fuckin' count on it!" yelled the Fatman getting abruptly to his feet. "You searched all round for the rucksack didn't you?"

"Yes boss, everywhere," answered Geordie. "It wasn't there."

"Ergo." The Fatman glared at the both of them. "That bloody cyclist found it and made off with it! Right, well we'd better find the bugger, and quick before he starts spending my money!"

"How the hell are we going to find him?" Oscar looked concerned.

"Well, there is one thing," Shorty looked up at the Fatman. "He was wearing one of those reflective yellow coats some cyclists wear."

"So now all we need to do is find some cunt wearing a yellow coat and riding a bicycle!" retorted Geordie. "That will be dead easy!"

The Fatman scowled at him. "Tell you what, you'd better find him, or your days will be numbered!"

10.

Julia rolled over in the bed. The young man beside her was asleep. For a brief moment she felt a pang of guilt. Whatever would William think if he knew about Philip. She looked happily at him as he slept. Philip was quite a few years younger than Julia. They had met at the gym. He had struck up a conversation whilst jogging on the machine beside her. Immediately, she'd been smitten by him. He had wonderful shiny dark hair, was tanned and handsome. He was athletic looking and played rugby. Julia loved stroking his bulging smooth muscles. He was just gorgeous! A cup of coffee after a work out had soon led to lunch and, in short order, here she was in his bed. This wasn't the first time either.

She slipped out from under the covers and looked out of the window. They were about half a dozen storeys up in his city apartment. It was getting dark outside. Down below in the street, Julia could just see where Philip had parked his silver Porsche 911. The yellow of the street lights made it look a marvellous golden hue. What a car! They had been out for a few short drives in it and she really loved it!

She knew she would soon have to go home or risk alerting William that she was up to something. He thought she was at the gym. She smiled to herself thinking that, at least, she had had a good cardiovascular workout!

"Juliet, Juliet, wherefore art thou Juliet?" a quiet dry husky voice was coming from below the covers. She looked to see his big brown eyes look admiringly at her. He smiled flashing a row of white teeth at her.

"It's Julia you twit" she smirked at him.

"I know. But Juliet sounds better, doesn't it?"

"You don't know too much about Shakespeare then do you?"

He looked momentarily puzzled and she laughed at his expression. He was so deliciously naive. She just wanted to eat him all up!

"Its Romeo, Romeo wherefore art thou Romeo!" She gave a lovely theatrical wave of her arm to complete the little quote.

"Whatever! Anyway." He patted the bed beside him. "Come here to we see you!"

She didn't take much persuading. A short run and then she jumped up onto the bed on top of him.

"I have to go soon." she whispered.

"That's good, because I need to come soon!"

"Can you give me a lift back to my car afterwards?"

"Of course I can." he smiled.

Gently, he stroked her long hair away from her face and kissed her. Moments later they were making love again. Julia just couldn't imagine this happening anytime soon with William. It was wonderful! She wrapped herself around this beautiful young man. He was all hers. As she lay there, she realised she just couldn't be happier.

11.

"Forty seven to Control. Forty seven to Control."

"Control forty seven, go ahead."

"Cartwright is on the move again. We're in pursuit. Forty seven out."

"Roger forty seven, understood."

Henderson set the radio handset down. He and Butler watched as the Fatman pulled out of the scrap yard in his ruby red Mercedes.

"Bet I know where he's off to." quipped Butler.

"Do you think so?"

"He has a sort of routine this guy. Most people do. I reckon he's off to see his fancy woman again."

"You could be right." said Henderson. "This is the night his wife goes out to see her ma. Gives the auld bugger an opportunity to slip off for a bit of nookey."

The Mercedes was about a hundred and fifty yards up the road by now. Henderson started the engine of the Vauxhall and slipped gently away from the kerb. He kept a discreet distance, not wanting to be spotted by the Fatman.

Ahead of them, the Fatman was purring along in his AMG Mercedes cabriolet. He loved this car. The soft mushroom leather seats were so comfortable and a pleasure to sit in. It was one of only fourteen ever imported into the U.K and thus very rare. He reckoned he was the only person in Northern Ireland to own one. The rarity of the car made it all the more special to him. He always enjoyed driving it.

He slipped his hand inside the armrest compartment and felt something cold and hard. It was his Glock pistol. He never went anywhere without it. These days you just never knew when you'd need it. Beside the gun he could feel a C.D. case. He pulled it out and looked at it.

"Ah ha!" he said aloud to himself. "That's where it is. I've been looking for that for ages!"

He removed the disc and slipped it into the CD player. A moment or two later the gently opening bars of Boston, 'It's More Than a Feeling' started to play.

"Always liked this album." he thought to himself and hummed the tune along with the CD as he drove along. He felt the tension of the last few days ease a little. It was about time. He knew he'd been very stressed since the money had gone missing. How the hell had he been so stupid as to come up with the daft idea of moving the money in a skip?

Initially, it had all seemed very clever. The Fatman remembered how it had all started. A detective in the Police force had made an approach to him. He had asked for a meeting in private somewhere away from everything. They'd met in a pub down on the shore of Strangford Lough. The detective said he was due for retirement within the next year. He had information Cartwright might be interested in.

The two men had sat outside, as it was a warm sunny evening. There were a few tables and chairs on a veranda, which overlooked a bay full of little sailing boats. In the distance, there was a muffled bang, a small explosion of some kind.

"Must be a race on tonight." said the detective. "That's the starting gun going off.

"Oh, wondered what that was." replied Cartwright. "What's your name?"

"No names. If anyone knew about this I'd be in really big trouble."

"Then what are you doing here and what makes you think I'm going to tell you anything."

"I don't want you to tell me anything Mr. Cartwright. I'm going to tell you something that will be highly beneficial to you. We must have an agreement though."

"What sort of agreement?" The Fatman looked suspiciously at him as he sipped a large vodka and coke.

"The sort of agreement where I give you information and you pay me for it."

"That type of agreement. Suppose I go along with it, what sort of information have you got for me?"

The detective looked around him uneasily. They were almost alone on the veranda. A young courting couple were sitting about thirty yards away, under a small oak tree. They were looking into each other's eyes intently and obviously were preoccupied with each other. He leaned forward towards the Fatman and half whispered.

"It's the sort of information that will help keep you out of jail!"

"O.K. I'm always interested in that sort of information. Let's hear what you have to say."

"Did you bring the envelope we discussed on the telephone?"

The Fatman looked around him now. Content that no one was watching, he slipped his hand into the inside pocket of his jacket and produced a manila envelope. It was pregnant with notes. He set it down on top of the table and, mafia like, slid it towards the detective.

"Five grand in there." he said.

The detective pocketed the envelope.

"O.K." he said. "The police are watching you as of tomorrow."

"For frig sake! Sure the police are always watching me. That's nothing new."

"No! I mean they will be really watching you. There will be telephone taps and intensive surveillance. Something or someone has alerted them. They are going to do a job on you."

"Why? All I do is run a scrap yard!" protested the Fatman.

"I think we both know you do a lot more than that. They are highly suspicious that you are trafficking drugs. You are under investigation!"

The Fatman sat back in his chair and stared suspiciously at the detective.

"I'm not saying a bleedin' word more. Are you wearing a wire?" He looked suddenly very alarmed.

"Cool your jets big lad. I'm not wearing a wire." He unbuttoned the front of his shirt carefully and quickly buttoned it again.

"I want to know why you're here talking to me. It's not just for five grand, sure its not?"

"You are a remarkable perceptive man." The detective smiled sarcastically at him. Then he turned serious. There was bitterness in his voice.

"I'm only here for the money. I'm retiring next year. I want to top up my pension plan. I've been doing the goody, goody detective bit long enough. I was in for a big promotion last year, which would have greatly increased my salary, my lump sum and my pension. They gave the job to some young upstart who knows bugger all about detective work in my opinion. If they decide to pass over me, I'm going to look after myself.

The Fatman seemed satisfied with this explanation. Either the detective was telling the truth, or he should be up for an Oscar award.

"I'll keep you posted as to what the police are up to regarding your case. Every move they make, I'll keep you one step ahead of the game. All you have to do is be careful and they won't be able to pin anything on you."

"How much is all this going to cost?"

"Plenty! Just think, you are not going to jail with me on your side!" The detective leaned forward and handed the Fatman a small padded envelope.

"There is a number in there for a Swiss bank account. Transfer fifty thousand pounds into it within the next three days."

"Away and fuck yourself!" The Fatman was outraged. "That's extortionate!"

"Bit like the profit margin you make in your own line of business? That's only the down payment. You will have to make further instalments Cartwright. But it will be well worth it I assure you"

"You're a bloody robber." The Fatman looked disgusted.

"And you're a bloody drug trafficker!"

"How will you keep in touch if the phones are tapped and I'm under surveillance?" asked the Fatman.

"It's all in there Cartwright." The detective pointed at the envelope.

That had all happened a few weeks ago. As the Fatman drove on towards Sylvia's house, he glanced carefully behind him. Sure enough, a dark grey Vauxhall car was shadowing his every move. He grinned to himself. They could watch all they liked; he wouldn't be doing anything that would incriminate himself. Even if he did, they wouldn't see it even if he did it right under their noses!

He pulled into a suburban driveway in East Belfast. He noted out of the corner of his eye that the grey Vauxhall had parked about fifty yards away down the street.

"Hello Sylvia!" He gave the lady who greeted him a big hug and a kiss. That's for the cameras he grinned to himself. Sylvia was tall with blonde hair. She had a slim attractive build and beamed happily at Cartwright.

"Oh!" he said. "I almost forgot the chocolates dear!" he dashed back to the car and lifted a large box of chocolates from the passenger seat of the Mercedes.

Butler's camera was whirring away as the motor drive caught all the action. He could clearly see Cartwright hand over a large box of chocolates with a huge pink ribbon round them. He also had a bunch of flowers.

"What a big smoothie." Butler said to Henderson.

"Absolutely." Henderson followed his gaze lost in thought.

Next moment, both Cartwright and his fancy woman were gone into the house.

12.

William had been awake quite a bit of the night. He'd had to get up and make a cup of tea about three in the morning. He just couldn't sleep. He knew all that lovely money was sitting at the back of his garage. He was just itching to spend it!

But William knew also that it wasn't as easy as that. He'd have to be very, very careful. His head was full of concerns. What if the money was stolen? Were the police looking for it? What if it was counterfeit money? Was the money marked? If so, what would happen if he tried to spend it?

It was the middle of the night and a deathly stillness had descended upon the house. Quietly he sat thinking in his living room. Upstairs, Julia was fast asleep. She'd been really tired after she returned home from the gym. Actually, she'd been in a good mood, almost happy. Anyway, as he sat there, he wasn't thinking of Julia. He was thinking about the money. He decided he'd have to carry out a test or two to see if the money was marked.

As he sat there mulling it all over, an idea came to him at last. It was pretty much foolproof and he would find out if the money was marked or not.

William had noticed that a local off licence, where he frequently bought some wine, always checked notes by rubbing a marker pen on them. They then held the note under a special light. He assumed it was an ultra violet light. He would conduct a test. In the next street, convenient to the off licence, he'd often seen a homeless man. He usually slept-off the previous night's drink in a doorway to a disused building. He decided to pay him a visit.

Later that day, after Julia was off to work, he went out to the garage. William had put a few of the notes from his lucky find into an old tin box, which he'd carefully hidden amongst the junk at the back of his garage. From this box, he withdrew a couple of nice red fifty-pound notes and set out on a mission of discovery.

The bearded old tramp was sleeping soundly. He had newspapers wrapped around his legs and, beside him, a number of bottles of fortified wine lay strewn in the doorway. They were all empty. William decided to make the old guy's day. He knelt down and carefully placed two fifty-pound notes in the old man's hand. He didn't stir at all. William grinned imagining the glee when he awoke to discover this surprise windfall.

The only problem now was that the old tramp might not waken for ages. William would have to be patient. After fifteen minutes, William's patience had already run out. He had to know the answer to his question. From a discreet distance, he started tossing pebbles from a nearby flowerbed at the tramp. He was a truly rotten shot and the first three missed by a big margin. Finally, the fourth pebble, which was by far the largest, hit the old tramp in the ear hole.

"Aw fuck!" He woke up with a start. "For fuck sake what was that?" He sat up and looked around him with a glazed expression. He was momentarily disorientated and confused. Eventually he started to settle down to sleep again. Just then, he realised there was something in his hand. From his slumped position, he stared at it in disbelief.

William was crouched behind a hedge and out of sight. He could hear the excited cries of the old tramp though. Like Lazarus, he had risen up from the dead and was dancing about and shouting.

"Yoooh! Praise the Lord. Thank you Jesus! Thank you! Thank you!"

It wasn't long before he had collected up the most valuable of his belongings and was ready to head off. William had a pretty shrewd idea as to what the first port of call would be. Sure enough, he was straight round to the off licence. William followed him inside the shop. He pretended to be browsing the shelves where all the up-market wine was.

The tramp lifted three bottles of a well-known fortified wine and staggered with them to the check out. The girl on the till eyed the old man with suspicion. He'd been in the shop many times before and often did not have the wherewithal to purchase his selections.

"Now Mr. Browne, do you really want three bottles of that. It's very strong you know." she said to him in a patronising tone.

"Yes! Three bottles! I'd buy more but that's all I can carry."

"Are you sure you can afford three bottles?"

The old man reached deep into the pocket of his filthy coat and after much searching about, he produced one of the fifty-pound notes. He slapped it down on the counter with a loud and triumphant thump!

"There you are my dear. I think that will cover it, don't you?"

The shop assistant's eyes bulged when she saw the fifty-pound note. This old critter usually turned out pocket after pocket full of coins to pay for anything. He seldom produced notes of any denomination, let alone a fifty!

She lifted the note warily and immediately reached for her felt tip-testing pen. She marked the note and held it under a little light under the counter. Just to be sure, she held it up to the light and looked for the watermark.

"What's wrong?" slurred the tramp. "My money's as good as any body else's!"

"You're quite right, of course it is." With that she opened the till and counted out change to the old man. William noticed the fifty disappeared into a security slot of some sort. The shop assistant saw William was watching and grinned.

"Can't be too careful these days. Lots of forgeries around! What can I do for you?"

William asked her if they stocked an obscure make of vodka. He knew they didn't before he asked. When she informed him that they didn't have any, he politely thanked her and promptly left.

He continued to follow the old tramp at a discreet distance. It wasn't long before he found his way into a local express style supermarket. He went up to the counter and ordered a hundred cigarettes. To William's delight, he used the other fifty-pound note to make his purchase. The man on the till checked the note very carefully before politely giving the old boy his cigarettes and change.

"Wow!" said William to himself. He was elated. The money had now undergone scrutiny in two places and neither had raised any alarm nor indeed even an eyebrow! This was great, but he would need one more test before he would be convinced that all was o.k.

13.

Shorty thought Oscar particularly restless to-day. He was pacing up and down the office. He glanced over at Geordie who was sitting at the next desk. Geordie was anxiously watching Oscar also. The girls in the office had just gone home for the day, so they were all alone.

"Right." Oscar addressed them. "Mr Cartwright and I have been thinking over what you guys told us yesterday. The way we see it, it must have been the cyclist that found the money. He almost certainly made off with it on his bicycle. At first, we thought it would be like looking for a needle in a haystack, but we think we can narrow the odds a bit by being clever!" He grinned maliciously at the two boys.

"What do you mean?" asked Geordie.

"Well, firstly, people who use that cycle path tend to do so on a regular basis. We reckon whoever lifted the money will probably be out cycling along it again. People are often creatures of habit. Take you Shorty." Oscar looked directly at Shorty.

"Every Saturday, at about one o'clock on the button, you're over to the bookies to place a wee bet on the gee gees. And you Geordie, every Friday night without fail, you're into Donovan's bar for a few pints."

"You're right Oscar. It's true," agreed Shorty.

"I think the cyclist who stole our money will return to the scene of the crime, so to speak. He will know that it's a very stupid move to make, but he'll do it anyway. He'll know that its risky, but he'll do it because he's a creature of habit and won't be able to help himself."

"I can see that it's possible Oscar, but loads of people use the cycle track and how will we know it's the right guy?" asked Geordie looking somewhat dubious.

"We're going to set a trap for him! Did you ever here that curiosity killed the cat?"

"Yes." Shorty replied. "Everyone's heard that one before."

"Well, that's what we are going to do. He'll probably be out cycling along the path on the same day of the week, at around the same time. From now on, we will be staking out that part of the cycle path on a regular basis. It may be that he doesn't come back for some days, maybe even a week or two, but he'll come back eventually."

Just at that there was a knock at the door.

"We're closed," barked Oscar. He was obviously annoyed at his briefing being interrupted.

"Its only me!" It was a boy's voice.

"Must be Cecil." said Geordie. "The boss had him cleaning and polishing his Mercedes." Cecil was Cartwright's sixteen-year-old nephew. He often came down to the yard after school to do odd jobs for his uncle.

"Come in." Oscar's voice was more tolerant now.

The boy came in. He was of a slight build and, if anything, looked younger than his sixteen years. His hair was all spiky and had blonde streaks in it, as was the fashion of the day.

"I've finished cleaning the car." he announced smiling.

"Well go into the kitchen like a good boy and make us three cups of tea, and one for yourself too. Close the door after you." Oscar instructed.

The boy walked across the office and into the kitchen. Obediently, he closed the door after him and Oscar continued.

"You guys will watch the cycle track every evening from around six until eight o'clock. From what you told me, Geordie, it was around seven when you and Shorty killed the badger and nearly crashed."

"And lost my bloody money!" It was the Fatman. He had emerged from his upstairs office and was coming down the open staircase into the general office. Immediately, the whole atmosphere changed. Up to now the meeting had been conducted in a reasonably relaxed manner, but now there was the ominous presence of this man. Everyone was instantly on edge.

"You'll take it in turns to stake out the cycle path and watch for this creep." Oscar instructed. "Hopefully he'll be wearing a yellow coat."

"What if we see someone suspicious?" Shorty nervously asked.

"Then you follow along after him on your bicycle," the Fatman interjected.

"How will we know it's him?" asked Geordie. "There are loads of cyclists."

Oscar grinned evilly. "We bait him! We will leave a big black bin bag lying on the track exactly where he found the money. It will not contain any money of course. But our man will have to have a look at it won't he?"

"What do you mean?" Geordie looked puzzled.

"The bugger will do a second take when he sees the bag. He'll have to go and have a peep inside. When he opens it up, it will be stuffed full of old newspaper all cut up in bundles to look like money. On top, he'll find a note, which will say 'You're a dead man if you don't give it all back!' He'll near shit himself and run away like a scalded cat! That sort of reaction will let us know we've found him!"

At that the kitchen door burst open and Cecil appeared with mugs of tea on a tray. He walked very slowly forward as if he was afraid of spilling any.

"Look at the floor of my office you stupid boy!" the Fatman suddenly yelled at Cecil. "Its all covered in mud off your dirty boots!

Cecil looked down at his shiny D.M. lace up boots. Although they were nicely polished, the bottom inch or so was caked in muck. He had left a trail of muddy footprints on the floor when he came in.

"Sorry uncle." the boy said. "The yard is very muddy outside. I've finished washing your car. It looks great!"

The Fat man was over to the boy in an instant. He had flown into one of his rages! He slapped the boy hard in the face. Instantly, blood trickled out of Cecil's nose and ran down his chin.

"Look at my bloody floor!" roared the Fatman. "Take those dirty boots off now before you take another step!"

"But uncle!" the boy started to protest, tears coming to his eyes. "Take them off now!"

The boy set the tray down on a desk and started to unlace his boots. Unhappily he slipped them off revealing that he was wearing bright pink socks. Aware that the men were all staring at him, he started to blush in embarrassment.

"What the fuck colour of socks are those?" shouted the Fatman. "Did you go to school wearing those?"

"Yes." stammered the boy between tears.

"Looks like something a poof would wear!" the Fatman added in disgust. The boy was doing a full roast now, his cheeks bright red.

"Leave the boy alone." Said Oscar. "The kids all do that sort of thing these days."

The Fatman glared at Oscar. He was not the sort of man who took kindly to any dissent amongst the ranks.

"You mind your own bloody business!" he snapped at Oscar.

Geordie and Shorty were shocked. Normally, the Fatman and Oscar saw pretty much eye to eye. This was highly unusual.

"I just think you're being a bit hard on the boy, that's all." said Oscar handing the lad a tissue from a box that one of the office girls had left on her desk. "Here, wipe the blood off your face."

"Thanks Uncle Oscar," he sobbed.

"Cecil, pick up your boots, son, and bugger off home!" ordered the Fatman.

The boy needed no further encouragement. Sobbing, he gathered up his boots and, holding the tissue to his nose, he hurriedly left.

For a few moments there was a very long, awkward silence. Then, Oscar continued almost as though nothing had happened.

"So that's what we're going to do. You guys will watch the cycle track every evening from now on until further notice. I'll make up the bag and the note for you. It will be ready for you in the morning."

Then, totally ignoring the Fatman, Oscar walked out. With an enormous crash, he slammed the outside door behind him. The glass in the door cracked with the impact.

The Fatman, with a slightly puzzled expression on his face, stared after him. Without a word, he turned and, somewhat painfully, heaved his huge weight back up the office stairs. Geordie and Shorty listened as the stairs creaked under the great strain they were being subjected to.

Outside they could hear Oscar's car engine start up. There was a screech of tyres and he was gone.

"Let's get the hell out of here." Shorty said.

"Motion carried." replied Geordie.

14.

Sylvia was upstairs in her bedroom. She looked carefully through the window blinds. Outside, it was a cloudy day but with no rain. Everything looked perfectly normal with the usual light traffic of cars and very little commercial traffic passing by. This was a quiet suburb of the city after all. After ten minutes or so, she was absolutely convinced no one was watching the house.

She went downstairs and opened up the box of chocolates the Fatman had brought her. Inside, as expected, there were two bags of white powder. It was uncut cocaine. She sealed up the box again and carefully placed it inside a supermarket shopping bag. As an extra precaution, she double bagged it.

Several minutes later, a man emerged from the rear door of Sylvia's house. He walked across the small lawn and unlocked a wooden door in the rear fence. Stepping through the door, he pushed his way through a dense overgrown hedge and bushes, relocking the door behind him. The casual observer would never even find the door.

He set off across a small field. Just beyond him, there was an ancient burial mound about forty feet high. Trees grew upon it and all around it. It provided great cover for this sort of thing. The man skirted the mound and left via a small pedestrian passageway. There, in a quiet street, he unlocked a Volkswagen car and drove off.

As he drove he made a short call using a hands-free bluetooth built-in phone kit. He had recently had this installed in the car. Grinning he thought to himself, *Can't have the police stopping me for talking on the phone now, can we?*

"I'm on my way now. Be with you in about fifteen minutes."

"How will I know it's you?" The voice had a slight Irish brogue to it.

"I'm in a black GTi Golf. I'll be in the car park. I'll open the bonnet and look in as if there is something wrong with the engine."

"O.K. see you there."

The black Volkswagen pulled into the small, secluded car park. It was a beauty spot at weekends, but mid-week, at this time of year, hardly anyone came here.

The man popped the bonnet catch and jumped out. He was dressed in fairly tight black jeans and wore a black quilted coat. He opened the bonnet and stared inside at the engine.

"Are you havin' a spot of bother?" The voice was Irish.

"What if I am?"

"Just thought I might be able to help you like." The Irishman was wearing a heavy green outdoor coat. It looked far too baggy for such a small man.

"Do you know anything about fuel injection?" asked the owner of the Volkswagen.

"Well, just that this might improve things a little." A parcel fell out of the Irishman's inside coat pocket and landed on top of the engine.

There was already a large box of chocolates sitting there.

"Better lift those quick or they might start to melt." The Volkswagen driver was wearily looking around the car park to check no one was watching.

The Irishman looked inside the chocolate box and smiled. "Jaysus! Now, that's just what the doctor ordered!"

The Volkswagen driver had opened the parcel and thumbed through the tightly packed euro notes. They were all hundreds as requested. That way, it kept down the bulk of the parcel. He nodded his approval and stuffed the parcel inside his coat.

"I believe that's solved your problem," said the Irishman.

"I'll try her and see if she starts. Maybe see you again sometime?"

"You never know." The Irishman was walking away in the direction of a dark coloured estate car.

Seconds later, the Volkswagen had started up and was driving away.

15.

Oscar drove out of the scrap yard. The Fatman had really annoyed him. He couldn't understand the cruelty of it. Why did the old bastard need to beat the hell out of the wee boy?

Once he was round the corner, he stopped his car for a moment or two to cool off and think things over. It didn't take him long to come to a conclusion though, and soon he was off again. Outside the rain had started. The automatic wiper on his Mercedes coupe began to sweep across the screen. Moments later, the skies absolutely opened and the rain became torrential. The wipers increased their frequency to an almost frantic tempo in an effort to clear the rain from the screen.

It wasn't long before Oscar found what he was looking for. There in the growing gloom of the wet evening was a sorry looking figure walking wearily along the footpath. It was Cecil. He was soaked to the skin by the unexpectedly heavy rain. It had further compounded the misery of events earlier that afternoon for the boy. He'd come home from school, changed quickly into his jeans and old T-shirt and rushed off down to the scrap yard. He'd washed and polished his uncle's car as well as he possibly could and all he'd got was a thumping and a bloody nose for his troubles.

"Cecil! Cecil!" Oscar stopped the car and shouted through the driving rain.

"Come over here and I'll give you a lift home, before you catch your death."

The boy ran across the road and jumped into the passenger seat.

"Thanks Uncle Oscar."

"You don't need to call me 'uncle' Oscar any more lad. You're nearly grown up now, so just call me Oscar."

"O.K. Oscar." The boy smiled back at him. "Thanks for the lift. It's fairly chucking it down out there."

Oscar glanced at the pale face beside him in the passenger seat as he drove off. The boy was shivering with cold.

"You look frozen wee man. Switch the electric heated seat on." Oscar pointed at a switch on the centre consul. "That'll soon warm you up."

"Thanks." Cecil pushed the switch. Soon, he could feel a most welcome warmth radiating through his buttocks and back. The soft black leather seats of the car were really comfortable. He started to relax and feel good.

"This is a really cool car . . . . Oscar!"

"Yes, I must say I'm very pleased with it."

"My mum's old car is a piece of crap compared to this."

"Well I'm very lucky. The scrap yard is making lots of money at the moment so I was able to buy this little beauty." beamed Oscar.

"One day, maybe I'll be lucky enough to own a car like this, but right now it seems a long way off. I was hoping to quit school and go to work for my uncle next summer. After what happened this afternoon, I reckon I'll be in his bad books for a good while." The boy looked very glum.

"Oh, I wouldn't worry about it too much Cecil. He's not been in a good mood lately. Something happened to annoy him and that has made him much more angry than usual."

"What happened?" Cecil asked naively.

"Sorry, it's a bit private and I can't tell you. Its nothing that you need to worry about though."

"Oh. Sorry. Didn't mean to pry."

"That's O.K. lad." Oscar comforted him. "Tell you what, when he cheers up a bit, and is in a good mood, I'll ask him if he'll give you a job next summer. I'll make a case that we could do with the extra help. That all assumes that we continue to be busy though."

"Would you do that Oscar? Would you really ask him!" The boy was bursting with enthusiasm at the prospect.

"You can count on it. That's a promise."

"Thank you Oscar! That would be really sweet!"

"Right now though, we need to get you out of those wet clothes. Is your mum at home?"

"No, she's out at work this evening. She won't be back until about nine."

As casually as he could, Oscar asked the question.

"How would you feel about coming back to my place for a while? You can dry off and I'll order a carry out Chinese or a Pizza or something. I'll leave you over home in time for your mum coming back home."

"Wow, sounds great to me Uncle Oscar! Sorry Oscar, he corrected himself."

16.

It was morning again at number 32 King's Wood Park. Julia was ready to set off for work at the supermarket.

"Please go to the job centre to-day William, will you?" she asked as she went out the door. "And dinner is at six sharp. This is my gym night remember?"

"No problem love, have a nice day!" It was as insincere as an American waiter's parting comment.

"Oh and fuck you very much too!" Julia caught the mood instantly. Again, she slammed the outside door behind her.

It wasn't long before he heard the engine of her little car fire up and then she was gone. Good, thought William to himself. Now I can get on with things.

He was starting to gather all sorts of bits and pieces into a file box. Chiefly, there was a document he had printed out on his computer. It was titled "The Master Plan." He needed to get rid of Julia out of his life. He now realised he didn't love her anymore, and probably never would again. He was also pretty certain that the feeling was mutual. Nothing that had happened in recent weeks could convince him otherwise.

He needed to get a divorce from her. Short of that, it had actually crossed his mind that he might have to do her in. He didn't favour this idea at all though. It would only be done as an absolute last resort. He wasn't sure that his conscience could handle such an action. No, no he thought to himself, I could never do that. It would have to be a divorce. He decided that he would ask her for a divorce in the very near future. He wrote it down on his Master Plan.

After he was separated from her, he would need somewhere else to live. He reckoned that a small, modest apartment or cottage would probably be best. He didn't want to have too high a profile for a long while. He really needed any trail to the money to go stone cold before he started spending it in a big way.

Having said all that, he had also decided that to-day was going to be a big day. He was going to try to spend some of the money and to hell with the consequences. The experiment with the tramp had worked well, so he figured the money probably was genuine and unmarked. In the final analysis, though, there was really only one way to find out. He caught a bus into town and made his way into the recently opened Prince Albert shopping centre. This was where all the best shops in Belfast were located. In his inside pocket, he had an envelope full of both hundred and fifty-pound notes. There was a total of some two thousand pounds in his pocket.

William sat down in a small café and ordered a Cappuccino coffee. He had tendered a fiver in payment. This was not part of his newly acquired stash. Outside, across the mall, he could see the shop where he would either begin or end his new life. The shop was brightly lit and smartly fitted out with nice modern tables. The tables were covered in computers and computing equipment. This was a new Applestore. William just had to buy an iPad. He'd wanted one for months now and this was an ideal opportunity to test out the money once and for all. It was do or die!

Bracing himself, he walked over and into the shop. He tried to act as calmly as possible. Inwardly, he was a complete jangle of nerves! Ten minutes later, there could be police cars everywhere. Sirens would be sounding. Blue lights flashing! He could be led away in handcuffs! Tried in court! Sent to prison! His stomach churned.

Eventually he gathered himself. A polite geeky looking young man, little more than a boy, introduced himself as "Todd." And asked if he could be of any help. William enquired about the iPad and soon selected a model, which he could use with his home Wi-Fi.

"I'll take this one please."

"That will be four ninety-nine please sir." said Todd. "How would you like to pay?"

"Cash." replied William with all the authority he could muster.

"No problem sir."

William counted out five one hundred pound notes and handed over the cash. Todd wandered off somewhere into the bowels of the shop. It was an anxious wait. Todd seemed to be gone forever. William was getting worried. He considered doing a runner as panic was starting to set in. He turned round to make for the door out into the mall.

"Mr. Forsythe" It was Todd back again. "Here's your new iPad! If you've got a few minutes, I'll go through the registration process with you?"

"Oh, yeah, that would be good." lied William who was practically shitting himself by now. Somehow, he was able to sit and listen as the young man politely and painstakingly went through all sorts of details about his new purchase. They registered the iPad with Apple and eventually, after what had seemed an eternity, Todd said.

"O.K. You're good to go. Enjoy your new iPad. Have a nice day!"

"You too Todd. Thank you!" William had at last lightened up. Relief was flooding into him. This was going to be all right. The money was O.K. to spend!

As he walked down the mall two police officers were suddenly coming towards him. 'Oh my God' he thought to himself. This is it. I'm going to jail. Somehow he managed to keep calm. The officers were now running towards him with their faces set hard. He was just about to give himself up to them when they ran past him one on either side. They ran just another ten feet and grabbed hold of a man.

"We are arresting you on suspicion of shoplifting." he heard them say. "You don't have to say anything, but anything you do say may be taken down and used in evidence." The caution continued.

William couldn't believe it. '*Wow!*' he thought, *that was a close one. That was lucky.* He walked calmly away and started back for the bus to go home. He was delighted with his new iPad, but the whole experience had taken a lot out of him.

He thought to himself that he would get used to it in due course. Near home, he went into his bank. When he got to the till, he produced the payslip for his credit card. He paid in the remaining fifteen hundred pounds against his outstanding balance. That would give him some low-key spending power. The bank teller never raised an eyebrow. Afterwards he was elated. All tests had been passed!

17.

The meeting was being held in a conference room at the P.S.N.I. headquarters on the Knock road in Belfast. Detective Superintendent Dobson was addressing the assembled Drug Squad detectives. It was progress report time.

"O.K. That brings us all up to date on the Johnston case so let's move on swiftly to our final subject." She paused to read a note on her schedule sitting on the lectern in front of her.

"Ah yes, the surveillance operation at Cartwright's scrap yard." She lowered her thin gold-rimmed glasses just a tad and stared over the top them. It was a mannerism many of her staff were well used to. It was, as they would say in poker, her 'tell.' It usually meant some one was in for a severe grilling!

"Sergeant Henderson. Where are you?" She peered around the auditorium.

"Over here." He stuck his hand up. He was hiding near the back.

"What progress have you and your team made with this?"

"Well, to be honest, not a lot really. We've been watching Cartwright's outfit very carefully. His telephones have been tapped and we've followed him about when he drives anywhere. So far though, zippo."

"Zippo?' questioned Dobson. "What's that supposed to mean?" Her voice was impatient.

"Nothing. It means we have absolutely nothing."

"Then just say nothing! This isn't a game sergeant. People die when thugs like these get away with supplying drugs to youngsters etc. Lives are destroyed so you'll just forgive me when I tell you, 'zippo' doesn't quite cut it!"

Her voice had increased in volume during this last discourse. Her broad Yorkshire accent assuring one and all that she didn't tolerate fools gladly. She continued:

"It's not good enough Henderson!" She looked threateningly over the thin-rimmed glasses at him.

"We have been conducting the investigation in a regular and thorough manner. So far, Cartwright hasn't done anything out of the ordinary. Are we confident about the source of information on this one?" Henderson queried.

"The answer to your question Henderson is that, yes, we are very confident!" She paused wiping some speck off her glasses with a soft cloth. There was dead silence in the room.

"So you're saying you have absolutely nothing further to tell me?"

"I'm afraid that's right."

There was a protracted pause terminating only with a look of severe disapproval directed solely at Henderson.

"O.K. folks, we'll break it up here," she announced. "You can go now."

Instantly, people were rising from their seats, scraping them occasionally on the parquet floor. A general murmur had set in.

"All except for Henderson and Butler that is. I would like to see you two in my office. Immediately please."

A chuckle or two came from some of the other detectives as they scurried off unscathed.

"You two are bloody well for it now! Headmistress has her cane out for you!" One of them joked as he passed by.

18.

Oscar parked his Mercedes in the underground car park of his apartment building. He ushered a still dripping Cecil into the lift. Cecil stood in silence as Oscar inserted a special key into a slot on the control panel of the lift. He pressed a button, and with a slight whirr, the car started to rise rapidly.

"What floor do you live on?" asked Cecil.

"Top floor."

"Wow! The penthouse!" Cecil was obviously well impressed.

The lift made a muted 'ding' sound and the doors slid open. There was a small vestibule with the front door of the penthouse opposite.

"Gee. Imagine having the whole top floor to yourself!" Cecil enthused.

"Well, there are actually two penthouses on this level. They're back to back as it were, so you never actually see anyone. It's as good as having it all to myself though.

As he unlocked the front door, Oscar said:

"I don't wish to sound like your uncle Cecil, but would you please take off the muddy boots before going inside?"

When Cecil looked at Oscar he was smiling broadly.

"Of course I will."

The boy dutifully unlaced his DM boots and set them to one side of the door. Oscar set an old newspaper under them to absorb any water that might otherwise mark the white marble tiles.

Cecil wandered into the penthouse apartment. It was amazing. Oscar gave him the tour. The penthouse was well over two thousand square feet. There were three large bedrooms each with en suite bathrooms. The master bedroom was the largest and most luxurious sporting a Jacuzzi in its en suite. The main living area was open plan with a kitchen bar separating the kitchen and lounge. There was a huge black leather suite sitting on a polished wood floor. Oscar picked up a remote control and pressed a button on it. An attractive life-like gas log fire crackled into life. It made a good vocal point in the room. It was only surpassed by the simply enormous flat screen television above it, which Oscar also switched on with a further click on the remote.

"Oh my God!" was all Cecil could utter quietly. He'd never seen such opulence before in his life.

"Uncle Oscar, this is absolutely fantastic! It is so cool!"

"Glad you like it Cecil. Better go and change out of those wet clothes though. There's a bathroom in there in the guest room. Take your wet clothes off you and put them in this basket. We'll bung them in the tumble drier. You could take a warm shower and that will put some heat back in your bones."

"Good idea." Cecil went into the bathroom.

"I'll leave you a towel and dressing gown hanging on the door. I'm going to order the Chinese, what would you like?"

"Sweet and sour chicken and rice would be great."

"Sweet and sour it is then."

Oscar picked up the telephone and ordered the carryout. He could hear the shower running when he finished. He opened the bathroom door and removed the boy's wet clothes from the floor. In a moment or two, he would put them all into the tumble drier. Now, though, he couldn't help but look through the shower door. Despite the mist, he could make out the naked body of Cecil. The slim figure was humming contentedly to himself, unaware of any attention he was drawing. Oscar watched for a few moments and then went off with the clothes.

Twenty minutes later, Cecil, wearing a thick towel dressing gown was sitting on the settee eating his Chinese off a tray. Oscar was sitting beside him. The gas log fire was at full tilt and the television was on.

For a while, both of them were lost totally from the world watching Arsenal play Manchester United. To Cecil's delight, Arsenal won two one. He was an Arsenal fan and didn't much like Man United!

All in all, it had turned out a much better end to the day than Cecil had thought it would. Oscar stopped outside the house where Cecil lived with his mother and momentarily put his arm around the boy's shoulders.

"I know it's been tough for you son, losing your father when you were only thirteen. Even though your uncle is hard on you sometimes, he does like you. He thinks the world of you. We all do, down at the scrap yard. If you ever need anything, all you have to do is ask. If you ever need help just ring me." With that he handed Cecil a business card with his mobile number on it.

The young lad smiled and carefully put the card inside a red fabric wallet he carried everywhere with him. Oscar heard the Velcro rasp as he opened it up.

"Here." Oscar opened his own wallet and handed the lad twenty pounds.

"What's that for?" The boy had a very puzzled look on his face.

"That's for cleaning your Uncle Cartwright's car for him. He never paid you. Don't worry; I'll make sure I get it back off him again. Now go on away into the house and tell your mother I said hello."

"Thanks Oscar. That's been really good of you. Thanks very much!" The boy smiled widely.

"Away you go!" Oscar wound up the window of the Mercedes and drove off.

19.

Detective Superintendent Dobson's office was immaculate inside. It was a larger office than most people would imagine. On television, it often looks like such people work in an office the size of a budgie cage, but not this one. The office had, as usual, a desk and chair and filing cabinets, but also a small conference table with several chairs around it for meetings. Large wall-mounted notice boards were covered in cuttings, pictures and notes relating to cases under investigation. This was her 'Ops' room!

Roberta Dobson had been born in Scarborough, North Yorkshire. She had been fortunate enough to grow up close to the seaside and was often able to play on the beach on the few fine sunny days that you get in that part of the country. Those had been far off carefree days. It had been a happy childhood. Happy that was until her younger brother had started using heroine during his first year at university.

John Dobson had led a fairly sheltered life. He had always lived in the shadow of his brighter and more athletically proficient older sister.

Once away from home for the first time at university, he had most unfortunately fallen in with a bad lot. John had been a good person. He had been the best younger brother any girl could ask for. Sadly, he had died of a drug overdose during his first term at university. The relatively well to do, salt of the earth, decent family were devastated. Roberta was in tears for weeks. Some said she never really got over the loss of her brother.

Now, miles and years away from the happy days of her childhood, she had settled in Northern Ireland. After graduating with a first in English at the University of York, she'd met Paul a really nice Ulsterman during a holiday in Majorca. They had had a whirlwind romance and she had ended up living with him in Northern Ireland. He was a policeman at that time serving with the Royal Ulster Constabulary. Two weeks before their planned wedding, disaster struck again. A stray bullet had killed Paul when some IRA terrorists had opened fire on a routine roadblock.

Roberta had been left completely numb after the funeral. At first, her parents had strongly advised her to come home to Scarborough. They were worried about her safety. But by then Roberta had already begun her own training with the Royal Ulster Constabulary. She had formed good friendships and discovered that she enjoyed living in Northern Ireland. For reasons that she couldn't quite put a finger on, after much soul searching, she decided to stay and finish her training.

After her graduation, she had rapidly risen within the ranks as she was so intelligent and indeed dedicated to her work. She now worked in the drug squad. A picture of her younger brother John, in a small silver frame, always sat on one corner of her desk. Many asked about him, but she just told them he had died before his time due to an unfortunate tragedy. She never elaborated on that story. The pain was too deep still. It was, however, this pain that drove her. It was this awful, terrible pain that motivated her in her work. At catching people involved in the trafficking of drugs, she was an absolute zealot!

She was tidying some papers away into a file when there was a knock on her door.

"Come in." The door opened. "Ah! It's you two. Have a seat over at the table. I'll be with you in just a moment."

Uneasily, D.S. Henderson and D.C Butler settled themselves at the table. There was a large scale map set on it. They could clearly see that it showed the location of Cartwright's scrap yard and the surrounding dockland area. The two pored over the map whilst they were waiting.

It wasn't long before D.I. Dobson joined them.

"Well, what do you two have to say for yourselves?" she peered at them over the trademark gold rimmed glasses. The distinctive Yorkshire accent, which she retained, added a certain piquancy to the enquiry.

"As we said earlier in the conference room, we haven't really got very far with this." D.S. Henderson answered.

"There must be something? You've been observing these guys for nearly two weeks now. You must have seen something unusual surely?"

"Just that Cartwright has a fancy woman living in a house up in East Belfast. He goes up there to see her, regular as clockwork, once a week."

"Really. What's the address?"

Butler pulled a notebook out of his pocket and flicked through it. "It's 37 Sandown Park East."

"What's the post code there? Do you know?

"It would start with BT5, but I don't know the rest of it."

D.I. Dobson pressed a button on her intercom desk telephone.

"Samantha, could you please check ownership on a domestic property at 37 Sandown Park East. Yeah. It's BT5. Thanks."

"What else is going on, anything out of the ordinary?"

Henderson described Cartwright's scrap business. "Lorry loads arrive regularly with scrap cars and engine parts etc on them. The cars are then dismantled and any useful parts kept to be sold on to the motor trade. The rest of the vehicles are then stripped and sorted into different types of metal and this is presumably sold as scrap metal.

"What do you mean by scrap metal?" Dobson enquired.

"Well, the old batteries are lead, the wiring looms are copper and sometimes certain parts are aluminium or even magnesium. They also recover platinum from the catalytic converter in the exhaust. The rest of the car, apart from glass and rubber, is usually steel. All the steel is crushed and shredded in a machine and then dumped on a piece of ground at one end of the yard. Eventually, when they have enough, they sell it. One lot about three months ago went onto a boat to go to China."

"That's all very interesting. At least you now know how a scrap metal business runs, even if you know bugger all about the drugs."

The intercom phone buzzed.

"Go ahead Samantha."

"The house is leased to a Mr James Cartwright. His own address is a farm at 107a Drumcarn Road, about eight miles south of Belfast in County Down."

"That's great Samantha. Thank you." She switched the intercom off.

"So, Cartwright is paying the rent on that house. What do we know about his fancy woman?"

"Not very much I'm afraid," answered Butler. "We just know she is called Sylvia Browne. She's a blonde and looks quite attractive from a distance. In fact D.S. Henderson here is developing quite a crush on her!"

"That's enough Butler!" Henderson said disapprovingly.

Despite herself, Roberta Dobson laughed out loud.

"That's rich that is, two eggs in a cup would be more appropriate for an old crumbly like you sergeant!"

"Gee thanks." Henderson said. "It's great to know everyone has such a high opinion of me."

"Right. Lets move on." Dobson was serious again. "We have it on good authority that Cartwright and his gang are trafficking drugs. They are probably receiving their supply from somewhere in the dockland area. As you know, the Harbour Police are very good and security is fairly tight, but always some drugs will find their way into the country. We have to find that source of supply. I have another team working on that one.

What you have to do is figure out how the drugs are arriving with Cartwright, and how he's actually distributing them. It may be they leave his premises in some of these parts he's selling. We need as much information as possible so that I can get a search warrant organised to check him out thoroughly. So go away now, out of my sight, and try a bit harder will you!"

Henderson and Butler got up to leave.

"Don't dare come back here with nothing again!" was her parting comment as they left.

After they were gone, she found herself staring at the small portrait of her lost brother. He had been about seventeen when it was taken. From the silver frame, he smiled at her. Sometimes, when she was alone, she did this. She just stared for minutes on end at the picture. It seemed to imbue her with some strange power of insight she didn't entirely understand. As she gazed at it, a thought slowly started to form in her mind.

There's something wrong here. Something just does not add up! The source of information regarding Cartwright was impeccable. Why were Henderson and Butler finding nothing? Something was definitely wrong with this picture!

She mulled it over for a while before deciding the best thing to do was to let the pot stew for a while. Eventually, whatever it was would come to the surface!

20.

Julia had arrived home from work. She didn't see the new iPad as William had taken great pains to hide it from her. He knew that, if she saw it, she would not only go ballistic, but there would be a court of enquiry to discover where he had got the money to buy it.

She hurriedly made dinner, which turned out to be cheese, bacon and tomato on toast with a bit of salad. Even when flooded with tomato sauce, it wasn't a memorable culinary experience as far as William was concerned. Apart from the meal, his digestion wasn't encouraged when Julia asked him about the job centre. Of course he hadn't been near it. This declaration started her off moaning and indeed shouting again. Happily, it wasn't long before she departed, as previously promised, for the gym. William was very well pleased to see the back of her.

After arriving back from his foray into town, William had again checked the newspaper for any news on a robbery. He'd been doing this since he had found the money. His concern had long been that the money he'd found was stolen. Perhaps the police were looking for it?

He used his newly acquired iPad to surf the Internet and look for any articles on a recent robbery anywhere in Northern Ireland. He could find nothing beyond the usual petty burglaries and robberies of a grocery store and a post office holdup. It increasingly looked like the money had not been stolen. It also appeared not to be marked and it obviously wasn't counterfeit either. The bank teller he'd lodged the money with earlier would certainly have noticed if it had been forged.

All in all, he was at last beginning to believe that this was real money that he could spend! He'd at last spent some of it today. This money would change his life. He was no longer a poor person. In recent months, before he found the bag of money, he had been extremely depressed. One very wet Tuesday morning, it had been so bad that he had briefly contemplated doing himself in. Two credit card bills had arrived that day. He was well overspent on both of them, and was worrying about how he would ever pay off the balances. The electricity bill and the rates were also both due that month. He was running out of savings and his financial prospects were looking increasingly grim. The worry of it all was dragging him down.

William had started to plan the whole final chapter of his life that day. There was a gas heater in the garage. He would go down to the off licence and purchase one of those large litre bottles of vodka and the best cigar he could find. He'd then take a comfortable chair out into the garage. Then, whilst enjoying the vodka he'd eat a few bags of crisps. The portable gas heater would keep him cosy. Once suitably anaesthetised by the vodka, the heater would be switched off and allowed to cool. He'd then switch it on again. That would allow the gas from the cylinder to leak out for as long as he could stick the smell.

At that stage, he would take out the cigar and light up! BANG! That would be it all over. He reckoned that if he had enough vodka, and allowed plenty of gas to build up in the garage, he probably wouldn't know all that much about it. Poof! Gone! Just like that!

Now, of course, things had all changed entirely. He had the money. Over a million pounds in notes and it was all his! That witch wife of his wasn't going to get a penny of it!

He was thinking about his darling wife as he went upstairs to change. He would take his bike out for a quick spin. Now that he was so unbelievably wealthy, he would have to keep himself fit. He needed to stay healthy so that he could enjoy the money!

He was just pulling on his tracksuit bottoms when he noticed something odd. Julia's training shoes were sitting on the floor at her side of the bed. She had gone off to the gym and left them there.

Now, he happened to know that these were currently the only trainers she had. There was a very old pair in the wardrobe she sometimes used for gardening, but, when he looked, they were still there.

"Now that is really very interesting indeed!" he grinned to himself.

21.

A telephone was ringing somewhere in the Fatman's office. At first, he was puzzled by it; not recognising the ring tone. Then, he realised it was the unregistered phone the detective informant had given him in the envelope. This phone could not be tapped or traced.

He reached into the desk drawer and grabbed it.

"Hello."

"Its me. We have to meet. Its urgent!"

"O.K. when and where?" asked the Fatman.

"Look at the note in the envelope. Use location 'A'. Can you be there in an hour?"

The Fatman looked at his watch. "Is this really necessary?"

"Yes."

"Right. See you there in one hour."

"Make very sure you are not followed!"

"I will."

The phone went dead. For a moment the Fatman stared at it, his mind momentarily blank. Then his brain kicked into gear. What was this all about? Why the urgency?

"Oscar", he shouted down the stairs to the general office.

"Yes boss, what is it?'

Oscar was climbing the stairs to the Fatman's office. Once he was within whispering distance the Fatman continued in a very quiet voice.

"Our friend has been in touch. I have to go and meet him."

Both men looked carefully through the venetian blinds of the office. Across the road a dark coloured Vauxhall car was parked in the shadow of a deserted warehouse.

"I can't have those boys see me leave, so here's what we'll do."

A few minutes later, Geordie reversed a small van into the warehouse. Unseen from outside he opened the rear door. The Fatman climbed inside and knelt down out of sight.

Geordie pulled out on to the road and gently drove away. The unregistered phone rang again. It was Oscar.

"That's ok. There was no response from our friends across the street."

"Good. See you later." The Fatman hung up.

Geordie drove the Fatman out to his farm.

"Come back for me here in two hours," ordered the Fatman.

Once Geordie was gone, the Fatman unlocked a garage door. He'd already decided to go in the Porsche. It was near the entrance of the garage. Besides, the Ferrari always attracted too much attention anyway. He unlocked the key box on the garage wall and lifted out the keys.

Moments later, the black 911 turbo was purring down the road. Location 'A,' as scheduled in a note inside his envelope, was some twenty miles away. He put the foot down and soon the Porsche was moving along at a rate of knots. 'Better watch out for the cops!' the Fatman chuckled to himself. He plugged in a dashboard mounted laser detector for police speed traps. 'Don't really want to get caught doing a hundred!'

Despite the undoubted power of the Porsche, the roads were windy and bumpy. It took the Fatman a good half hour to reach his destination. It was a little car park up near Slieve Croob. The mountain itself was an unremarkable one thousand feet high. It did however provide commanding views over the surrounding countryside for many miles in all directions. It was also the source of the river Lagan that eventually reached the sea at Belfast Lough.

Today, however, there would be no lovely view. It was absolutely lashing with rain and a murky mist shrouded the summit of Slieve Croob. Lurking in the drizzly gloom, the Fatman could see there was only one other car in the small car park. It was a dark coloured saloon hiding in the shadow of an old dry stone wall.

As the Porsche came to a halt some yards away, the Fatman could see someone get out of the car and start walking towards him. Despite the remote location, the man was looking all round him in a wary fashion. It was his man O.K.

The informant got into the car and sat in the passenger seat beside him.

"Hello Mr. Cartwright. Terrible day isn't it?"

"Dreadful," agreed the Fatman.

"Sorry to have to bring you all the way up here, but in this game, I think you'll agree it's in both our best interests."

"Yeah," the Fatman sighed. "What is so bloody urgent anyway?"

"I have to warn you, the surveillance operation watching you guys is stepping up a gear or two. I don't know where my top brass are getting their information from, but I'm told it's from an impeccable source."

"Shit. I'd love to know what the 'impeccable source' is. If I can find out who's squealing on us, his frame will fuckin' float, I can tell you."

The Fatman was grim faced. For the first time, at close quarters, the informant could sense the terrible menace latent within this man. He shuddered, as he perceived the malevolent evil that was manifest beside him in the car.

"Are you cold?" the Fatman had noticed the man shivering. "I'll turn on some heat." He adjusted the fan settings on the digital control. "I'd better demist the windows too. Don't want anyone creeping up on us here do we?"

"You need to be very careful. They are watching you closely. They are just waiting for you to make a mistake. Once you do, they'll pounce on you with search warrants and all sorts. I don't know who it is that's providing the information," the detective said quietly.

"Then I suggest you take steps to find out!" The Fatman looked at him menacingly. "What I'm paying you for is information after all. You'd better go away and bloody well get me some!"

"I'm doing my best Mr. Cartwright," the voice sounded frightened now, intimidated by this crook.

"Well it's not good enough!"

There was an uneasy pause in the conversation. The detective felt distinctly uncomfortable. A violent scud of rain hit the windscreen with incredible force. It was misting up again. The Fatman turned up the fan to clear it.

Eventually, the Fatman reached into his inside pocket and produced an envelope full of notes.

"Here," he handed it to the detective. "I'll be careful what we do for a while, but I need you to find out who's squawking on me. Get back to me as soon as possible!" he growled.

At that, despite his vast bulk, he reached across in front of his informant, almost crushing him into the seat in the process. He opened the door of the car. The cold air outside was a severe shock and rain pelted in.

"Get out," said the Fatman gruffly.

The detective did so willingly. The instant he closed the door, the Porsche spun its rear wheels, savagely spitting a hail of small stones at him as it left.

For a moment, he stood stunned, the relentless rain pelting into him and then he made a run for his own car.

22.

William was out for a ride on his bicycle. It had been a while. He hadn't been out on it since he'd found the money that night. He was of a mind to go back to where he'd found the bag of money inside the bin liner.

He pedalled along steadily. It felt good. It was just marvellous to be able to whiz along and be free, out in the fresh air. 'Problem is it rains far too much in this country,' he thought to himself. By now he was only a couple of miles away from where the bridge was. He kept thinking about the money and how it must have been in the skip lorry that nearly fell on top of him that night. He wondered why on earth the bag of money was in a skip lorry anyway. Had someone lost it? Would it have been dumped if it hadn't fallen out down onto the cycle track? Perhaps he'd never know.

Anyway, he had to have a look at where it had all happened. He realised there was a certain amount of danger involved in this. It had taken a great deal of self-discipline since finding the money. Firstly, he hadn't spent much of it. At least he wasn't splashing it all around and drawing attention to himself. Also, he'd resisted the temptation to return to where he'd found it. Now, two weeks had passed since he'd found the rucksack. He reckoned it was probably safe enough to at least ride past without stopping.

Two miles further up the path, Geordie Taylor was hiding in some bushes. He sipped a cup of coffee from a flask he had with him. The coffee tasted rotten. He'd forgotten to put sugar in it, but it tasted horrible anyway. He had a little fold up chair to sit on but, after two hours, he was frozen stiff. This was a miserable job.

"Oscar, its Geordie." He was on his mobile phone. "There's no sign of anyone here again. How much longer do we have to keep up this stupid charade?"

"As long as it takes Geordie. Just stay patient. If it helps any, just picture the scene where you tell the Fatman we've lost his money for good and all leads have been exhausted. Imagine his response to that!"

"Aye, right enough. You're right Oscar."

"If I were you, I'd just sit tight and wait for this bugger. Sooner or later he'll show his ugly mug and then we'll have him!"

"Fair enough. Reckon I can sit an hour longer, even if it is freezing. It will be better than explaining it to the Fatman I suppose."

"Cheerio Geordie." Oscar hung up.

Geordie peered out through the bushes. The black bin bag was in the middle of the path. There was no sign of anyone. It was cold and starting to get dark. He was sure no one would come now.

Meanwhile, William was only a few hundred yards away. He was thinking about Julia. He couldn't get the training shoes out of his mind.

'She isn't going training that's for sure. Not without her training shoes. She's must be getting a work-out elsewhere. She's probably horizontal jogging. I wonder who with?'

At that he had a thought. He brought the bike to a smart halt and pulled out his phone. He spent a few moments searching through the contacts menu and then pressed send.

"Hi James. It's William. Yes, it has been a long time hasn't it? I was wondering if you still have that old Vespa scooter of yours? Could I borrow it for a few days? I'll give you a hundred quid if you lend it to me for a week or so. You're probably not using it much, anyway, in this weather?"

James agreed to the proposal. William arranged to come around and collect it later. He hung up the phone and then stared up the cycle track towards where he could just make out the bridge in the distance. He thought about it for a moment. 'Na, leave it. I'll do it another night. Right now, I'm more interested in what Julia's up to!'

He turned the bike around and pedalled in the direction of home.

23.

The Fatman was at his desk. It hadn't been a particularly good day. Generally drug dealers expect to be making serious money and organising beating the shite out of people who mess with them. He just loved his job!

Today, though, was not one of his better days. Firstly, he'd had to pay out a small fortune to some drivelling little squirt of a copper for the privilege of discovering the police were on to him. Next, he'd just had wee Geordie on the phone to report that, after two weeks of watching the cycle track, no one had appeared back at 'the scene of the crime.' It wasn't looking good in terms of recovering his money.

Oscar had walked in and was hearing all the bad news.

"To bloody well top it all," the Fatman continued, "we daren't do anything at all in case we get rumbled. The cops are watching us. One false move and the bastards will be in here with a search warrant."

"What about the deliveries?" asked Oscar. "Do you want me to send them out?"

"No!" was the terse reply.

"I had Sylvia on earlier, needing stuff urgently."

"She'll just have to bloody well wait like the rest of them. As I said, one false move now and we're all fucked!"

"What do you want me to do then?" Oscar asked.

"Nothing! We suspend our activities. We'll just close things down for a while and bide our time. I've absolutely no intention of going to jail. I take it you're not keen on reacquainting yourself with it either?"

"Definitely not," replied Oscar.

"Then I suggest you do exactly as I say."

There was a pregnant pause for effect and then he continued.

"I want you to go and find big Bill."

"Are you serious?" a look of abject horror had come over Oscars face. "Big Bad Bill?"

"The very same!"

"But he's a complete psychopath! Are you serious?"

"Yes. I want you to go and find him. I want my money back. If Bill is working for us, it will put the fear of God into everybody. Everyone in the underworld has heard of him. No one; and I do mean no one, fucks with him!"

"Yes, I hear what you're saying, but the man's a lunatic! We would have to be insane to have him near us. It would be like setting off a bomb to light a cigarette! Are you sure about this?"

"Very sure. Believe me, I've thought it all through, Bill is the very man we need. If we can't sell our drugs, at least we can divert our energies into looking for the money! Go you now and find him and bring him here to me."

"Your wish is my command, but just remember I told you I'm not happy about this."

"Oscar, it may come as a complete surprise to you old son, but I couldn't care less whether you're happy or not! Now, just go and find him!" he barked.

Oscar left without a further word. The boss had lost his marbles. This was an act of desperation, of lunacy! He had a very bad feeling about this.

24.

Paddy Rooney was loading some old gearboxes onto his pick up truck. He ran a small garage business, which serviced mostly German made cars. His clients were all people who tended not to buy new cars. Instead they would typically buy a good second-hand car which was already several years old. They mostly drove Volkswagens, BMWs and Mercedes cars. Paddy made it his business to keep them serviced and on the road.

Paddy's workshop was on the outskirts of Belfast, up a quiet lane, close to his father's farm. He was a hard working, honest man. He was certainly just about as straight as anyone in the motor trade!

A mobile phone was ringing.

Paddy answered it. "Hello, Paddy Rooney," he chirped.

"Hello, its me." The voice had a broad Yorkshire accent. He immediately knew it was D.I. Dobson. "Would it be possible for us to meet up please?"

"Yes. I'm going to be busy for the next couple of hours, but after that, yes certainly."

"Could you meet me in the upstairs bar at the Europa Hotel, say about five thirty?"

"Yeah that's fine. See you then." Paddy hung up. He wondered what Dobson wanted. He'd already done his best to help. What more could he do?"

25.

William had feigned complete disinterest as Julia left to go training yet again. This was the third time this week. He'd pulled her leg about entering the marathon and thus utilizing the high degree of fitness she would be obtaining through her recent dedicated training regime. This suggestion had been met with a smirk. It was complimented by the usual contemptuous remarks, which would be unhelpful to the perpetuation of a happy marriage.

The exchanges between them each added to a growing sense of division. It was becoming increasingly clear that the marriage was in danger of a terminal derailment. It now seemed only a matter of time.

William was surprised, in some ways, that he felt a complete lack of emotion about the whole thing. He remembered back to the happy times when he and Julia had met. It had all been so wonderful! He really enjoyed every moment with her in those early days. When he was away at work, he thought about her all the time. He couldn't wait for five o'clock to arrive everyday, so that he could go home to be with her. He reminisced upon the romance of those happy times, the flowers, the perfume and the special dinners together, when they had shared their dreams with each other. The sheer ecstasy he had felt making love to her had been so incredible. Where had it all gone? Sadly, he just didn't know.

As soon as Julia had closed the front door, he ran out the back door, quickly putting on his crash helmet and gloves. Hidden at the side of the garage, the Vespa scooter was sitting all ready to go. The key had been left in the ignition. It started instantly on its electric start and William was away after Julia. Initially, he had to travel rapidly to catch up with her. It wasn't long, though, before he saw the unmistakable profile of her small white Fiat 500 car ahead of him. Once he'd caught up, he fell back and followed at a discrete distance.

At first, it appeared Julia really was going to the gym. She was following the logical route to go there. William was starting to feel unsure of his suspicions about her, then, without warning, she turned left and off the by-pass and drove in the direction of the city centre.

William fell back further behind the Fiat. The bright streetlights here would highlight his presence, and he feared Julia might spot him if he followed her too closely.

A few minutes later she arrived outside a tall apartment building, only a few hundred yards away from the city centre. She stopped and made a phone call. A couple of minutes passed and then a metal, electric garage door started to clank open. This permitted entrance to the private underground garage of the building. In the dimly lit interior of the car park, William could make out the profile of a young man waving to Julia. The Fiat 500 disappeared into the bowels of the garage and the metal door clanked and clunked its way closed again.

William parked across the road. For a moment, he was in a state of denial, of disbelief. He had suspected Julia was up to something, but to have it now indisputably confirmed was a cold shock. He paused for a minute, allowing himself to absorb the fact, to take it all in. Coming abruptly to his senses, he looked up. A noise above him had attracted his attention. A balcony door had opened. The street was quite quiet and he could distinctly make out the tones of Julia's voice.

About five floors up he could make out the soft red glow of a cigarette lighting up. Caught in the light of the window behind her, he could make out the profile of a woman. It was unmistakable to him. It was Julia.

"The rotten bitch!" he whispered to himself between clenched teeth. "But I've got you now!"

26.

Detective Superintendent Dobson was in the upstairs bathroom of the Europa hotel. Only a few years ago, you would have needed to think very carefully before going in there. It was once the most bombed hotel in Europe or possibly even the world! Now that the troubles had substantially abated, it was deemed as safe as anywhere else within reason.

The bathroom was very luxurious with its marble floors, mirrors and subdued lighting. Piles of soft white hand towels and perfumed soap added to the pleasant ambience. She was making a few subtle improvements to her make up before meeting Rooney. It wasn't that she wished to impress him, she was just freshening up so that she felt on top form herself. She glanced at her watch as she headed towards the door. As always she was early for her meeting. It was something she had learned from her family in Yorkshire. Show up on time and show some respect.

As she stepped out of the bathroom, she could see Rooney was already there. She smiled to herself thinking that a man who would appear on time could probably be relied on. She strode confidently across the polished tiles of the floor and onto the thick luxurious carpet of the lounge bar area Rooney was sitting at a quiet table in the far corner. The table enjoyed the advantage of the seclusion afforded by a large potted plant. It was a table they had used on an earlier encounter.

"Hello Paddy. How are you?" she asked as she sat down opposite him.

"Nervous!" He rose to shake her hand politely.

"Don't think you need to be. It's probably not very likely that you'd find any of Cartwright's lot in here."

"Nervous all the same," he smiled weakly. "What can I do for you?"

"Well, firstly I'd just like to thank you for your help with all this. We are very much appreciative. I'm really just after an update on our first meeting. Have you heard anything further about what's going on?"

"I'm afraid I don't really have much to add at the moment." Paddy Rooney shifted uneasily in his chair. He looked around wary that someone might be watching.

"It's O.K." assured Dobson.

"Aye, its O.K. for you. You're used to this sort of thing. It's your job after all! I'm not used to it and frankly I'm worried about being found floating face down in a pond or something."

"It's all right. You'll be all right. Don't be afraid. Besides we are doing something here, which will help to save countless young lives. Not only are we saving them, but avoiding the grief of family and friends. What you're doing here might be the greatest service you will ever make to your fellow man."

"Gosh, you should be in politics or something, making a speech like that." Paddy was impressed.

"Sorry," she smiled. "Didn't mean to get up on my soapbox. I'm afraid I am just very passionate about my work."

"Nothing wrong with that." Paddy managed a weak smile. "I think what Cartwright is doing is sending out consignments of drugs inside engine parts. These scrap dealers are always dismantling old crashed cars and then selling the parts. Sometimes, for an extra charge, they'll deliver them to people like me."

"That's interesting. Have you got any evidence of that?"

"Well, I didn't give you all the details the last time we spoke. About two months ago, I had a ten-year-old Mercedes in for a new starter motor. The customer didn't want to pay for a new part so I phoned Cartwright's for a second hand one. I had a lot of work on that day, so I asked if they could deliver it out to me."

"Yes. Go on," encouraged Dobson.

"Well, when it arrived, I noticed the starter motor felt lighter than it should have done. Suspicious about this, I tested it on a battery before fitting it. It was a dud! It didn't work. I decided to open it up to see if the inside of the motor was O.K. When I opened it up, there was a big bag of white powder inside it!"

"What did you do?"

"I put it all back together again sharpish, and phoned Cartwright's up. I told them the starter motor was a dud and asked them to come and collect it and bring me another one."

"So you didn't tackle them about the white powder?" enquired Dobson.

"Definitely not! I was shit scared of what would happen if they knew I'd found it. None of the other mechanics working for me saw it. I've told no one about it. You're the only one that knows about it."

"That's really useful Paddy. So do you think that Cartwright might be using similar parts to deliver his drugs to avoid detection?"

"Absolutely! I reckon that's what he's doing. For instance, he could be using the like of an old gearbox. All you'd need to do would be to remove the innards and you could stash a fair old quantity of drugs in there."

"Does Cartwright often deliver parts to you?"

"Yeah. They have a van out on the road every day. I just have to lift the phone and the van can deliver, usually within a couple of hours. The driver is called Geordie Taylor. We sometimes give him a cup of tea. He once told me he covers the greater Belfast area. He could be delivering drugs all over the place!"

"He could indeed, but let's not jump to conclusions about this just yet. It's possible that this Taylor fella doesn't even know what's in the packages. He might just be the deliveryman."

"You really think he doesn't know?" asked Paddy

"Very possibly not."

"I think he knows and I'll tell you why. He's usually a very bubbly sort of person. Often wants to tell the mechanics some dirty joke when he calls with us, that sort of thing. The time he called to replace the duff starter motor, he looked very worried. He was far more concerned than he should have been at just delivering a dud part. I remember distinctly that he examined the faulty motor very carefully before he went off. He asked me if I'd had it apart."

"What did you say?"

"I lied through my teeth. Told him he must be joking. Did he really think I had time to start carrying out post mortems on his duff starter motors! I tried to make a joke out of it."

"Do you think he bought it?"

"Yeah. Pretty sure he did. Seemed happy enough when he left. Actually, thinking back on it, he was definitely vastly relieved!"

"Thanks very much Paddy. That's been very useful. Let's just keep this between us in the meantime."

"Don't you worry Superintendent Dobson, I'm not going to tell anyone, even if they're pulling my toe nails off!"

"I trust it won't come to that," she smiled as she got up to leave. "Don't hesitate to call me if you hear anything more and thanks once again."

27.

Oscar parked up across the street from the Rosie bar. He was reticent about what he had been instructed to do. He didn't much like Big Bill and he was fairly certain the sentiment was mutual. Outside, the rain was on again. Oscar grimaced as he stared out the window of the car. He felt that maybe, in a previous incarnation, he must have been a cat because he hated getting wet.

The Rosie Bar was close to the docks and was not noted as a good place to go if you wished to return home again with a complete set of teeth entirely intact in your mouth. This didn't bother Oscar in the slightest; he was big and strong and could handle himself in any fight. Big Bill though, Bill was a different kettle of fish. Oscar was convinced Bill was mad in the head. Any dealings with him were bound to be fraught with trouble. He felt it was like approaching a grizzly bear from the rear and poking him up the orifice with a sharp stick. Considering the circumstances, the response elicited from the grizzly bear would obviously be violent, but quite expected, deserved, and not at all unreasonable. With Bill, all the uninitiated needed to do was to bid him good day to end up nursing a sore jaw! He was quite the most bad tempered, and entirely unpredictable individual Oscar could think of.

Oscar remembered the time some years ago when Bill had worked at the scrap yard. That had been an experience! Even the Fatman had been shocked at his antics. One day a chap had come into the yard and seen Bill working away at some old car. From a distance, Oscar had overheard the exchange between them. The customer had been reasonable enough, Oscar had thought. He remembered, the man had a wee squeaky voice as he'd said:

"I was in here yesterday and I bought this starter motor for my car because it wouldn't start. I later discovered it wasn't the starter motor at all but the battery that was dead."

"Oh aye," said Bill, disinterestedly working away with a socket spanner on something in the engine bay of an old car.

"So I bought a new battery for the car and it's workin' just fine so it is. So I don't need the starter motor anymore."

"Right."

"Would you be able to take it back and refund me the sixty pounds I paid for it, as it's no use to me now?"

"No."

"But its no use to me now. I don't need it."

"Tough. You bought it, you own it."

"All I want is a refund. The motor is no good to me!"

"I don't care." Bill continued all the while working away in the engine bay without even directing his gaze at the customer.

The customer was stunned by his bluntness and indeed rudeness. He looked around the yard for inspiration.

"I might as well just take it and throw it away. I might as well throw it over there into that pile of scrap metal!"

At that, Bill stood up; wearily wiping away the sweat from his brow. He walked slowly over to the man, looking him straight in the eyes. There was an expression of outright rage on his face. He grabbed the starter motor out of the man's hand and, giving an enormous grunt like a shot putter, he threw it an unbelievable distance and it landed in the pile of scrap.

"There you are!" he yelled. "That will save you the bother!"

"But, but, ... what about my refund?"

Bill completely lost the bap. He felled the man with one almighty blow. The guy just lay there on the ground holding his face in his hands. When he eventually struggled to his feet, blood was pouring out of his nose. It was everywhere, dripping off his hands and all down his shirt.

Bill just glared at him as if he was making the yard untidy. He pulled a filthy rag from his pocket and threw it at the man hitting him in the face with it.

"There," he said. "Clean yourself up and fuck off home!"

Oscar remembered it all as if it had only happened yesterday. As the manager of the scrap yard, he had experienced plenty of problems with customers over the years. Many such disputes ended unpleasantly, but none of them had ever ended quite as badly as the way Bill had dealt with the purchaser of the starter motor!

He was bearing all this in mind as he entered the Rosie Bar. This was the fourth such establishment he had checked out in his quest to find Bill. As he opened the door, he half hoped there would be no sign of him here either. It would be just fine with him if he had to report back to the Fatman that he was nowhere to be found. No such luck however. Oscar could make out his unmistakable bear-like profile, sitting with his back to him, at a table at the far end of the lounge bar.

Oscar pushed his way through the crowd of boozers and skirted the table. Then Bill saw him.

"Ah Oscar! What a pleasant surprise," the friendly greeting immediately indicated he'd had a few jars. "Sit down here me old son and have a pint with us."

Bill pushed some wee man, sitting to his right, clean out of his chair and onto the floor. "Here's a seat for you."

Oscar sat down noting the indignant but totally resigned expression on the face of the chair's previous occupier. Oscar wasn't a big drinker and all he wanted to do was get out of the pub.

"Oi Dickie!" shouted Bill "Bring a pint of Harp for the big man here."

The barman immediately nodded and set down a shot glass he'd been about to fill for another customer. He started pulling the pint of Harp instead. He knew well to keep Big Bill happy, as the consequences of annoying him were unthinkable!

Shortly the Harp arrived on the table and Oscar said cheers and raised his glass to Bill. He took a great swig of the beer, just to pass himself, and then set the glass down again. *That's enough of that swill he thought to himself.*

"The Fatman wants to see you," he whispered in Bill's ear.

"Fuck him!" was the short answer.

"No, he really does want to see you."

"Why?" Bill took an enormous drag from a cigarette he'd just lit. He blew the smoke out all around Oscar.

"Thought you couldn't smoke in here?" said Oscar waving away the smoke as it curled around, acrid, under his nostrils.

"Do you see anyone objecting?"

Oscar knew no one would dare to tell Bill to put it out. Last time anyone had made such a suggestion, Bill had put them out. Out for the count that was!

"The Fatman wants to see you. Now!" Oscar was a little more insistent this time.

"I've already told you. No!"

"You'd enjoy it. He wants you to scare people, to hurt people. He's prepared to pay you well."

"How well?"

"There's five hundred quid waiting for you in an envelope on his desk, as a little introductory taster for you." Oscar smiled at him encouragingly.

There was a great scraping noise as Bill stood up, pushing his chair away from beneath him. He stubbed out his fag and lifted his glass of beer, emptying it hurriedly down his throat.

"Come on. What are you waiting for? Lets go."

28.

Julia had just woken up. She had been making love with Philip all evening. It had been absolutely wonderful. He was asleep beside her on the bed. She caressed the beautiful shiny black curls in his hair. She softly stroked the golden brown skin of his muscled arm, which lay out on top of the cover.

A brown eye opened gently as Philip became half conscious again.

"You can stroke all you like woman, but that's it for tonight!"

"Aw, what's wrong with you?" She put on a mock sympathetic voice, "Has it all been too much for the poor boy? Can he not handle a real woman yet?"

"I'm going to have to phone Arnold Palmer up soon."

"What do you mean?" Julia looked puzzled.

"Didn't you ever hear that old golfing joke?" he giggled.

"Don't think so."

"Well a young golfer was in bed in a hotel room with Arnold Palmer's wife, or maybe it was his girlfriend or something. Any way, he makes love to her and is getting up to go home when she says 'Arnold wouldn't do that!'

So he says, 'What would Arnold do?'

'Arnold would have done it again!' So the young golfer beams on again and when he'd finished, he gets up to go.

'Oh!' she says, 'Arnold wouldn't have done that!'

'Well, what would Arnold have done?'

She replies, 'Arnold would have done it again!'

So he gets back into bed and this time, by the time he's finished, he's really knackered.

He's just about to get up and crawl away home when she starts into him again.

'Oh! Arnold wouldn't have done that!'

So this time, he reaches over and picks up the telephone.

'What are you doing?' she asks him.

'I'm ringing up Arnold to find out what's par for this hole!'

Julia chuckled. "That's funny," she laughed. Then she jumped on top of him and started nipping him. "I'll teach you not to take the piss out of me you naughty boy you!"

"Ow! Ow! Stop! You mad bitch!" he struggled free and then, naked, jumped out of the bed.

"Are you going to phone Arnold then?" she asked giggling.

"I'm going to take a pee!" he laughed and disappeared into the bathroom. She heard him lock the door behind him as a precaution, to prevent any further molestation from her!

Julia giggled again as she opened a sliding door and went out onto the balcony. She was only wearing her nightdress, but, as she was about six floors up, no one would see her. The floor tiles were cold against her bare feet. She lit up a cigarette and took a deep draw. Just at that, there were three or four brilliant bright flashes of light, all in quick succession. They appeared to have come from a multi-storey car park across the street from her. She was momentarily blinded by the intensity of the flashes and couldn't see a thing. She rubbed her eyes with her hands and then peered across at the multi-storey car park.

"That's odd," she whispered to herself as her eyes became gradually accustomed to the light again. She screwed up her eyes slightly, attempting to focus on the level of the multi-storey car park the flashes had emanated from. There was no sign of anyone there. Maybe someone had taken a photo of something and she had just seen the flash from it. That must have been it, she mused to herself as she took a drag from her cigarette.

29.

"Oscar said you had five hundred quid for me."

It was Bill's opening statement. He didn't ask about what he was expected to do. All he was interested in was the money. It was typical of Bill.

"Hold on a minute," said the Fatman, "You're putting the cart in front of the horse and you're hardly even through the door!"

"He said," Bill pointed at Oscar, "you had five hundred quid for me. Is that true or am I wasting my time here?"

"Sit down a moment and listen to me will you."

"What about the money? Where is it?"

"Will you for fuck sake sit down and shut up!" The Fatman was becoming irritated.

Oscar was very surprised when Bill obeyed and quietly sat down.

"Thank you. Now, let me explain what I want you to do for us," began the Fatman. "We have recently lost a significant sum of money."

"How much?" Bill asked.

The Fatman sank back into his soft, green, leather desk chair. It creaked noisily under the enormous strain.

"One point one million pounds."

"Holy Mother of God!" Bill let out a big whistle. "That is a large sum of money alright!"

"Well, we're lookin' it back again." The Fatman's voice was full of its usual menace. "And that's where you come into the picture. I want you to use your considerable charm to scare people to death. I need people crapping themselves with fear! I want someone to start talking and telling me where this money is. If they aren't willing to speak voluntarily, I want you to hurt them bad until they squeal with agony. Badly enough that they'll spill the beans!"

"Now you're talking turkey," said Bill, "I'm the man to do that sort of thing for you."

"I know you are. But there's something you need to know. The police are watching us. We need to conduct this whole investigation very discreetly. Any inquisitions need to be carried out somewhere quiet. I don't want any neighbours, or passers-by, hearing people screaming out in agony. Is that totally clear?"

"Ah sure the police are always floating about. That doesn't worry me in the slightest. I know a nice quiet place where we can torture people in private. It's a remote farmhouse miles from anywhere." Bill paused for a moment and then continued. "It's nice and quiet. Do you remember the film 'Alien?' They had an advert for it when it came out at first that said:

'In Space no one can hear you scream!' Bill grinned maliciously!

"That's just what we need." Oscar agreed.

"That sounds good Bill, just the ticket. I want you to work closely with Oscar on this one. He'll fill you in on all you need to know. Are you happy enough about that?"

"Aye, that's fine. Only thing I need to know now is what's in this for me? Much as I enjoy tormenting people, I need to be well paid for it."

"There will be a good bung it for you Bill. If we recover the money, I'll give you a bonus of ten grand."

"Fifty," countered Bill immediately.

"Wise up! No way am I giving you fifty thousand." The Fatman paused to think for a moment. "How about twenty?"

"Thirty."

"Too much!" yelled the Fatman

"Twenty five. I won't do it for any less." Bill was suddenly very serious and grim faced.

"Alright, twenty five it is," agreed the Fatman.

Oscar watched on with incredulity. He wanted to say something, but knew he'd be wisest to keep quiet. It wouldn't be good to get caught up between either of these two!

Bill stood up to go. "I'll start on this in the morning. By the way, where is the five hundred quid?"

The Fatman reached into a drawer and tossed an envelope across the desk in the direction of Bill. It slid onto the floor. Bill picked it up and gave the Fatman a very dirty look.

"I'll help you find your money. Just one thing though, don't either of you two fuck with me!"

The Fatman nodded.

Bill went out the door closing it heavily behind him.

"What a nice chap he is," Oscar commented.

"Yeah, isn't he just?"

"You do know the guy is completely mad in the head don't you?"

"Yeah, but, as a means to an end, he'll do the job rather well I think," concluded the Fatman.

30.

"What are these? the corpulent solicitor asked politely in his very upper crust accent.

"They're photos of that bitch wife of mine. She's pretty much been caught in the act, don't you think?" said William.

The solicitor spread the photographs out over his green leather desktop and carefully studied them for a few minutes, his immaculately clean pudgy fingers moving them about until he was content that he had thoroughly examined them all.

"I see a woman dressed in a night dress, a very attractive looking woman actually. Is she your wife Mr Forsythe?"

"She is indeed, but not for very much longer!"

"Well," James Harrington the solicitor continued, "I see a lady wearing a night dress. She is standing on a balcony smoking a cigarette. What conclusion do you expect me to draw from these?"

"This is my wife. She is standing out on a fifth floor balcony of an apartment in Matthew Street in central Belfast. She has been making love to some young man in the apartment. Judging by the length of time she spent, they probably did it several times. She has then stepped outside to have a smoke."

"What precisely do you want me to do with these photographs?" Enquired Harrington.

"I would like to instigate divorce proceedings!" replied William, using his best legal speak.

"These photographs would probably be useful as part of a case, but I can see how they could prove to be insufficient as stand alone evidence. I'm talking about what would happen if the case were to come to court. Do you see what I mean?"

"Yes, I think so."

"What other evidence do you have to support your case?"

William explained about the training shoes being left behind when his wife was supposedly away at the gym. He told how he'd discreetly followed his wife and discovered that she was visiting this young man.

Harrington asked William for the exact address of the apartment and noted it down on the legal pad before him.

"What's this young man called?"

"Philip Thompson. He's an estate agent working for a large company in Belfast." William gave his solicitor further details.

"How did you obtain these photographs?" asked Harrington.

"I used a small digital camera I own. I went up to the sixth level of a multi-storey car park that is opposite the apartment building. The photos were taken from there."

"Have you mentioned anything, about any of this, to your wife yet? Have you told her you want a divorce?"

"No. I wanted to speak to you about it first to see what my options are."

"Very wise. Well, I'll tell you what I think. I believe we need more conclusive evidence. What I would suggest here is that we contact this chap," Harrington pulled a card out of his desk drawer and slid it across the desktop.

William examined the card as the solicitor continued.

"He's a private detective who's also a very competent photographer. He has all the correct telescopic lenses, etcetera, that are needed for this sort of job. If you're content with this, I'll contact him and brief him as to our exact requirements."

"What are our exact requirements?"

"In short that he photographs the two of them, excuse the French here, 'focking' the living daylights out of each other!"

At this William laughed. It was not just at the suggestion, but also at the politely, well spoken solicitor using the word 'focking' and how he had pronounced it!

"Once we have the photographs, we'll be in a much stronger position to issue divorce proceedings. We'll have to build up a bit of a dossier documenting all her infidelity. Is this the only recipient of her amorous affections?"

"Yes, as far as I know anyway," replied William looking suddenly doubtful.

"Let's see what our friend here," Harrington patted the business card on the desktop, "let's see what he can discover. He's been very thorough and revealing in other cases he's done for me."

William got up to leave.

"Remember, keep this all under your hat for now. The element of surprise will prove crucial to our success."

"I understand. I'll keep up the pretence that I'm as stupid and as naive as she thinks I am!"

"Good man!" The solicitor smiled approval.

31.

"Hi there Big Boy! It's Sylvia. I was hoping you could come and see me this afternoon? I've got something for you Big Boy!"

"Hi Sylvia, I'm actually very busy. It doesn't really suit. It's absolutely bedlam here today. You should see the yard outside. There are lorries coming and going like crazy."

The Fatman glanced out into the yard. There was an unusual deathly still about the place. Nothing was happening at all!

"I'd still like to see you Big Boy!" Sylvia was fairly laying it on. "I hope you're not neglecting me, besides I'm absolutely out of choclates!"

"Hold on just a moment love." The Fatman set the phone down on the desk and thought. He was weighing up the risk-involved versus his inherent greed. He knew Sylvia would have a bag of money for him. After a moment or two, he picked up the receiver again.

"Maybe I could nip over about three-ish. It will have to be quick though," he said.

"How quick will all depend on you Big Boy!" she chuckled.

"O.K. I'll be over about three. Make sure you have the kettle on. Love you!"

"I can't wait to see you! Love you too!"

The Fatman put the phone down. "Fuckin' tart," he muttered to himself.

32.

"Where did that scooter come from?" Julia's voice was even more strident and unpleasant than usual.

"What scooter?" William decided to be purposely awkward.

"The bloody scooter that's down outside our garage! I do hope you haven't been stupid enough to buy it!" she shouted.

"Oh that scooter." William was reading a newspaper.

"Yes that scooter. Where did it come from?"

"Actually I borrowed it."

"Where from?"

"Do you remember James?"

"James who?" Julia was rushing about the kitchen wiping surfaces in her usual manic way.

"The James who went to school with me. The same James Graham who was best man at our wedding! Do you even remember that?"

Julia stopped wiping the breakfast bar and glared at him.

"Yes, of course I remember, worst thing I ever did!"

"Sorry you feel that way. I still love you, you know." William said it with a totally straight face, lying through his teeth.

Julia looked at him with a deeply puzzled expression.

"Love? What do you mean love? You don't love me at all!"

"Of course I do," he looked at her putting on a face as if she had hurt him by the very suggestion. He decided he'd messed with her enough though and changed tack.

"By the way, I have got myself a part time job."

"I don't believe it!" Julia looked amazed.

"Yes, James now has a little garage which sells second hand cars. He's been very busy lately and asked me if I would help him out with cleaning the cars and also with some of the sales."

"That's great!" Julia was suddenly enthusiastic.

William instantly sensed the change in her attitude. All she was really interested in was the money. He knew from hard experience that she was a money-grabbing, greedy little bitch. He was able to predict the next question with unerring accuracy.

"How much does it pay?"

"What pay?" William was being deliberately obtuse again. He studied the newspaper feigning disinterest in the conversation.

"The job at the garage you idiot!"

"Oh yes. Well I'll get a hundred and fifty a week . . . ."

"A measly hundred and fifty. Is that all?" she interrupted.

"If you'd just let me finish. That's a basic amount. I'll get much more if I sell a few cars. I'm on a bonus for anything I sell."

"Then you'll only be getting a hundred and fifty a week. After all, you've never been a great salesman!"

"Thanks for the vote of confidence! You may remember I was, until quite recently, selling medical products to the National Health Service. Experts say they are one of the most difficult customers to sell anything to. I reckon I should be able to sell a few old cars to unsuspecting punters!"

"That remains to be seen. I suppose time will tell."

"It certainly will," he smiled at her knowingly. "You never spoke a truer word." He paused for a while, again pretending to be absorbed in his newspaper. The next statement was important to him. It was important that she swallowed it whole, and fell for his little subterfuge entirely.

"I'm also able to get a nice Company car with the job. James has said he'd sort me out with an old car that's been lying about unsold for ages. He's said I can use it for a few months, until things improve for me."

"Oh. What sort of car is it?"

"He hasn't actually told me yet. I'm going down to the garage soon to see what it is."

"We wait with bated breath," Julia sarcastically teased him.

33.

Detective Superintendent Dobson was sitting at her desk thinking. She was mulling over the whole Cartwright situation, trying to figure out how she was going to catch them out. Big problem was, if she made a move and got it wrong, that would let the cat out of the bag and give the game away.

She buzzed her secretary and asked her to send in Henderson and Butler. It was several minutes before the two appeared.

"What took you so long?" she asked.

"Sorry." said Henderson. "We were away down at the canteen having some lunch."

"Right enough," Dobson checked her wall clock. "It is twenty past one after all. Sometimes I forget all about lunch and then feel hungry noticing it's about four o'clock!" she chuckled.

"Anyway, I wanted to talk with you two about Cartwright. Since our last meeting some fresh information has come to light. Cartwright's dismantle old cars and sell the parts. That much is pretty obvious. What I didn't realise until recently is that they sometimes deliver these parts to their customers."

"Pardon me for asking, but so what?" Butler wanted to know.

"Butler, that's why you are still a detective constable, one, you don't think and two you then just blurt out the first thing that comes into your thick head!"

Butler looked very subdued. "Sorry, I was only asking."

"Well let me tell you then! Cartwright's deliver parts to their customers. Recently, a starter motor was delivered to a garage owner. It didn't work. He took it apart and found drugs inside it."

"Ah so that's how they're doing it!" Henderson was quick on the uptake. "They could be sending out deliveries of drugs all round the Province inside engine parts."

"Exactly!" said Dobson.

"Who was the garage owner?" Henderson wanted to know.

"Sorry. Can't tell you. He's pretty much shit-scared of what could happen to him if something leaks out. I've agreed to keep his identity secret, at least at this stage of the investigation."

"I don't blame him for being cautious," Butler interjected. "Do you remember what happened to that poor guy last year, when that lot from west Belfast found out he'd squealed on them!"

"Aye that was terrible," recalled Henderson. "They cut off his willy and made him eat it before they shot him!"

"After that, shooting him was a kindness wasn't it?" Butler replied.

"Aye, well it certainly saved him from suffering indigestion!" chuckled Henderson.

Butler started to laugh. "It's like that fast food restaurant down the road. They always ask you, 'Would you like fries with that sir'?"

Both Butler and Henderson laughed, imagining some unfortunate wee man being asked if he would like fries to eat with his willy!

"I see you two have reached your usual infantile level again. Could you just pretend for at least the rest of this meeting that you are actually professional police officers!" Dobson was now shouting. She definitely didn't suffer fools gladly.

"Our major problem here is that, if we do a raid and seize some of these engine parts, and then discover they are clean, with no drugs in them, we've given the game away and shown our hand. Cartwright would realise we knew what they are up to, and then quickly go to ground and we'd have nothing. We'd have blown it." Dobson got up from her desk and began to pace about the room. She was obviously deep in thought and seeking inspiration.

"I had hoped that either of you two might have had an intelligent suggestion to make about this. I now realise how foolish I was to harbour such a notion!"

"I don't have an immediate answer for you, but let me think about it. If I can come up with something I'll come back to you." Detective sergeant Henderson was serious again. "There is bound to be a way of increasing the odds in our favour."

Dobson nodded her head in agreement.

"O.K. Keep watching them. You think about it and so will I. We'll meet again on Friday and see what we can come up with. We've got to get this right first time. That's absolutely critical"

Henderson and Butler got up to leave. As they went out into the corridor Butler asked. "Are you going back to the canteen to finish lunch?"

"No. You go on ahead. I've just remembered I should have phoned my wife. I'll join you soon."

34.

The Fatman pulled up outside Sylvia's house. He was driving his AMG cabriolet again. Its ruby red paintwork had been burnished up to a fine sheen, which shone radiantly in the bright sunlight. He stepped back to admire the car briefly. Cecil had done a really good job polishing it this time. He opened the boot of the car and lifted out a big box of chocolates. A huge bow of ribbon completed the romantic picture.

A hundred and fifty yards away, the police surveillance team were watching carefully, their camera capturing images of the entire event. It wasn't long before the tall leggy Sylvia appeared and gave the Fatman a big hug and a kiss.

"That's for the cameras," she whispered in his ear."

The Fatman responded by returning her kiss, but it was just a peck on the cheek.

"He didn't look too enthusiastic about that!" said Butler.

"What do you mean?" asked D.S. Robinson who had stepped in for Henderson who was apparently off ill that day.

"Just wasn't the sort of kiss you'd give a girl you were keen on. I mean, he's doing the dirty on his wife here. He's risking her wrath and divorce if she ever found out, right? You'd think he'd be more enthusiastic than that!"

"Good observation young Butler. That's a very good point. Note that down in the log," replied Robinson. They both watched as the two disappeared into the house.

"I take it that's them down the road in the dark coloured car?" said Sylvia.

"Yes. That's them. They're watching every friggin' move I make. I can hardly take a leak these days, and I'm not looking to see is there a hidden camera watching me!"

The Fatman rapidly opened up the box of chocolates to allow Sylvia to inspect the contents. There were several cellophane bags inside full of white powder.

"Oh that does look lovely!" she said.

"Cut the crap. Nobody is listening in here. Where's the money?"

"Don't get your knickers in a knot!" Sylvia pulled the curtains closed. "Let's keep the boys outside guessing," she grinned!

She opened a drawer in the sideboard and lifted out a large manila envelope and tossed it onto the table.

"Aren't you going to weigh it first?" the Fatman asked.

"Oh no ducky. I trust you implicitly," she fluttered her eye lashes at him smiling. "Besides, as we discussed before, I'm not a one night girl. I'm in this for the long term!"

The Fatman nodded as he opened the envelope. It was stuffed full of notes. Many of them were fifties and hundreds. He folded over the top of the envelope and stuffed it into his jacket pocket.

"Oh, aren't you going to count it?"

"I trust you too Sylvia," he replied keeping a straight face. "Besides, if its not all here," he patted the pocket with the money in it, "I'll come back and slit your fuckin' throat!" he grinned evilly.

He could see from the expression on her face that she knew he meant business.

"Right, we need to put in a bit of time for the benefit of these boys outside. Put that kettle on till we have a nice wee cup of tea. Unless that is, you want to go upstairs and let me give you as they say in England, 'a bloody good seeing to!'

"Bugger off!" was Sylvia's reply to that. "You're bloody lucky to be getting a cup of tea!"

35.

The Fatman was on his way home when the call came. It was the unregistered phone ringing. He knew instantly who it was.

"Hello."

"Hello yourself," the Fatman answered.

"We've got to meet up, it's important."

"Where and when?"

"Location 'B.' Can you be there in an hour?"

"No. Your lot are following me up the road at the moment," the Fatman glanced in his rear-view mirror. The dark coloured car was about two hundred yards behind him. "I need to take a few precautions and get rid of my tail. Give me two hours and I'll see you then.

"O.K."

36.

William knocked on the door of the house. A lean, smartly-dressed middle-aged man opened the door a few moments later.

"Hello, I'm William. I telephoned earlier. I've come to see your car."

The man smiled and shook his hand. "I'm Andrew. The car is out in the back garage. Follow me please."

The large red brick house had a rear courtyard with garages and stables. Andrew approached one of the garages and unlocked the door. He pulled open the two wooden doors and carefully removed a dustsheet to reveal a gleaming white Porsche 911 Carrera cabriolet.

"Don't forget it's now just over twenty five years old," said Andrew.

"It doesn't look it!" said William enthusiastically.

"Well it has been very well looked after. I've had it almost from new. It was a Porsche demonstrator. Only had about two thousand miles on it when I bought it. Its been pampered and used sparingly."

William was pleased with the spotless paintwork. He felt the treads of the rear tyres.

"Those tyres were all new about a year ago. The car has probably only done about five hundred miles since. I just drive her about once or twice a month and even then, it's usually a fairly short journey."

"How many miles are on the car?" William asked.

"Have a look at the clock," the proud owner smiled.

William opened the door and climbed inside. The blue leather upholstery was sumptuous and still looked in very good condition despite the fact that the car was now a quarter of a century old. Having given the interior the once over, William's eyes came to rest on the odometer. Twenty six thousand seven hundred and eighty one miles it read.

"Wow! It has a very low mileage. Is that for real?"

"Yes it is. I have a complete service history for the car. It's all with Porsche. The service book and MOT certificates authenticate the mileage."

Andrew had a file with him, which detailed the entire service history and had all the old MOT certificates. The file bulged with documents. William had a quick look through it and felt convinced by its sheer comprehensiveness.

"Will it start up? Can we take it for a test drive?"

Andrew chuckled. "Course it will start up! Try turning the key."

William did as he was asked. There was an initial metallic chu, chu, chu, noise as the starter turned the engine. It fired into life and was soon running smoothly with its characteristic whirring noise.

Andrew got into the driver's seat and took William as a passenger. A few minutes into the drive, he stopped and allowed William to take over.

"I've always wanted one of these!" William beamed. "Ever since I first saw one, and then read about it in a car magazine."

"She's warm enough now. You can give her a bit of throttle," encouraged Andrew.

William pushed the pedal nearly to the floor. The car took off like a scalded cat! The acceleration was incredible. It was all William had hoped for and more. The two hundred and thirty one horsepower would allow the car to rocket to sixty in about five and half seconds. William was smitten and just had to have the car.

"How much do you want for her?" he asked.

"In view of the exceptionally low mileage, and the car's superb condition, I want seventeen thousand for it. You won't find another one in this good condition in a month of Sundays!"

William knew he was right. He'd spent hours on his iPad surfing the net and looking for a suitable dream car. It had to be exciting to him and also believable to Julia that it was on loan from James at the garage. This one might just about fly.

"It's a very nice car. I'll give you thirteen thousand pounds for it. That's a genuine offer and will be paid to you in cash."

Andrew looked a bit crest fallen. "Sorry. I won't let it go at that," he looked sadly out the windscreen for a moment. "My wife died a few months ago. She had cancer."

"I'm really sorry to hear that." William interjected.

Andrew nodded acknowledgement. "We had many happy days out in this little car. I'm really going to miss it, but I need to move on. I'm moving back to the south of England. I've enough stuff to take with me as it is." He paused, momentarily lost deep in thought.

"Tell you what, you seem like a nice chap and I think you will really enjoy driving this Porsche. I'd like to see you in the car! I'll split the difference with you. Give me fifteen for her and she's yours."

"Done!" William shook hands with Andrew. He left a thousand in cash, as a deposit, promising to return with the balance once the Porsche was insured for him to drive it away.

He then went to his friend James' garage and explained that he'd bought a Porsche and that Julia would kill him when she found out!

James being a long-standing friend readily agreed to cover for him. The official story was that William was working in the garage and that the Porsche was on loan to him for a few weeks until it was sold. William even agreed to come up to the garage and wash a few cars to add to the subterfuge.

37.

The Fatman drove into the little car park and allowed the black Mercedes SL 55AMG to roll to a halt as he turned it round to face towards the sea. Location two was another little-used car park. In the summer it would be teeming with people but now, late in autumn it was deserted. At the far side of the car park, he could make out a dark coloured Vauxhall car.

"That's my man," he mumbled quietly to himself and waited. Sure enough, the door of the car opened, and a familiar looking figure strode towards him, casting concerned furtive glances to left and right as he came.

"Get in." The Fatman opened the passenger door.

"Frig me, its windy enough isn't it?" His informant climbed into the Mercedes.

"Aye, not a very nice day. In fact, recently, many days haven't been very nice," the Fatman scowled at him. "Hope for your sake you've something good to tell me. You've no idea of all the buggering about I've had to do to make sure no one was following me here."

"I appreciate it Mr Cartwright, can I call you James?"

"No! Just call me Mr Cartwright, we're not getting engaged here or anything."

"I do have something very interesting to tell you, actually."

"Well I hope so, I'm certainly nor here for my own amusement. What is it?"

"Cough up first. It will be worth your while, I promise."

The Fatman reached into an inside pocket and pulled out an envelope. He handed it, somewhat reluctantly, to his informant.

"Five grand there," he grumbled. "This had better be worth it!"

"I've done some research for you. Apparently a van of yours delivered a starter motor to one of your customers."

"So what?" growled the Fatman.

"Well, firstly, it didn't work. Secondly, when your customer dismantled it to find out why, he discovered it was full of drugs!"

"Ah!" The Fatman was instantly excited. "That must be the wee bastard who's squealing on us! What's his name?"

"Unfortunately, I don't know."

"What the fuck good are you to me if you don't know!" yelled the Fatman outraged. "Call yourself a detective! You couldn't find the zipper on your trousers, on a dark night, if you had a whore on heat with you!"

"Calm down a bit."

"I'm perfectly bloody calm." the Fatman barked at him.

"All you've got to do is question the van drivers who work for you. Obviously, one of them messed up, and delivered this starter motor to the wrong garage."

"Obviously!"

"One of your drivers knows which garage it is, because he went back again to collect it once he realised his mistake."

The car was misting up. The Fatman opened one of the windows to allow air in. The wind was blowing strongly. Out in the bay, small yachts were bobbing up and down. There was a pronounced ding, ding, ding, ding noise as their halyards beat manically against their metallic masts in the wind.

"O.K. I'll question the van men and find out which idiot delivered the starter motor to the wrong place. Then I'll know who's squealing on me!"

"What will you do when you find out?" asked the informant.

"We'll have a wee chat with him and decide on a course of action as a result of what he tells us."

"What makes you think he'll tell you anything?"

"Oh!" chuckled the Fatman maliciously, "he'll talk all right! I can guarantee it!"

"What happens to him if he tells you he has been squealing on you?" The informant was suddenly worried about the ramifications of the information he was divulging to this thug.

"Firstly, he'll squeal a lot! A hell of a lot! After that, believe you me, you don't want to know what will happen to him."

The informant said nothing and just stared out the window of the car. The wind had picked up even more and the halyards on the yachts were now beating an insane percussion on their masts. The rain was driving strongly across the small car park. A squall in the bay made the little boats bob up and down precariously.

"Looks like a storm brewing up." The Fatman narrowed his eyes as he gazed out at it.

The informant kept his silence, thinking that it was probably an ominous harbinger of what was to come.

38.

"Wow!" was all Julia could muster as she looked out of the window. William had just arrived home in the Porsche. "That's a lovely little car!"

"Isn't it just!" beamed William.

"You're telling me James has lent that to you!" Julia was incredulous.

"Yeah, it's over twenty five years old and its not worth that much any more," he said carefully playing down the whole deal.

Julia had to go outside to look at it. She walked all around it twice and, clearly, was in admiration of the car.

"Its certainly very smart! You're lucky James has allowed you to borrow such a nice car." Julia stroked the paintwork admiringly.

"Good, isn't it!" William grinned.

Julia opened the door and jumped inside.

"Nice seats." she said looking around the interior. "Gosh, there's only twenty six thousand miles on the clock!"

"Well, not really. It's actually been round the clock so it's a hundred and twenty six thousand." William had carefully rehearsed his lies in advance.

"Gosh! It's been well looked after then hasn't it?" Julia was obviously well impressed.

For just a moment she smiled at him and it was almost as if the present had been forgotten. The normal animosity somehow dissolved. They were living briefly in the past again. It was as if all was well. All was rosy in the little garden again. Totally forgetting herself she got out of the car and put her arms around him and kissed him. Despite himself, he kissed her back and suddenly felt the urge to go much further as he did so. To his surprise the feeling was mutual and they were both instantly borne away on a tide of urgent and primeval need to make love.

Moments later they were running up the stairs to the bedroom. Julia had the presence of mind to close the curtains and then, in a sheer frenzy, they were pulling each other's clothes off as they embraced. For William it was all happening as if in some trance-like dream. He didn't want to do this and yet he couldn't stop himself. He was powerless to wake up. It was insane! He didn't love her anymore and yet he couldn't help himself as he pushed her naked onto the bed. It was as if he was part of some ritual being performed in an unstoppable hallucination! Once initiated, the end was as inevitable as sky diving out of an aeroplane.

For a few minutes, they were both lost in the ecstasy of a fantasy world. Transiently wonderful, beautiful and ending in the physical release that brings contentment, and an all too short sense of tranquillity and fulfilment. Soon it was all over and as the rapture started to wear off, reality came crowding back into their confused minds. William decided to make light of the whole incident.

"Do you remember the old joke I once told you about the guy who bought a Porsche? It rambled on a lot, but the bottom line was that the guy got the girl, and the moral of the story was: 'You don't need to have a big prick to pull a bird if you have a Porsche!'

Julia gave the merest of chuckles and got up out of bed. As was her wont, she opened a window and lit up a cigarette. Holding it between two fingers, she inhaled deeply whilst looking out upon the world outside. Its banality was somehow suddenly harsh, cruel and cold.

It was highly significant for William, as images of her smoking on the apartment balcony, in Belfast, rapidly rushed back into his mind. She was still that same adulterous bitch he thought to himself. All that had just happened was an automatic response to the pushing of an emotional button. A sequence of events had been initiated by something that was purely and solely instinctive and indeed animal based. The distillate of all this was, unfortunately, that it was entirely meaningless. He looked at her as she smoked. What on earth went on inside her tiny mind he wondered?

Without warning she swivelled round to face him.

"I want a divorce," she said starkly.

"You are of course joking!" He attempted to look as surprised as he could possibly manage. In reality, he felt as though all his birthdays and Christmases had come all at once! Instantly the thought ran through his mind. The money is all mine. I've got rid of her.

"Despite the Porsche, which isn't even yours anyway, you are still a complete loser. I'm moving on." She paused briefly before she said, "I want the house, and half of all that's in your savings account."

39.

A rather dirty looking white van came tearing up the worn gravel drive way towards the old deserted farmhouse. Bill heard it coming long before he could see it. It was like music to his ears! He rubbed his hands together with glee, giggling fiendishly to himself in anticipation of what was to come.

"I just love my work!" he shouted out loud, even though there was no one there to hear him. At the first sound of the rumble of tyres on the driveway, he opened the Judas door in the gate and stepped out into the yard.

The filthy white van came screaming into the yard and screeched to an abrupt halt a few yards away from him. Oscar and wee Geordie Taylor got out of the front of the van.

"Did you get him?" asked Bill.

"He's in the back," Geordie half whispered, as if he didn't want the man in the back of the van to hear him.

"Come on in." Bill was obviously in good form as he pulled out a packet of fags and offered them all round. "We'll have a wee smoke first before we start." He chuckled with malicious anticipation.

Oscar politely declined, explaining that he was currently working out in the gym a lot and had given them up. Wee Geordie willingly lit up and offered his match up to Bill's cigarette. Unfortunately, the match slightly singed Big Bill's nose. Bill gave a yelp of pain. Incensed, he grabbed the small man by the lapels of his coat and threw him unmercifully into a pile of old buckets and junk that had accumulated in the corner of the large shed.

Wee Geordie landed with a terrific great crash amongst the rusty buckets and detritus, looking totally stunned and bewildered.

"What the hell did you do that for?" he shouted angrily

"You near burned the frigging face off me with that match, you stupid wee cunt you!"

Geordie got up to his feet and was so enraged that he was obviously just about to try something really silly. Hit Bill. Luckily for him, Oscar intervened to prevent it happening.

"Now! Now! Girls! Let's stop all this and behave properly! We've got a job to do here, so no more messing about."

Wee Geordie started to calm down. Perhaps he had come sufficiently to his senses to recognise the insanity of what he had been going to attempt. He realised that if he'd hit Bill, he would likely have woken up in hospital, and that was if he'd been lucky. He started to wander off to explore the inside of the shed, as much to put some distance between himself and Bill.

"What exactly are you going to do to him?" asked Oscar.

"Terrible things!" Bill laughed horribly. He stared at Oscar. His wild looking eyes were wide open, clearly showing their whites.

It was at that precise moment that Oscar realised something he'd long suspected was true. Big Bill truly was mad in the head. Not just mad but completely and utterly insane!

"Bloody hell! What's happened back here?" It was Geordie. His voice was full of horror.

"Ah, that was an experiment," Bill answered sheepishly. "I was doing a wee test using electricity as a means of torture. The idea was to put just enough electricity through someone's body to inflict great pain, but not enough to kill them."

"So what happened then?" asked Geordie aghast staring in horror at the wall in front of him.

"I tried it out on a live rabbit but I think I over did it just a tad," conceded Bill.

"Just a tad!" Geordie couldn't believe it. The wall in front of him was covered in bits of rabbit, which had been liberally distributed around the entire area. Blood, guts, fur, you name it, it was there!

"Aye, all right. It didn't work the best. The fuckin' thing just sort of exploded," Bill admitted and then burst out laughing in a clearly deranged fashion.

Oscar started looking around the inside of the shed. It was like a veritable chamber of horrors. Everywhere there were rusty looking chains attached to the walls, obviously meant to restrain people. An ancient wooden beam had more chains hanging from it. Everything was festooned with cobwebs. There was a huge heavy wooden chair with leather restraining straps. Knives, saws, hammers and instruments with sharp points and cruel curves, intended to do God only knows what, sat on a massive wooden table. They were laid out like the operating theatre of some deeply disturbed psycho surgeon from the worst imaginable horror film.

Nearby sat the apparatus, complete with electrical dials and electrodes, where the unfortunate rabbit had met its demise. The whole place was kitted out like a torture chamber!

"What in hell are you going to do to him?" Oscar asked, almost trembling himself at the thought of it.

"You'll see." Bill was suddenly serious now. "Bring him in here."

Oscar and Geordie brought in the man who had been in the back of the van. His hands had been tied behind his back and a hood had been placed over his head.

"Bring him over here," commanded Bill.

The man was brought over and Bill strapped his wrists to the arms of the huge wooden chair. The chair itself was bolted to the floor so it wouldn't move about. Once the straps had been tightened up, Bill ripped the man's hood off. It was, Paddy Rooney the garage owner.

"We're going to ask you a few questions now old son, and you're going to answer them," Bill said in a deep and ominous tone. "If you don't answer the questions quickly, this is going to hurt very, very badly indeed."

"I'm telling you nothing!" the man said defiantly.

"We'll see about that. Take his shoes off," he ordered.

Geordie got down on his knees and untied the laces of the man's oily work boots. He removed them and took his socks off too. Whilst he did this, Bill had gone over to a wood-burning stove. He opened the door. The coals inside were a glowing orange inferno.

"Ah good," he said, "They're red hot now alright!"

He lifted a long poker out of the embers and came over to the man in the chair. Briefly, he held it up under Paddy Rooney's nose. Paddy recoiled violently attempting to escape. The long tapered tip of the poker was a bright glowing orange colour.

Bill knelt down quickly and applied the red-hot iron to the sole of one of Paddy's feet.

There was an almighty yell as the pain struck home. Forget all those war films, where you see someone being tortured and stoically refusing to speak, putting up a brave resistance. Forget the images of the hero, with his jaws clamped closed, refusing steadfastly to cry out in pain. The man in the chair yelled and screamed out in agony! He writhed, suffering sheer purgatory, stretching his restraints fit to break! He shrieked, squealed and howled with pain!

"Are you talking to the police and giving them information about our activities?" Bill started his interrogation.

"Why don't you go fuck yourself! Rooney screamed defiantly.

"Oh good!" cackled Bill. "It's no fun at all if they give up too easily!" He smiled wickedly at Oscar who was watching with a growing sense of horror. Oscar couldn't care less about this Rooney fellow. If he'd been grassing on them, well, serve him right! What Oscar didn't approve of was the obvious pleasure Bill was taking in tormenting the little man. That was just sheer cruelty and, as a thug, he thought it thoroughly unprofessional.

"I'm going to ask you again," Bill said gruffly. "Have you been speaking to the police? What do they know about our activities? Are you the reason they've been watching us?"

"I'm telling you nothing you big bastard! Rooney uttered a little weakly.

Bill knew he was close to breaking. He knew most men couldn't suffer too much in the way of pain and agony without cracking, especially the sort that squealed on people.

Bill undid Rooney's trouser belt and roughly pulled down his trousers and underwear to his ankles.

"Oh look at that! Same as a willy, only much smaller!" Bill mocked him as he returned to the stove and withdrew an even larger poker from the flames.

"Now, as the doctor would advise you, this may sting just a little!"

At that, Bill shoved the red-hot iron poker up between McAuleys legs. It went under his most delicate parts and up into the entrance of his rectum. To say that this caused great distress would be to grossly understate the reaction to this most unwelcome insertion!

All the time, Bill was laughing in a totally demented fashion and twisting and forcing the poker further into his victim. The screams yells and wails of the man were nothing short of horrendous. It was as if someone was entering hell! Geordie was so overcome by the whole scene that he had to run out into the yard and have a nervous smoke.

It wasn't long however before, mercifully, Rooney passed out with the pain. Watching on, Oscar was greatly relieved.

"He'll talk now alright. Just you wait until he wakes up. He'll talk and no mistake. If I'd done that to you, would you let me do it to you again or would you talk? Bill asked Oscar.

"Oh I'd talk alright! But if you ever come near me Bill, I promise you I'll kill you stone dead!" Oscar patted the Glock gun he had tucked inside his coat, and gave Bill a look that made even him look away.

Bill was right. Once Rooney came-to again, he gave up all the information: the starter motor full of drugs, talking to Dobson and what he knew about the surveillance operation. Oscar made brief notes, in a small notebook, to relay later to the Fatman.

When he'd got all he needed from Rooney, Bill went out into the yard. A couple of moments later a diesel motor chugged into life. It sounded to Oscar like a cement mixer. Then Bill came back in with two old steel buckets. He set them down on the floor.

"There," he said to Rooney, "that wasn't too bad after all was it? I mean like, I did make it fairly quick for you. I've sometimes tortured people for hours or even days! You got off easy!"

"You're a sick fuck!" gasped Rooney who was still writhing in agony.

"I know." Bill pulled out a gun from inside his coat and coldy shot Rooney between the two eyes. The crying and screaming abruptly stopped and that was the end of the interrogation.

"What the hell did you do that for?" Oscar yelled outraged.

"No witnesses. I'm not ever standing up in court in front of any judge whilst some wee pipsqueak tells everyone how I tortured him by shoving a red-hot poker up his arsehole!"

Oscar disapproved strongly, but he had to admit that there was a certain cold logic to this line of thought.

"Aye," he muttered reluctantly, "dead men can't talk I suppose."

"That's right," said Bill, putting Rooney's feet into the two buckets.

"What are you going to do now?" Oscar enquired.

"Rule number two of interrogation. No dead bodies are ever to be found by nosey policemen. I'm going to pour the concrete that's mixing outside into these buckets."

Bill disappeared outside and, after a couple of minutes, the mixer stopped. He reappeared with a wheelbarrow full of cement. With the aid of a small shovel, he soon had the two buckets, with Rooney's feet in them, full of cement.

"That's quick drying stuff so a couple of hours should see it hard as rock." said Bill.

"What then?" Oscar asked.

"There's a deep pond in a quarry, about a mile away. Once it's dark, we'll take him up there for a wee swim!" Bill grinned evilly. "Come on," he ushered Oscar outside and locked the Judas door with a strong looking padlock.

Bill looked over at Geordie who was still smoking. It was about his sixth fag in ten minutes. The wee man was white and shivering.

"Come on and we'll go get something to eat. All that torture has made me feel hungry!" laughed Bill.

40.

Dobson had called an emergency meeting in her incident room. She had asked Henderson and Butler to attend. They had been on stake-out duty opposite the scrap yard, and had needed to get a relief crew to take over before they left.

"Come in and close the door after you." Superintendent Dobson was shuffling some papers on her desk. She looked worried.

"We have a problem gentlemen," she addressed the two detectives.

"The informant who has been giving me information about the Cartwright case has gone missing. He went out from his business after lunch, going to lodge money at the bank, and he never came back.

"Was he robbed?" asked Butler.

"No. We found his van in a ditch on a quiet lane in the Castlereagh hills. The lodgement book and money were still in the van inside the glove compartment. That's why I'm worried!"

"Are you going to tell us his name now?" asked D.S. Henderson.

"His name is Paddy Rooney. He owns a little specalist garage that services mostly German cars. He's the one who got the starter motor delivered to him, the starter motor which turned out to be full of cocaine."

"What do you think has happened to him?" Butler asked.

"I think they have him," replied Dobson, "I think some one has leaked information to Cartwright and he has grabbed him. God alone knows what they'll do to him!"

"Wow!" said Henderson, looking just a little uncomfortable about all this.

"I really don't know how this could have happened," Dobson continued, "I told no one his identity. No one! I promised him no one would ever know he had given me information about

Cartwright. I feel terrible about this. What if they've tortured him or even killed him?"

"How on earth could anyone have found out his identity if you told no one?" Butler asked incredulously.

Henderson was silent lost in thought.

"What do you think Henderson?" she asked.

"I really don't know," was all he could say. "I really don't know." His voice trailed away.

The atmosphere in the room was downbeat for a few moments.

"I'll have to put more men on this case," said a grim faced Dobson. "If we've got some sort of a leak here, I need to find it fast!"

There was another prolonged silence in the room as everyone thought about the ramifications of all this, especially Henderson!

A few moments later, Dobson seemed close to losing her temper completely.

"I've had just about enough of this Cartwright and his bloody gang. It's time to spring a trap on him and take him down!"

41.

William had been on the phone to his solicitor. He had hastily arranged a meeting at his office.

Harrington had been quite pleased to hear that Julia wanted a divorce. He did, however, start the meeting by producing a set of photographs taken by the private detective they had earlier engaged.

"I believe these graphically display your wife's infidelity Mr Forsythe!" Harrington could not resist grinning as he spread out the photos on the green desktop for his client to view.

"Wow!" was all William could say. A series of slightly grainy, black and white images left little to the imagination. "I'd say she is well and truly caught in the act there!"

"We do actually have an unofficial legal term to describe someone who is the victim of such damming evidence." Harrington grinned.

"What's that?" asked William.

"She's focked!" laughed Harrington.

The two men laughed out loud. Again William could not help but find the very well spoken solicitor's turn of phrase very amusing!

"This actually makes things easier for you doesn't it? I mean, due to your current employment and financial situation, you aren't going to lose much by walking away from the marriage?"

"No. Not a lot. We have very little equity in the house anyway. If she wants it she can have it, as far as I'm concerned."

"What about personal savings?"

"I don't really have very much in the way of savings. Since I became unemployed, I've been eating into that in a big way. There's probably only about three thousand pounds left."

"You did tell me, at our first meeting regarding this matter, that you don't have any children, isn't that correct Mr. Forsythe?"

"Yeah. That is correct."

The corpulent solicitor sat back in his chair and clasped his hands behind his neck. He looked relaxed and about to pronounce a verdict upon the situation.

"As I see it, this is all very simple really. Your case is most uncomplicated and I see absolutely no reason why you shouldn't comply with your wife's wishes. After all, you have told me previously that you'd be quite content to escape from the marriage anyway. Under the circumstances, I see no necessity to bring up her infidelity, unless you particularly desire to do so. In my opinion, all that might do, would be to protract the matter and introduce a whole series of expensive costs. Let's keep the photos up our sleeve for now, and only produce them if things turn nasty. Better to agree to her request for the divorce and have done with it. Do you see what I mean?"

"Whilst I would love to haul her over the coals about her affair, I think what you say makes sense. Yeah, let's just get rid of her and make the break as clean as possible."

"Good man! I wish everyone had as clear vision as you do. Too many people become insanely bitter and get tangled up in the emotions of it all. They suffer unwanted and needless pain. Better just to make a clean break as you yourself can see."

William was thinking about the money. Now it would all be his. This was a whole new lease of life for him!

42.

The Fatman was having a meeting with Oscar and Bill. The court of enquiry was officially open and the Fatman was interrogating them.

"What's happening about the money? Are we still staking out that damn cycle track in case that bastard ever shows up again?"

"Yes Boss." Oscar replied. "There has never been any sign of him. I'm beginning to think it's a waste of time. He won't come back."

The Fatman chuckled softly to himself.

"That's why you won't ever make it into the master criminal bracket Oscar." He relaxed back into his seat, clasping his hands behind his neck, conjuring up an image of supreme power, menace and, indeed, even some sort of wicked wisdom.

"He'll be back." The Fatman uttered the words softly in a deep insightful manner. "I just know he will. It's instinctive and almost primal or some shit like that. He'll just have to come back for a wee look at the scene of the crime. He's done well to avoid giving in to the desire so far, but, you mark my words, he'll be back!"

He glanced over at Bill who was sitting in an armchair at the back corner of the large office. Bill was unusually quiet and looking thoughtful. He was obviously mulling over the whole situation.

"What do you think Bill? Will he show up again?"

Bill screwed his face up into a pensive considered look.

"Yeah. Actually I think he will turn up again. It's just as you say, he won't want to, but, by sheer instinct, he'll just have to. He won't be able to help himself. Like curiosity killed the friggin' cat!"

"Well if he shows up, we'll be waiting for him." Oscar added.

"Good," replied the Fatman. "How did your interrogation of that squealing wee rat Rooney go?

"Well he did plenty of squealing alright, but I can assure you he won't do any more!" Big Bill was rocking with mirth, chuckling wickedly.

"Just who exactly was he squealing to?" asked the Fatman

"Some detective woman called Dobson. She's the one who's heading the enquiry into your affairs. She's drug squad. They know you're moving drugs about, concealed inside motor parts."

Bill stood up and moved over towards the window. He parted the venetian blinds and stared out grimly across the street.

"See that old brick building over there? The bastards are set up in there, with binoculars and cameras, watching everything that goes on. You can't do diddlysquat without them knowing about it. In short, your whole operation is fully fucked."

"Pretty much as I thought." The Fatman looked ruefully out the window. "Just as well we moved all the stuff off site, aye Oscar?"

Oscar nodded agreement. "Pity we were not as successful when we moved the money."

"Well, that's what we are concentrating on from now on. The money. I want it found."

43.

Cecil knocked the door of the office and walked in.

"You wanted to see me Uncle Oscar?"

It was after five and the office girls had already gone home. Oscar was sitting at a desk checking some invoices. He looked up as the boy came in.

"I told you that you didn't need to call me Uncle Oscar." He scolded.

"Sorry Uncle Oscar . . . . I mean Oscar," the boy stammered apologetically.

Oscar smiled at him. "I have a wee surprise for you. Come with me."

Cecil followed Oscar outside and over into the parts' shed. It was the cleanest bit of the whole operation. The floor was always well swept, and parts were packaged in bags and neatly arranged on grey metal shelving. Oscar walked over to one corner and removed a tarpaulin from over something. Cecil gasped when he saw what it was, a brilliant white shiny scooter!

"This is for you Cecil. Happy birthday!"

"You're joking aren't you?" gasped the boy.

"No. This is yours. You are seventeen now, so you're legally entitled to be able to ride this. You'll just have to stick an L-plate on it."

Oscar handed Cecil a plastic packet with two L-plates in it.

"I talked to your mother about it and she's happy that you have it. It's not quite brand new, but it only has a thousand miles on it. It's insured, taxed and ready to go. You're really supposed to go and do some stupid test riding around a playground full of plastic cones, but you can ride it home and do that next week sometime."

"Wow!" was all Cecil could say. "This is absolutely fantastic."

"There are two conditions attached to this." Oscar suddenly looked very serious. "First, you always wear this helmet and the gloves inside it and ride carefully. Secondly, instead of coming to work here next year, I'd like you to consider going back to school and finishing your A-levels. You are a very bright young man and I think it would be much better for your future prospects than running about here wearing oily overalls."

"I really don't fancy going back to school again. I hate it!" The boy looked crestfallen. "Does that mean I can't have the scooter?"

"Of course you can have the scooter! It's your birthday! I just wanted you to consider some further education as I think it would be good for you. Maybe you could go to the Tech or something. Let's talk about it another time. Happy Birthday Cecil! I just want to see you happy!"

"Thank you so much Oscar!" The boy came over and shook his hand. Then, almost to Oscar's embarrassment, Cecil gave him a big hug. Oscar cast his eyes left and right, but luckily no one was in sight to see it. He gave the boy a quick hug in return.

"Right. Let's see if this powerful machine goes. Take it for a ride around the yard first, before you go home. I want to make sure you are not going to crash into anything!" said Oscar.

44.

William pumped up the tyres of his bike. The pressures were a little too low and that always made it more difficult to ride. He pumped them up to over sixty pounds per square inch. He had installed a cycle carrier rack on the back of the Porsche, which enabled him to take the bike with him. This allowed him to avoid busy suburban traffic, which he deemed dangerous to the leisure cyclist. He parked up in a quiet cul-de-sac and quickly unloaded the bike. He donned his reflective yellow jacket and cycle helmet and rode off.

Soon he was out on the cycle path, which followed the line of a long-disused railway track. Here, green trees and hedgerows flanked the path as he rode along. The sun was out for once and all seemed well with the world. He could smell a sweet perfume briefly as he passed some wild flowering shrub. It was a wonderful scent that could only but enhance the happy mood he was in.

William pressed a button and activated the electric motor. This just made progress a little faster and easier. Soon the bike was simply gliding along. As he pedalled, he began to really appreciate how lucky he was. Only weeks earlier, his whole life had seemed like a total disaster area. He remembered how he'd lost his job and his car.

He'd been depressed and initially upset at his ruined marriage. Now things were taking a turn for the better! He was retired, extremely wealthy, had a Porsche and was also free of a woman he no longer loved. Now at last he could plan for the future!

The cycle path led down through an industrial area near the docks and eventually out along past the motorway. Without stopping, he cycled past the spot where he'd found the money. On he went along the shore of Belfast lough eventually stopping at a little coffee shop near the end of the track. It was situated on an elevated site with good views across Belfast Lough. He parked up and went inside.

He ordered a Cappuccino and some rather delicious looking coffee cake. Sitting looking out across the sea, he started to formulate a plan. It was time to make a fresh start. Time to go away and live someplace else. His folks were both dead and he had no siblings. Now that he was divorcing Julia, there was nothing to keep him here.

He decided he would go to England in the Porsche. He'd head south. Why not? The weather was known to be just a little warmer and drier there. He had happy memories of holidaying with his parents in Dorset. He'd always intended to go back someday and relive those carefree days. Now he could afford to entertain such a notion.

William unzipped a small leather envelope type pouch he'd brought with him in the saddlebag of his bike. He whipped out his iPad and joined the free Wi-Fi connection the coffee shop offered it customers. He started to look for bed and breakfast accommodation in Dorset. After a bit of searching he found one he quite liked the look of. It was a lovely looking large thatched cottage with extensive gardens and a pond. They offered comfortable rooms with en-suite and the option of evening meals if required. It sounded just perfect to William. He bookmarked the page and finished his coffee whilst reading a newspaper on the iPad.

He was so absorbed reading that he wasn't really thinking about anything else. A loud voice nearby brought him back to reality.

"Oh look at him! He's gorgeous!" It was a young teenage girl. She had a couple of friends with her.

"Do ya see him in the pink." She yelled loudly.

She pointed at a handsome young lad serving coffee at the counter. The young man was wearing a pink T-shirt and his blonde hair did make him stand out a bit.

"I fancy him. He's gorgeous!" the kid shouted again in a loud voice. Everyone in the shop followed her gaze and embarrassed the young lad blushed.

Giggling, the girls ran out of the shop. William couldn't help but chuckle at the amusing scene. It brought him back to reality and he decided it was time to set off homeward.

He was planning ahead all the while as he rode. It would definitely be easier to take the Porsche to England on the ferry. No way could he take that amount of money through an airport and onto an aeroplane! What if security stopped him? No, he'd go in the car. Much less likely anyone would discover the money. He could hide it in the spare tyre well in the boot. He thought about a puncture and decided to take two canisters of that rubber solution you could use to re-inflate a burst tyre in an emergency. That would cover that contingency.

He'd have to tell Julia he was moving out of the house. He'd give her the details of Harrington Solicitors and she could contact him through them. He wouldn't tell her exactly where he was going though. Better to keep that to himself for now.

Just at that, he heard a loud thud! Alarmed, he looked to his left to see what it was. He was much relieved to discover it was only a wooden door in the fence along the shore that had banged in the wind. It unsettled him though and highlighted an underlying feeling of tension within him. He suddenly had a strong sense of de-ja-vu. He realised he was close to the underpass where the bag of money had fallen out of the skip lorry. This time he would stop and take a look. He could stand it no longer. He'd have to take a look.

There was a slight bend in the track where it approached the underpass. As he rounded the corner, shocked, he did a double take! A large black bin bag was lying right in the middle of the track. It was pretty much exactly where he'd found the bag of money! Astonished, he braked to a halt and dismounted. He went straight to the bag as if drawn by a powerful invisible force. When he opened it, he was flabbergasted to discover it was full of currency note sized pieces of newspaper. They were in stacked bundles inside clearly mimicking the money he'd found. There was a note inside the bag stuck to one of the bundles. William couldn't help but read it.

"WE KNOW WHO YOU ARE AND WE WANT IT BACK!"

William jumped away in alarmed astonishment. He could hear a noise. He turned round behind him recognising instantly that it was the motor drive of a camera. There were a series of clicks. He was being photographed! Just at that a small rough looking man came tearing down the bank from beside the underpass. It was Geordie Taylor.

"Oi. You! Stop right where you are! I've got you now!"

William jumped back onto the bike and pedalled off like mad!

"Stop you robbing bastard. Stop!"

William didn't stop. He pedalled as hard as he possibly could. His heart was pumping fit to burst. He pedalled as if the banshees of hell were pursuing him. He'd only gone a short distance when in a state of panic, he lost control of the bike. It had run over an empty glass bottle lying on the path. He came down with a great crash landing heavily on his right side. There was a sharp pain in his wrist.

Oh no! He thought. I've broken my wrist!

As he lay writhing in agony he heard a voice.

"Stay where you are you big bugger ye! I want to talk to you!"

He looked up and was greatly alarmed and dismayed to see the ruffian now on a bike himself tearing up the cycle path towards him!

Like Lazarus arising from the dead, he got up and despite the pain he remounted his bike and got going again.

"Stop you thieving bastard! I've got you now!" Yelled the rufian.

It was hard work pedalling the bike. His right foot had taken a bad twist when he went down. The pain was preventing him from going as fast as he needed to.

"Stop you big fucker you!

The man was catching him quickly. Panic stricken he became aware he wasn't going to get away. Then he realised he wasn't using the electric motor! He quickly pressed a button and instantly the machine leapt forward with renewed vigour. But it was too late. He felt a hand grab him from behind!

"I've got you now you bastard. Stop!

William flailed out desperately with his right arm and more by luck than anything else his fist connected with the wee man landing him a severe blow on the nose. Geordie squealed out sharply in pain and momentarily eased his grip. It was just enough for William to break free and with the electric motor now engaged he soon began to pull away.

Adrenalin had kicked in now and he found he was able to go at what seemed like a superhuman speed. He kept going as fast as he could possibly go. In the end, he felt ready to pass out. The exertion was killing him. He could go no further. Eventually, panting hard, he turned around to see where his pursuer was. A good two hundred yards away the wee man had dismounted his bike exhausted.

"We'll get you, you great cunt ye! You're a fuckin' dead man!" He shouted.

Despite the threats, William knew he had escaped, at least for now. The little man was all done in; finished! He pedalled away like fury again putting a safe distances between himself and the foul-mouthed little man. Twenty minutes later, lathered in sweat he arrived back at the Porsche. His head was spinning, his thoughts racing in a sheer frenzy.

Hurriedly, he loaded the bike on to the cycle rack and drove off. This had changed everything. He would have to greatly expedite the execution of his plans. He now needed to get the hell out of Dodge quickly!

45.

The Fatmans phone was ringing. It was the phone the detective had given him.

"Yeah." He answered gruffly.

"You guys are in big trouble."

"Do we need to meet up?"

"No. There's no time for that. The heat is really on here and I couldn't risk it. They know someone's been talking to you. They've found the empty van Rooney was driving. They know he's gone missing and suspect you have him. What happened to him?"

"No comment."

"Is he O.K.?

"I'm saying fuck all on this phone to you."

"Understood. Look I think a raid on your premises is due any time now. They'll be coming with a search warrant. You need to be prepared for that. I'll give you a ring to tell you when it's going down."

"You do that." The Fatman pressed the end key and set the phone down on his desk. He was deep in thought.

"Oscar!" he yelled out.

Moments later Oscar came into the office.

"I need you and Geordie to go out to the farm and do what we discussed earlier. Take plenty of old tyres with you and make a really good job of it!"

"No problem. I think Geordies staking out the cycle track. I haven't heard from him this afternoon at all. I'll give him a call." Oscar replied.

46.

"Shorty, you'll never believe what's just happened!" gasped Geordie still short of breath.

"What?" Shorty looked disinterested as he supped a pint of beer.

They were in McMorrans bar just a short distance away from the scrap yard.

"I saw the guy we're after! He came cycling along the track wearing that bright yellow coat, stopped and looked into the bag just as the boss and Oscar said he would.

"You're codding me!" Shorty was amazed.

He read the note and he nearly fuckin' shit himself. Literally jumped near out of his skin!"

"What did you do?"

"I photographed him with the digital camera Oscar gave me. Look at the pictures of him!" Geordie said excitedly as he scrolled through images on the tiny screen on the back of the camera.

Shorty inspected the pictures with great interest.

"Boy! The Fatmans going to be well pleased about this! But why didn't you catch him?

"I nearly did you know, but the bugger landed a punch on me and then he pedalled off on his bike. I chased him but I couldn't catch the bastard.

"Thought you used to be a boxer. Thought you were still fit!" Shorty jested.

"Ah for dears sakes! He had an electric motor on the bloody bike! I couldn't keep up with him!"

"Here wait a moment, let me have a deco at them photos again . . . ." Shorty motioned for Geordie to hand over the camera.

He looked very carefully at the cyclists face.

"I think I've seen that guy somewhere before." He said.

"Where?"

"Shut up a minute. I'm thinkin!"

After a few moments, Geordie was about to get up and go. Shorty wasn't too bright and he really didn't expect anything to register in his memory.

"Hold on a minute." Shorty was sitting with his eyes closed and his head clasped between his hands. This was obviously a supreme effort to draw some memory from the vague virtually vacant recesses of his tiny brain.

"Yes!" shouted Shorty triumphantly. "I remember where I saw him!"

"Are you serious?"

"It was at an off licence at Gleesons corner in East Belfast. I go over there because wee Willy Wylie works there on Saturdays. I know him these years. I buy my beer there. He always slips me a few extra bottles for free!"

"So what?" said a bored Geordie. "As the boss would say, will you get to the effing point!"

Shorty scowled at him looking somewhat aggrieved.

"That's where I saw him. I think he buys his wine there. I've actually seen him on a bike there too. He must live close by!"

"Well that's a turn up for the books, you remembering something."

"What do mean?" asked Shorty.

"Well, I bet you don't remember that fiver I lent you last Wednesday?"

Shorty laughed seeing the funny side of it. "No not at all!"

Then Shorty looked serious again. You could almost hear the cogwheels going around inside the little man's brain.

"I've had an idea!" he announced. "Lets go and see wee Willy Wylie."

"Why?" asked Geordie.

"Because the off licence has a really super C.C.T.V. system. It records everything onto VCR tapes. Willy showed me how it all works. I'll bet with the aid of a few pound, we can talk Willy into lending us the tape!"

"Shorty, have you just been eating brain boosting tablets or something! That's just plain and simple, probably the best idea I think you've ever had!"

Shorty beamed at the compliment.

"Lets go." he said. I think Willy should be there today.

47.

AN ESTATE AGENTS OFFICE IN BELFAST.

"Stupid bitch!"

Philip had just come off the phone.

"What?" James his astonished colleague said. "Keep it down! There's a lady looking through some brochures over there."

"Stupid bitch!" Philip said again. This time it was slightly more muted, but not much.

"Is something wrong?" James asked concerned. Philip never usually used such appalling language in the office, especially in front of customers.

"Yes!"

"Look, lets go somewhere a bit more private."

He pointed over towards a side office they reserved for meetings with important clients. Obediently, and obviously in a state of some shock, Philip walked over in the direction of the office.

The office was unoccupied and in darkness as they entered. James touched a switch and instantly, powerful fluorescent lights began to flicker into life. Soon the opulent office with a lovely oak wood conference table and leather bound chairs was bathed in a soft white light. They both sat down and for a moment all was quiet.

"What on earth is wrong with you mate? You know we can't use language like that in the office. If old Harrison heard you doing that, he'd probably sack you on the spot!"

"I just don't believe it!" Philip was gazing intently at a large oil painting of a local landscape on the wall opposite. Staring at it helped him to focus just a little and compose himself.

"What's wrong?" James asked again.

"Its that stupid bitch Julia! You know I've been having a bit of a fling with a bird I met whilst working out at the gym?"

"Yeah."

"Well, we were always joking and flirting a bit. She seemed like good fun and then one night, we went for a drink after a training session."

"And?" prompted James, even though he knew where this was probably going by now.

"Well it all seemed a bit of a laugh. I took her up to my apartment and we had a few more drinks. Listened to some music. You know how it is. One thing led to another and we ended up in bed. It was all good. Just a bit of harmless fun."

"Fair enough, we've all done it haven't we?"

"Well, it became a bit of a regular thing recently. I guess we were both enjoying it and it was easy for me, like I knew I was on a sure thing. I wasn't chasing woman round the nightclubs or anything just as hard as usual."

"It all adds up." James encouraged him to continue.

Unbelievably, Philip was suddenly almost in tears!

"She's just phoned me!" he sobbed. "She's just phoned to tell me. I mean I didn't even know she was married! She never even told me!"

"Didn't you see her wedding ring?"

"No I did not! She definitely never wore one!"

"Well so what?" James was getting a tad fed up with all this. "If its getting too hot for you walk out of the kitchen. Tell her to fuck off!"

Philip looked up, a glazed look on his face.

Just at that the phone buzzed. James answered it. It was Helen, one of the telephone receptionists at the front desk.

"There's a call for Philip on line three. Mrs Johnston wants to know about her offer on 143 Woodstock Park."

"Tell her Mr. Thompson is in a meeting and we'll get him to call her back later." James set the phone down again.

"Go on."

"Well, as I was saying, I didn't know she was married. She's just phoned to tell me she is leaving her husband and she wants to move in with me!"

"Yeah right on!" replied James. "What age is she?"

"She must be definitely mid to late thirties."

"And you are remind me?"

"Twenty six."

"Twenty six." Repeated James walking around the office. It was so simple for him. He could see it all in razor clear light as one always does when totally uninvolved emotionally. "Twenty six. Look you are still young and virile and you should be out there playing the field for all you're worth! Unless she really is one hell of a honey with film star looks, I refer to my earlier comment. Tell her to fuck off!"

"It's not as simple as that." Philip paused before delivering the bombshell. "She's pregnant!" He looked absolutely desolate.

"Oh." Replied James looking a little concerned now. That's a pig with a different snout.

"Yes. It bloody well is. Life as I know it is all over." He looked utterly resigned to his fate.

"Don't be so bloody stupid!" shouted James. "You've lots of options here. You can tell her to have an abortion. Pay for it yourself if it makes you feel better. Or as I said earlier, tell her where to go.

"I can't do that!" protested Philip.

"Look, you're not married to this woman. She misled you by hiding the fact that she was actually married. She has obviously, stupidly not been taking any form of birth control medication. You owe her nothing! She's clearly a conniving duplicitous bitch. Probably planned all this just to trap you! I'd leave her in a heartbeat!"

Philip stared at James in disbelief. He'd worked with him for a couple of years now. He was a senior colleague and indeed mentor. In all that time, he'd never picked up on this cold, callous streak he was now clearly manifesting.

"So that's your advice. Just leave her?"

"Yes it is." Replied a grim looking James.

"Really! Just like that!"

"Just like that. Life's too short." James looked at his watch. "Anyway, its nearly six o'clock. Why don't you go on home and think about it. I'll get Helen to ring Mrs Johnston.

"O.K. thanks." Philip replied weakly as he got up to go.

James watched him gather his belongings and walk away wearily towards the car park. "What an idiot!" he thought to himself. "He's young, good looking, got a Porsche and a nice apartment. Why the hell give it all up just because some bitch gets herself pregnant?"

48.

THE FATMANS OFFICE.

The Fatman looked at Geordie and Shorty with some degree of bewilderment as they marched confidently into his office.

"I didn't realise we had a meeting scheduled today gentlemen!"

It was about as close as Cartwright ever came to joviality.

"Boss, can we plug this video machine into your T.V. set please?"

It was Shorty asking almost apologetically.

"Listen guys. I'm too busy today to watch porn so just bugger off and get on with your work. I believe Oscar is looking for you anyway Geordie. He needs you to help him burn some old tyres out at the farm."

"This is important!" Shorty looked deadly serious.

"What!" The Fatman reddened at the gills looking set to go off on one.

"Boss he's right. It is important." Said Geordie. "Just sit down in your chair and listen to what Shorty here has to say. You are going to want to hear it believe me!"

Somehow, the Fatman realised this really was important and incredibly, he obediently sat down to listen.

"Firstly," announced Geordie "You were right. That cyclist cunt came back to the scene of the crime. I photographed him with this digital camera."

"Let me see the pictures!" demanded the Fatman.

Geordie handed over the camera and the Fatman scrolled through the images on the cameras tiny screen.

"This is good boys!" he laughed. "Where do you have him? I would like to ask him a few questions as you can imagine!"

"Ah, we don't actually have him. The Bastard escaped," admitted an embarrassed Geordie.

"He what!" Screamed the Fatman incredulous. "You had the fucking bastard that stole my money and you let him get away!" He was going white in the face now. The boys knew this was a bad sign. Red in the face, not good, but when he went white in the face, that meant he was really pissed at them!

The Fatman reached into his desk and pulled out his black Glock pistol.

"Tell me how he escaped Geordie. Just tell me!" he yelled pulling back the slide mechanism of the gun.

Trembling with fear, Geordie told the whole sad story of how the cyclist got away using the electric motor on the bike.

"I don't believe it! I just do not bloody believe it!" Yelled the Fatman.

He started to point the Glock at Geordie and was taking aim when Shorty said.

"There is some good news though!"

Lowering the pistol in disbelief, the Fatman glared at the wee man. His ears were flared wide just like the open doors of a taxi. What a stupid looking wee man he thought to himself.

"And just exactly what the fuck do you have to add?" he yelled.

"Chill out boss! Don't shoot till you hear what we have to tell you!" pleaded Geordie.

"Aye." Said Shorty. "Just cool your jets and listen will you!" he shouted sounding actually rather irate.

This amused the Fatman slightly, the cheek of this wee runt standing up to him. Intrigued he enquired,

"O.K. Shorty you have the floor son. But this had better be good or I'm probably going to shoot the pair of you!"

Shorty explained that he'd recognised the man Geordie had photographed. He went on to tell the Fatman about wee Willy Wylie and the off licence where he had seen the cyclist.

"Then I had an idea," Shorty beamed proudly.

"And it was a good idea; a real brainwave!" Geordie added.

The Fatman looked at the two of them dubiously. He employed these guys to carry out his instructions. He didn't really expect them to think, just do what they were told. Not in all the years they'd worked for him had either of them ever had anything remotely like a brainwave.

"C.C.T.V!" said Shorty excitedly.

"What about it?" the Fatman asked becoming exasperated. It was always like drawing teeth!

"The off licence where your man goes to buy his drink has a fantastic C.C.T.V. system fitted. It's a modern, state of the art job. It even records video in colour!"

"Interesting, continue!"

"Well," Shorty went on, "You know wee Willy Wylie?"

"Yeah."

"Well, you know he went to school with me years ago? Well you know I was telling you that he now works in an off licence so he does."

"So fucking what!" the Fatman's blood pressure was rising again!

"Well you know . . . ."

"Don't start telling me I know! Remember we talked about this previously?" the Fatman growled in a deep menacing voice.

Shorty paused gulping air like a goldfish. The wide spread ears looked particularly ridiculous today and the Fatman was really struggling to take him seriously.

"Look" said Shorty finally gathering himself, "I gave Willy £50 to lend me these tapes."

He held them aloft. "I spent hours looking through them last night and finally. He pushed a tape into the VCR player Geordie had by now wired into the Fatman's TV set.

"Finally Geordie and I have him for you. Hit play Geordie."

With a great flourish, Geordie pressed the button on the remote control of the VCR player. For a brief moment there was a whirring noise and a series of crackles and all that appeared on the screen were black and white dots. Then, as if by magic the image of a man appeared on screen. He had his back to the camera.

"There he is!" said Shorty pleased with himself.

The man on the screen was wearing a bright yellow reflective cycle jacket. He was carefully selecting a bottle of wine from the shelving. After about thirty seconds he turned round facing the camera and Geordie froze the frame.

"That's him!" Geordie announced. "Shorty you're a genius!"

"Well, well." The Fatman said shaking his head in astonishment. "I must say I am amazed! Well-done guys and particularly you Shorty! It really was a brainwave!"

Shorty smiled really pleased with himself.

The Fatman stared intensely at the image of the man.

"Who is he?" he asked.

"We don't really know yet. But, he'll almost certainly return to this off licence as wee Willie Wylie says he often comes in."

"Does Wylie know anything about him?" Queried the Fatman.

"He just knows him to see. He's apparently not the talkative type."

Geordie and Shorty looked at the Fatman expectantly.

"Right." The Fatman leaned back in his leather chair characteristically clasping his hands behind his head. "This is what we're going to do."

49.

SUPERINTENDENT DOBSON's BRIEFING ROOM AT POLICE HEADQUARTERS.

D.I. Dobson had assembled a team of eight detectives around the conference table in her office. Behind them, sat around a dozen or so uniformed officers.

"O.K. listen up people." She said. "The subject of our attention to-day is a certain Mr. James Cartwright alias the Fatman. Most of you are already well aware of his operation, but for those of you who are not, I'll give you a bit of background. Cartwright and his gang operate out of a scrapyard business located here in Capstan Street in the docklands."

Dobson used a large wooden pointer to show everyone the location of the scrapyard on a very large-scale map on the wall behind her.

"The scrapyard is however only a front for the criminal activities we have reason to believe these chaps are involved in. Cartwright, Oscar Jamison, Geordie Taylor and Shorty Thompson are the main targets of are investigation.

"Are there others working in the yard?" Asked detective constable Hudson a fairly new face amongst the drug squad.

"Don't interrupt me at this stage." Dobson said sternly, "I'll take questions at the end of the briefing."

Dobson outlined the activities of the villains including the concealment of drugs within motor spares like starter motors, exhaust systems, oil filters etc. She explained that a delivery van frequently delivered parts to various garages and other locations on a Province wide basis. This was all a cover for distribution and sales of drugs to other dealers.

"These guys think that they are very clever and that they won't get caught. We're going to prove them wrong! A few months ago we got a break when an informant came to us and gave us information which led to the start of this investigation.

We have had the whole operation under surveillance for some weeks now, but recently several things have happened. Most importantly, Paddy Rooney, our main informant went missing last Tuesday. His van was found in a ditch just South of Belfast here."

Dobson referred to a smaller scale map of Northern Ireland which was beside the main map on the wall behind her.

"We suspect, I think with good reason that the gang have captured Rooney and are questioning him. This is the best case scenario. Rooney was very concerned that the crooks would get him if he gave us information about them. As a result of his fears, I gave him an assurance that we would be very careful indeed. The interesting thing is that no one except myself had ever met Rooney or knew any of his details.

This afternoon, we are going to pay a surprise visit to the Cartwrights operation. This will be the main target. We will also be doing a raid on a house in East Belfast. The house is rented out in the name of James Cartwright so we suspect it is being used to distribute or sell drugs.

Dobson went on to outline the details of the raid. There would be two teams. She herself would lead the main team going to the scrapyard and Detective sergeant Nelson would take a smaller unit to the East Belfast address.

"One final thing. This operation is not to be discussed with anyone outside of this room. It is imperative that we have the advantage of total surprise when we go to search these premises. Is that clearly understood by all here?"

There was a general murmur of concurrence.

"I'm going to ask you again to make sure that everyone is absolutely clear on this point. No one is to discuss anything about this operation with anyone outside of this briefing room. Understood?"

"Yes everyone shouted back."

"Thanks for that. On this particular occasion, I am also taking the added precaution of asking you to hand over your personal mobile phones. This is unfortunately necessary."

There was a general muffled grumble of disapproval from the assembly, but everyone complied putting their phone in a basket passed around for the phones to be collected into.

"Thank you everybody. We will be going in thirty minutes so gather up all your gear and be ready to go at three o'clock on the dot."

At that, Dobson brought her briefing to a conclusion.

50.

THE FORSYTHE HOUSE.

William was eating his usual breakfast of coffee, toast, butter and marmalade when Julia eventually came in. She was dressed for work and ready to go off to the supermarket.

"I'm leaving tomorrow morning," announced William dispassionately taking a bite of toast.

Julia was momentarily dumbstruck. She was well aware that they were splitting up but suddenly the finality of it all was hitting home.

"Oh," she stammered. "Didn't realize you would be leaving just quite so soon."

"Well there you go. All good things come to and end. It shouldn't be any surprise to you anyway. I told you that you could keep the house. Said I'd go."

"I thought you were staying until the end of the week though." Julia seemed almost disappointed that he was leaving so soon.

"Well my plans have changed and I'm going tomorrow morning now."

William was greatly surprised that she actually seemed to care. Apart from the brief frolic in the bedroom last week, they had barely spoken to each other.

"Fair enough. Suppose that's it then." Julia said almost tearfully.

For just a moment, William felt almost sorry for her. He was going off to a new life and she was still working at the supermarket.

"Lets have dinner together here tonight," he said "Just one last time, nothing grand, just a carryout Chinese or something simple. I'll get a bottle of wine and we'll finish our relationship on a high and civilized note." He was half expecting her to say no.

"O.K. That would be nice. Lets do that." She replied pleasantly. "I have to go now. I'll be late for work."

"See you later." William flicked the T.V. on to watch the morning news as she left by the back door. He waited until the engine of the little Fiat started up and she had driven off. Quickly he sprang into action.

Out in the garage he removed the spare wheel of the Porsche from its wheel well. He rolled it away into the darkness at the back of the garage and hid it under an old tarpaulin.

He opened the safe and packed all the money neatly into a large soft conformable luggage bag. There was a problem though. It didn't quite fit properly into the wheel well. He had to resort to stashing some of the money below the passenger seat. Eventually, he was reasonably happy that if a security man at the ferry took a cursory look at the car he'd find nothing.

He locked the car up and armed the expensive alarm and immobilizer system he'd had fitted just a few days before. The horn of the alarm would waken the dead if it went off. He wheeled his bike outside and closed and locked the garage door behind him.

As he walked back towards the house to pack everything else, he realized the spare key for the Porsche was still hanging on a hook at the back of the garage. He didn't want to leave without it and was about to walk back to retrieve it when he had second thoughts. He felt it unlikely anyone would find it as the hook was in a dark corner of the garage and hidden behind some old paint tins. No, it would be safe enough there. Returning to the house, he went upstairs to pack.

51.

"Hi Philip." Julia was on a break from the till at the supermarket. "How's your day been darling?"

"Fine, just fine." Philip was just about to dash off for an eleven o'clock viewing of a house. On top of everything else, it was a bad time.

"How are you fixed at lunch time to-day. I can pop over to see you for half an hour or so. We've so much to talk about!" she said enthusiastically."

"Yes. You're right there," replied Philip. "There's plenty to talk about alright. I can't do lunch time though. I'm way too busy I'm afraid. What about tonight?"

"Oh." Julia was obviously disappointed. "I can't do tonight. I've agreed to have dinner in with William just one last time. He's leaving in the morning. After that we'll have the house to ourselves."

"Yeah. We need to talk about all this. This is all moving way too fast for me." Philip sounded a bit weary.

"Well what about tomorrow?"

"Tomorrow is much better." Replied Philip. "I can get away early tomorrow night I think. I'll ring you."

"O.K! Love you lots!"

"Love you too." Philip tried to sound enthusiastic and hoped he'd got away with it.

"See you tomorrow! Bye!"

Philip had already hung up. Momentarily, Julia stared at her mobile phone surprised that Philip had cut her off so suddenly.

52.

William had cycled around to some nearby shops. He bought a newspaper and read it in a local coffee shop. As usual, he scanned all the headlines and stories looking for some mention of a robbery or anything to do with missing money. As usual, there was nothing.

Earlier, he had bought his ferry ticket to take the Porsche over to England. Tomorrow, he would be out of here. He'd got most of his gear packed already. The money was safely stowed away in the Porsche. All was going according to plan.

He sat drinking his coffee and in his mind, he went through things carefully. He wanted to avoid any problems and possible glitches in his plans. He was thinking about the lunatic ruffian he had met on the cycle path. That was the only thing that really worried him. He was obviously the guy who had lost the money. William involuntarily shivered with fear. If that guy found him before he got on the boat, he was in big trouble. There and then he decided to go off home and lie low until the morning.

The good thing was, they didn't know where he lived. After all how could they possibly know? The thought was haunting him now. The madman had chased him on the cycle path. He remembered the motor drive of the camera whirring. He shuddered as it registered that they had a photo of him. That was definitely not a nice idea!

William decided to go back to the house. He'd stay there until he left for the boat. If no one saw him out and about, no one could recognize him no matter how many photographs they had of him. The house was only about a mile away. He could pedal back there using side streets and indeed a very secluded alley way and was confident no one would spot him.

Outside, he was climbing onto his bike when it suddenly struck him he was just about as low key as a belesha beacon. The bright yellow reflective coat he always wore for safety purposes was now a liability. He stood out like a sore thumb! Hurriedly, he took it off and stuffed it away into the tail bag on the bicycle rack. That would certainly help when stealth was at a premium he thought. Crossing the road, he started down an alley that ran for about a quarter of a mile behind a row of terrace houses. This was clever enough he thought. No one would see him here. He was well on the way to the house when he remembered something important.

"Oh blast! I've forgotten to get the wine." He said to himself.

He stopped for a moment and then taking everything carefully into consideration, he turned the bike around. A quick trip to the off licence would not constitute a major de tour.

Soon afterwards, he emerged from a side street at Gleeson's corner. The off licence was just across the street. He parked the bicycle carefully locking it to a railing. Feeling somewhat more uptight than usual, he looked across the road. He viewed the whole scene with some trepidation. After a minute or so, everything looked perfectly normal. He crossed the street and entered the off licence.

At the rear of the shop was an area, which proudly displayed a sign proclaiming "Fine Wines." He had over the years developed a taste for some of the lesser Burgundy wines. He selected a bottle labeled Chablis Premier Cru. "That will do very nicely!" he grinned to himself.

As he paid for the wine, he imagined the wiry little man behind the counter stared at him just a second too long. Then, the little man smiled cheerfully and said "Have a nice day Sir." Moments later, after the shop door closed, Willy Wily lifted his phone and made a quick call. "That's your man now. He's just leaving on a bike. He's wearing a blue polo shirt. You'll need to be quick Shorty."

"Thanks!" came the reply as the phone went dead.

William left and after quickly unlocking the bike, he was on his way.

My imagination is just too fertile he thought to himself. After all there is nothing to worry about! "Its all in your head!"

he said out loud to himself. "Speaking to yourself, the first sign of madness!" He laughed out loud as he rode along. Smack! Something struck him an almighty blow on the back of the head and neck. The pain was intense and losing control of the bike, he slammed hard into the back of a parked car.

He lay there totally dazed. What had happened he wondered? He was in a complete state of bewilderment. There were two men, one with a baseball bat. The men grabbed him and bundled him into the back of a van. Next thing he knew, a piece of cloth was being held over his mouth and nose.

"Don't give him too much of that!" a voice shouted out alarmed. "We don't want to kill the bugger!"

The cloth had a strangely familiar medical smell to it. "Ether!" William recognized it. He struggled desperately to free himself but soon everything went into a void of utter blackness.

53.

Oscar was up at the farm. He was annoyed that he hadn't been able to locate either Geordie or Shorty. In the end, he'd enlisted Cecil to help him. He'd thought very carefully about this. Eventually he decided there was no harm in it as the boy wouldn't really understand what was going on anyway.

"Right Cecil, let's get these tyres out of the back of the van."

"O.K." Cecil was pleased to be able to help. It gave him a chance to earn a few extra pounds. He was saving up to buy a decent motorcycle jacket to wear on his scooter. It always seemed to be raining and he was fed up with getting wet!

Oscar rolled a tyre over to one side of the yard and dumped it on top of some very heavy steel plate sheeting. Cecil noticed the plate was nearly an inch thick.

"Bring all the tyres over here Cecil. When you've unloaded them all, we'll burn them. I'm going into the house to talk to Maureen."

"No problem!" Cecil answered obediently wondering what was under the steel sheeting. It never ceased to amaze him that Oscar seemed to think he was so naive!

Meanwhile, Oscar knocked the back door of the house. After a minute or so, a very overweight looking woman appeared at the back door. Oscar hadn't seen her for some time now and was astonished that she now seemed even heavier than when he'd last saw her. It was the Fatman's wife, Maureen.

"Hi Oscar. "She said with a slightly suspicious look. "What brings you up here?"

"Hello Maureen." Oscar smiled pleasantly. "Anybody else here?"

"No. The housekeeper is off today. Do you want to come in?'

"Yes please love."

"How about a cup of tea? Maureen was already putting a kettle of water onto the Aga in anticipation.

"Yeah that would be good." Oscar looked around the kitchen. It was fairly tidy looking due to the attentions of the house keeper he suspected. Maureen wasn't noted for having everything spic and span. There was the after smell of some sort of greasy cooking or something hanging in the air. It was an unpleasant sort of odour.

"Maureen, I'm up here to burn some old tyres."

"Oh. Why on earth are you doing that!" Maureen looked surprised and not too pleased at the prospect of black smoke all round her house for hours on end. "Last time you did that it stank for days!"

"Has James told you about the situation?"

"Yes. He tells me pretty much everything."

"Then you know what's under the steel plating?

"Yes" she replied.

"Well, we are going to burn the tyres on top of the plating. That way, if anybody of a nosey or suspicious disposition comes up here, they won't find anything."

"Sounds like a good idea to me. Leave some of the tyres over to one side will you? That way, every now and then, once they are nearly burned out, I'll add another couple on to keep the fire burning."

"That's a good idea Maureen." Agreed Oscar.

The kettle was already starting to whistle that it had boiled.

"That was quick!" said Oscar.

"I always keep the water warm on the side of the aga." Maureen grinned.

"There's milk and sugar on the table and here are some biscuits." She said handing Oscar a steaming mug of tea. "Who's with you today? Would they like a cup of tea too?"

"It's just young Cecil."

"Cecil!" Maureen looked astonished. "Why the hell did you bring Cecil! He shouldn't know anything about this!" Maureen was annoyed. Her shocked wide-eyed look was reminiscent of her husband when he was angry.

"Cecil knows nothing. He's only here to burn tyres as far as he knows!" Oscar defended himself.

"Does my sister Aggie know about this?"

"About what?"

"About you involving Cecil in our business. About putting him in danger. If the police came up here while he was here what would happen?" she yelled accusingly.

"Well, James has him down at the yard washing the cars and sometimes stacking batteries and the like, so what's the difference?" Oscar had always found Maureen to be a right pain in the arse. No matter what you did she was always questioning and objecting.

"You know fine well what's under that steel sheeting Oscar! That's a very big difference in my eyes."

"Neither Cecil or Aggie know anything about what your husband and I really do for a living and that's the way its going to stay! Now please leave this to me and don't interfere!" Oscar had already had enough of her. He took a big slug of tea from the mug, slammed it down on the counter and left by the back door.

Maureen stared angrily after him. Oscar had just pushed the wrong button and rage welled up inside her. After a few moments thought she lifted the phone. It rang for quite a while before there was any answer.

"James!" she yelled. "Oscar is out here burning tyres!"

Outside in the yard, Maureen could see Oscar pouring petrol liberally over the tyres. Next thing, there was a great woooof! They were lit and burning.

The Fatman was sitting at his desk. He rolled his eyes when he heard who was on the phone. Biting his tongue and trying to be patient he answered.

"Yeah. I know Oscar is burning tyres. I sent him and you know why he's doing it so what's your problem?"

"He has your nephew young Cecil with him. That's my problem! I just don't like the idea of him being involved in all this. The boy has only just turned seventeen for dears sakes!"

The Fatman was momentarily caught off balance.

"I didn't know he had Cecil with him. I told the idiot to take Geordie with him to burn the tyres. Only thing is, Geordie hasn't been seen all day and he isn't answering his mobile. Maybe Oscar couldn't find Geordie and enlisted Cecil as there was nobody else."

"Why couldn't Shorty have helped?" Maureen wanted answers.

The Fatman was mindful of the fact that it was possible his phone had been tapped.

"Could be he's away helping Geordie with whatever he's doing. Now will you just go away and bake wee buns or something and give my head peace!" With that he slammed the phone down cutting Maureen off.

Maureen was seething by now! She was just about to phone the Fatman back when another idea occurred to her.

She went through the menu on her phone until she found the number. This time, the phone rang only twice before it was answered.

"Hello."

"Hello Aggie, how are you.?"

Aggie was quite surprised. Her sister hadn't been in touch for quite a while now. Recently, she'd been upset that neither she nor James had bothered to even send Cecil a card for his seventeenth birthday.

"I'm fine Maureen, just fine. How are you dear?" Aggie knew her sister only usually rang her when she wanted something. Aggie was altogether different from her sister being modest, quietly spoken and polite. Maureen had always spoken her mind and to hell with it if you didn't like what she had to say.

"I'm grand. Did you know that your Cecil was up here at our place burning tyres with Oscar?"

"No!" Came the surprised reply. "I thought he was at school today. What's he doing burning tyres?"

"Well that's what I wondered. I thought he ought to be at school too. Didn't you know about this?" Maureen was really winding her sister up now. It wasn't for amusement. She just had a thoroughly bad streak in her.

"Obviously I didn't know. What I do know is that Cecil has been spending a lot of time with his Uncle Oscar. Oscar takes him down to his gym and they do weight lifting together. He's a very nice man. He's taken an interest in the boy and even bought him a scooter for his birthday. I was very pleased, because as you know, I don't have much and couldn't really afford to buy him anything like that."

"So Oscar bought him a scooter!" Maureen was surprised. "That's a turn up for the books. James has always told me that Oscar's a real tightwad. Said he wouldn't spend Christmas!"

"Well he's been very good to young Cecil. Even told him he should continue his studies and do his A levels at school. Cecil was ready to leave school you know. Now, because Oscar talked to him, he's thinking about staying on. He's like a father to that boy."

Maureen was most annoyed by all this. This wasn't the reaction she'd hoped for. She couldn't help but throw a spanner in the well-oiled works.

"Maybe Oscar is just a wee bit too nice! James told me he was never much of a man for the ladies. Maybe he prefers little boys like Cecil. Maybe he's gay!"

"That's a horrible thing to say! You really are rotten to the core. Just because you have no children of your own and are a miserable old cow doesn't mean you have to go casting aspersions like that."

"Well you have to look at the evidence don't you? Has Cecil been round at Oscar's apartment yet? Maybe they've been at it already!"

Maureen was really spooning it on.

"How dare you say things like that about my son! Just you keep your big mouth shut and your opinions to yourself. Don't ring me again!"

Aggie hung up. She walked back into the living room of her small semi-detached house. Sitting down on the sofa, she noticed for the umpteenth time the threadbare carpet on the living room floor. She sat there thinking about what Maureen had said. Oscar had been like a light in the darkness. In a world where nobody cared, he had taken an interest in the wee lad. He had recently been like a father to her son, always helping and advising. What a nice man he was.

As she sat, she found herself starting to sob. What if she was wrong? What if Oscar was really some monster with hideous plans for her polite pleasant little innocent son? The doubts were beginning to crowd into her mind. Her sister was a right bitch no doubt, but what if she was right? She felt a cold shiver run down her back.

54.

If you had asked him afterwards why he'd done it, he couldn't have given you an answer. The Fatman had a secret safe in his office. No one knew about it, not even Oscar his most trusted companion. The safe was hidden behind some wood paneling in the wall. It had been concealed so carefully that it was very difficult to spot. The special trick was that he had another safe hidden behind a picture. That was obvious. Everyone knew about it.

The Fatman pressed the panel in just the right place and slid it open. Quickly he opened the safe and stowed his glock pistol away inside it. He briefly caressed a stack of bright red fifty-pound notes. There were many such bundles in the safe. This was his own emergency stash. He locked the safe and slid the paneling carefully back into place.

He was just about to sit down at the desk again when he glanced out into the yard. Suddenly all hell was breaking loose. Even though he'd been half expecting it to happen sometime, it came as quite a shock. His jaw sagged down in surprise.

Outside, half a dozen police cars and vans had come charging into the yard sirens blazing, blue lights flashing. They screeched to a halt scattering gravel as they did so. It was like something you'd see in a film on the television. It all had an air of surrealism to it! There was a great crashing sound as they broke down the front door of his office building. He couldn't understand this at all. He was certain it hadn't actually been locked!

Downstairs he could hear his office girls shrieking and screaming in terror. He opened the door of his own office and started down the stairs.

"What the bloody hell do you lot want! How dare you come charging in here like this scaring the shit out of my secretaries!"

An officer wearing a flack jacket and helmet came forward. "Are you Mr James Cartwright?"

"Yes. What is going on here?" He purposely put on an act of surprised innocence."

A detective approached. She looked very determined and serious. It was Superintendent Dobson. "We have a warrant to search your premises. No body is to attempt to leave this office without our permission." Dobson held up a document for the Fatman to inspect. He gave it a cursory glance and then resignedly sat down at a desk.

"Don't worry girls." He reassured his office staff. "This is all a total load of balls. We've done nothing wrong. This is all some sort of stupid mistake."

A policeman was pulling out the drawers of a nearby desk and turning everything out onto the desktop. Samantha, his office manager was giving off hell to him. The officer totally ignored her.

"What's all this about anyway? Haven't we paid our VAT or something?" the Fatman asked looking at Dobson. This was all for the benefit of the office staff. It was well known that Cartwright never paid the VAT until Her Majesty's Customs and Excise had virtually threatened him with jail first!

Two policemen raced up the stairs and into his office. There was lots of noise and he could hear things being broken and thrown about. Infuriated, he got to his feet. He could stand it no longer.

"Stop it!" He yelled. "You're wrecking the bloody place!"

"Mr Cartwright." It was one of the officers up above in his office. "Could you come up here please.

Obediently, the Fatman waddled upstairs. The sight that met him was terrible. The whole office had been upturned and papers were lying everywhere. It was as if a bulldozer had been running amok!

"You bastards! Look at my office! Who's going to tidy all this up again!" he yelled florid with rage.

"Mr. Cartwright." An officer had removed a picture from the wall. "Could you please open this?" he pointed to a safe.

"Why the hell should I?" he barked defiantly.

By this time, Dobson had joined them.

"Either you open it up or we will open it by force. It's your choice." She starkly informed him in her broad Yorkshire accent.

Cartwright pretended to be really upset about it all. He should have been nominated for an Oscar. In reality, he wasn't the least bit concerned.

"People have safes like this to keep their private possessions in. Its not fair. You have no bloody right to come in here threatening me!" he protested.

As he did so, he glanced out the window into the yard below. It was a scene of utter chaos. Every building was being searched. There were men with sniffer dogs ranging back and forth. The mechanics had been lined up against a wall and were being searched at gunpoint. It suddenly occurred to him that no one important was here. Oscar, Geordie and Shorty were all currently off the premises. What a stupid lot these police are he thought to himself.

"Mr Cartwright, this is your last chance or we'll blow the door off the safe with explosives." Dobson was clearly losing patience.

"Alright, alright. Don't get your knickers in a knot wee girl."

Cartwright turned the knob on the safe rotating it back and forwards as he dialed in the combination. He pulled a lever and released the locking mechanism. An officer pounced on him quickly pulling him away as the other officer opened the door of the safe.

The Fatman could barely conceal his amusement at the look of utter dismay on Dobson's face. The safe contained a stack of papers and a few hundred pounds, quite a lot of it in bags bearing pound coins and fifty pence pieces.

Two officers were rummaged about lifting the documents and a couple of small notebooks out and packed them into plastic evidence bags.

"Oi!" Shouted the Fatman. "Where are you taking that?"

"You'll get it back later after we've examined it all." Said Dobson.

The Fatman wandered over to the window and anxiously looked out. He was greatly relieved to see looks of exasperation on the faces of the police search party.

Dobson joined him at the window. "Where is it Cartwright?"

"Where's what?" the Fatman put on a puzzled expression.

"You know bloody well what!" Dobson shouted in frustration. "Where are the drugs?"

"I have no idea what you're raving about dear." The Fatman's expression was poker faced.

Dobson stood back a pace or two and regarded him. "Oh you're good." She mocked. "You really are good. You're a piece of work you are."

She opened the window and shouted down to Henderson who was by now looking up at the windows of the Fatman's office. "Anything?"

"Sorry. Nothing Ma'am." Came the reply.

Dobson turned to the Fatman who was grinning smuggly.

"You're very lucky this time Cartwright. But I'll be back again!"

"What for? To personally bring me a cheque for all the bloody damage you and your lot have done to my offices? Just look at the mess!" the Fatman made an expansive gesture holding out his arms.

Dobson glared at him. She was very close to completely losing her temper. She lent forward. Shoved her face so close to his that their noses almost touched. Their eyes met. Hers were blazing with hate.

"Cartwright I'm going to get you. I promise you that. I'll have you behind bars. Its people like you who are responsible for killing innocent kids and ruining lives. You're totally oblivious of the heartache and damage you cause. You are a complete moron. I'm going to have you. I will from now on make it my mission in life!"

The words were delivered in such a vehement manner that even the Fatman was temporarily rendered utterly speechless.

He stared back at her and then callously said.

"Aye, you and whose army? Just get out of here. Go outside gather up that pack of bloody hoodlums and bugger off!"

She walked away. At the doorway, she rounded again to see his face staring after her. It was cold, hard, dispassionate and filled with a terrifying malevolent evil. She went down the stairs and away.

Outside, two officers were searching one of the vans and even had the rear seat out of Cartwright's Mercedes car. Despite the thoroughness of the search, it had revealed nothing.

Dobson wandered hopefully over to the warehouse where the spare parts were. Her men had disassembled several starter motors and opened up all manner of boxes and cartons and packages. Nothing! They had found absolutely nothing.

She allowed the search to continue for fully a further half hour. Occasionally she looked up at the window of the Fatmans office. He was looking down at her sneeringly. Later, she could see him laughing, mocking her.

Eventually, Dobson had had enough. She leaned inside a car and withdrew a loud hailer.

"O.K. folks that's it. Lets call it a day."

She didn't look up at Cartwright this time, but just climbed into the back of a van beside Henderson. Her expression resigned, defeated.

55.

Geordie and Shorty had arrived up outside Bills shed. Shorty had tried knocking the door several times. No answer. Bills car wasn't there anyway so he was probably out somewhere.

Geordie was trying to get him on the phone. It rang for ages. Then eventually.

"Who's this?" an irritated voice replied.

"Geordie"

"What do you want?"

"We've got the bastard who took the money! He's inside our van. We're outside your shed. Where are you?"

"Well bugger me senseless with a wet lettuce!" came the surprised reply.

"Are you anywhere close by? Said Geordie. "We need you to have a wee chat with our new friend and find out where he's got the money."

"Aw shit!" came the reply. "I'm away in the west of Ireland fishing with a few buddies. It's a trip I do every year. Trust you to catch the bugger now!" Bill sounded completely pissed off.

"When are you back again?"

"I'm not back until tomorrow night."

"What the frig are we going to do until then? The Fatman will go absolutely spare when he hears this!" Geordie was exasperated.

"Let me think a moment." The phone went quiet. Geordie could hear muffled voices. Bill was obviously talking to his fishing buddies. Gradually the conversation got louder.

"Its not my bloody fault! Sure you know, you can never get a moments frigging peace to yourself! Sorry boys I'm going to have to go home, damn it!"

After what sounded like a mild argument, Bill eventually came back on the phone.

"Listen Geordie. This is a bloody nuisance. You've gone and picked the one and only weekend I go away all year!"

"I didn't pick anything. We've been fortunate enough through a bit of cunning detective work to find this twat. You did nothing. It's the least you can do to come up here now and interrogate him! I gather you're getting paid plenty if the money shows up."

"You just mind your own business about what I'm getting paid!" came the angry reply. There was silence for a moment then Bill continued.

"I'll tell you what you'll do. Take the bugger into the shed and put him in my interrogation chair. Strap him into it. There's some chain in a box near the door. Take the padlock off the diesel tank and chain his ankles up with it so he can't get away. I'll leave shortly and I'll be back with you first thing in the morning."

"O.K." said Geordie. "What time will you be back?"

"Probably about eight o'clock in the morning. I'm about three hundred miles away. I'm away down in county Kerry for dears sake!"

"Do you think you can make him talk and tell us where the money is?" Geordie asked anxiously.

"I can guarantee it. He'll talk alright. I'll think up something so terrifying for him that he will definitely talk." Bill paused a moment thinking.

"Now," he continued. "You tell him I'm coming to have a wee chat with him. Tell him about me! Suggest to him that if he's suffering from amnesia or anything like that, that he'd be well advised to have a miraculous recovery before I arrive. Scare the shit out of him. That way he'll have all night to sweat about it. It will make it easier for me in the morning. One more thing, listen very carefully. Don't try questioning him yourself! You'll only cock it up. Leave him for me. Is that clearly understood?

"Yeah Bill. No problem." Bill rang off.

Geordie made another call.

"Boss, good news! Shorty and I have caught our cyclist friend!"

"Bloody excellent! Well done! Where is he?"

"We have him up at Big Bill's shed."

"Where is Bill? Is he going to interrogate the bastard? I want my money back as soon as possible!"

"That's the bad news, Bill is away in the west of Ireland fishing with some buddies. I rang him and he's on his way. Only thing is though, he won't be here until eight o'clock in the morning."

"Bugger! Isn't that just typical. I remember Bill did that a couple of years ago when I wanted him to shoot someone who hadn't paid me. He's a bloody unreliable big bastard. Never here when you need him"

"It's certainly most inconvenient." Geordie admitted.

"Listen up, you and Shorty tie that bugger up and keep a very close eye on him. Make bloody sure he doesn't waltz away off somewhere before Bill gets home. Is that totally clear.

"Yes boss, totally clear."

56.

Dobson looked utterly dejected as they drove back to towards the police station.

"That could have gone better." said Butler.

"Yes not half!" replied Henderson.

"Wonder where the Dickens they had the drugs stashed." Mused Butler.

"Well, they were a couple of steps ahead of us." Dobson said sadly.

The Radio crackled into life.

"Control two three."

"Two three control" replied Dobson "Go ahead."

"Two three, we have two four for you."

"Patch them through." Dobson said.

"Two four. We have found nothing at Cartwright's farm. The whole place is shrouded in smoke. They have been burning old rubber tyres up here. Its absolutely stinking! We can get Environmental Health onto them if you want Ma'am?"

"Don't bother Two Four. Just leave it and return to base."

"Bloody hell! Where do they have the drugs?" Dobson was really frustrated and disappointed. "They must have known we were coming. There was nothing there to find. Cartwright was tipped off and obviously moved it all somewhere off site. No sign of Rooney either sadly."

"At least we had a result at the house in east Belfast!" said Butler.

"Oh! What was that?" asked Dobson perking up a bit.

"Didn't you hear?" Butler looked puzzled as Dobson was shaking her head. "Came through on the radio just before we left Cartwright's yard. That fancy woman Cartwright goes to see every week. She had a kilo of uncut cocaine hidden inside a box of chocolates in her living room!"

"Really!" Dobson's face lit up.

"Yeah. It was very funny actually. When our lads arrived, she scarpered out the back door. They chased her but she escaped into the woods at the back of the ancient burial mound behind the house. The lads radioed Traffic and they caught her getting into a Volkswagen car in the street just beyond the mound.

"Brilliant!" Dobson was really excited now.

"There was a further twist too!" Butler started giggling. "When they grabbed her, her wig came flying off and guess what?"

"What?" said Henderson joining in now.

"She is not a she, but a he!"

"A tranny! You're joking me aren't you?" Henderson was chuckling.

"Nope! Totally serious! All the proper man parts but dressed up like a woman. The wardrobes in the house had loads of woman's clothes and boots with high heels. All of them too big a size for a lady!"

"Wow!" enthused Dobson. That's a turn up! So we've got something after all!" Soon they were all laughing and cheering.

The celebrations were suddenly punctuated by a mobile phone ringing.

"Where's that coming from?" Dobson was irritated. "I distinctly said no phones!"

Everyone in the van including the uniformed officers looked around.

It soon became obvious that it was Hendersons. Sheepishly, he fished for it in his pocket and brought it out.

"Hello?" he answered it. As he did so, he was shocked to discover it was not his own usual phone. The reply was just audible to the others inside the van, which had just stopped at a traffic light.

"You bastard! Thought you were going to warn us you useless great twit you!" said a gruff irritated voice.

"Sorry!" Henderson stammered realizing every one was looking at him and intensely focused on the conversation.

Butler touched the arm of their driver and whispered. "Stop the van. Switch the engine off." The van pulled into the side of the road and stopped.

"What happened? Why didn't you call me?" A gruff voice on the phone said.

Instantly, Dobson recognized the voice. It was Cartwright! She momentarily looked in a puzzled fashion at Henderson and then realized what had happened.

"Give me that!" she snatched the phone from him.

"Hello." She said. Dobson deliberately lowered her voice in disguise.

"Who is this?" the Fatman said astonished.

"A friend."

"I have no friends now bugger off. I want to speak to Henderson."

"No! Henderson won't be speaking to you anymore." Dobson gave Henderson a look, that would have turned cream. Henderson knew he was in very big trouble.

The Fatman was getting concerned about this now, but his curiosity was too much for him. Who was this?

"However," Dobson assumed her normal Yorkshire accent. "You can come and talk to me if you like?" The phone suddenly went dead. The Fatman had twigged on.

Dobson let out a great laugh. It was as much in relief as anything else.

"We've got the blighter now!" She giggled. "Butler, get on the horn and organize getting the chocolate box and its contents found at the transvestites house finger printed as a matter of priority. I bet it's all covered in Cartwright's finger prints." She paused thoughtful.

"And as for you D.S. Henderson, you and I are going back to the station to have a nice long chat about all this. I'm going to nail you to the bloody wall!" She yelled at him.

Butler couldn't contain himself either. "You complete bastard! You traitor! You told me we'd catch these guys and no mistake. All that guff you told me about your nephew taking an overdose and dying! Was it even true? Was that all just a sop to fool me?"

Henderson said nothing but resignedly hung his head and stared despairingly at the dirty floor of the van. He knew he was finished.

57.

Philip was sitting at his desk reading his e-mails. His iPhone rang. It was Julia. He let it ring out and ignored it. What was he going to do about her he wondered?

He started to type a reply to one of the e-mails when the iPhone buzzed a notification that an SMS message had arrived. He paused curious to read it.

"HI PHILIP. WILLIAM HAS STOOD ME UP! BASTARD! ARE YOU ABOUT THIS EVENING. FEELING A BIT DOWN. PLEASE CAN WE TALK?"

Philip put the phone down on the desk and continued answering his e-mails. After about five minutes he could stand it no longer. He just couldn't shut it out. He'd have to man up and face this square on. He typed an SMS message on his phone.

"STILL WORKING. COULD MEET YOU LATER AT THE CHINESE IF YOU LIKE. I'M REALLY BUSY SO WOULD YOU PLEASE RING THEM AND BOOK IT AND LET ME KNOW IF THAT SUITS? LOVE YOU!

He pressed send. Moments later the phone bleeped the message had been sent successfully. His desk phone rang and soon he was chatting away to a man who wanted to buy a property to rent out as an investment. In the midst of the conversation his mobile phone buzzed. As he talked, he picked it up and looked at the screen.

"CHINKY BOOKED FOR NINE. COME TO HOUSE FIRST. LOVE JULIA."

58.

Geordie and Shorty dragged William out of the back of their van. William was still very groggy. They frog marched him inside the big shed in Bill's Yard.

"Lets get him onto the chair." Geordie said.

"Come on, move you stupid bastard you." Urged Shorty.

William was staggering along unsure where he was. What was happening to him? He was set down in a chair. Geordie gave him another whiff of the ether. Moments later he drifted off into a state of anaesthetized oblivion again.

It was some time later that he began to recover consciousness. It had started to get dark by now. He had no idea where he was. There was a glimmer of light from a couple of fluorescent tubes hanging from the tin roof high above him. Somewhere, not too far away he could hear voices. His head hurt badly. He could feel the mother of all headaches was setting in.

He started to take stock of the situation. He was sitting upright in a sturdy wooden high backed chair. He couldn't move his arms. He looked at them and discovered leather straps restrained them. His feet felt heavy and cold. Eventually, he realized someone had wound a length of heavy looking chain around them. He was inside some sort of barn or shed.

The whole place was very untidy with loads of old junk lying about. Most of it was rusting away with neglect. In one corner he could make out what looked like an ancient tractor. It was covered in cobwebs and obviously hadn't moved in years. Chains hung down from a nearby wall. They had fittings on them that indicated their purpose was to restrain people.

Most concerning of all however was a stout dusty looking wooden table which stood nearby. Its surface was covered in a terrifying variety of implements. There were huge sheering scissors, hammers, tongs, hideous looking curved knives, an axe, several iron pokers, medical scalpels and a huge saw. There was much more besides all laid out like surgeons instruments ready to operate.

"Ah, the sleeping beauty awakes." Shorty said mockingly.

"Who are you?" William asked puzzled by all this.

"Remember me?" Geordie asked.

William groaned recognizing him instantly. It was the rough looking baldy wee man who had chased after him on the bicycle.

"What do you want?" he asked weakly. "Why have you got me tied to this chair?"

Geordie looked over at Shorty. "Its amazing isn't it? I mean Big Bill did say we'd find he was suffering from amnesia!"

Shorty cackled evilly.

"Let me help to refresh your memory." Geordie said. "You may recall riding your bike along the cycle path up near the Mahon road underpass. You heard a noise and looked up to see a skip lorry nearly crash over the edge."

Geordie stopped. He looked at William to see if there was any trace of recognition. There was no reaction. Geordie went on.

"Then after the skip lorry was gone, magic! You found a big bag of money inside a bin bag had fallen out and landed right at your feet! You must have thought it was friggin' Christmas or something!"

William felt really scared now. He was in deep, deep trouble. What he had most feared could happen, had happened. He'd always known there was a risk. He thought he'd been so clever. He hadn't gone on a spending spree or anything foolish like that. He'd taken great care not to draw any attention to himself. Despite all his wise precautions, they'd caught him. How the hell had these guys found him he wondered?

"Well!" yelled Geordie, "Where is it?"

"I have absolutely no idea what you're on about." William answered poker faced.

"Is that a fact now. Well, well well." Geordie looked at him. "A huge big bag full of fifty and hundred pound notes. Over a million pounds and you know nothing about it!"

"That right." Williams's expression was one of pure innocence.

"You're certainly a cool customer alright. Question is though, how long will you remain that way?"

Geordie was silent then. He just paced up and down the room. His tread was deliberate, quiet, and thoughtful. Several minutes passed by. Eventually, William could stand it no longer. The silence and palpable tension were too much for him.

"What happens now? I've told you I know nothing about it. You obviously have the wrong man. You must be looking for someone else. Are you going to let me go then?" It was worth a try William thought.

"This might come as a big surprise to you mate." Geordie scowled at him, "but I don't believe you. I know you have the money. You've hidden it away somewhere oh so carefully. Oh so very carefully!"

"I haven't the foggiest clue what you're talking about. I was out riding my bike. I stopped to buy a bottle of wine. I'm due to be having dinner with my good lady wife right now. She'll probably call the police when I don't turn up."

"Oh we are so scared!" Shorty said. "Sacred, scared scared!" He pretended to bite his nails. "Those bastards couldn't find their arse pocket with both hands on a sunny day!"

"Anyway," he added. Its just a matter of time as far as you are concerned."

"What do you mean?"

"Well," continued Shorty. "Big Bill is on his way here."

"Who's big Bill?"

"Your worst possible nightmare!" laughed Shorty.

"We were here with another chap recently," Geordie took up the running again. "Bill asked him a few questions. The chap was suffering from amnesia. But Bill helped him remember everything though!"

Shorty and Geordie were both laughing now. Geordie picked up a huge iron poker from the table. He approached William and held the poker up under his nose.

"Can you smell anything?"

"No." William answered.

"Well you should be able to. It should smell of burned shite. Bill heated this up until it was red hot."

"Red hot!" repeated Shorty. "Never saw anything looking so friggin hot in all my life."

"He then took it and shoved it up the mans arsehole!" Geordie explained.

"It's a miracle!" Shorty was dancing around laughing and waving his arms about like someone who had just seen the light at an evangelistic meeting. "All of a sudden, he could remember everything very clearly!"

"Very clearly indeed." Geordie added nodding.

"Yes, first he remembered finding cocaine inside a starter motor. Then he remembered telling the police all about it!" Shorty was cackling ecstatically.

"So this money you're looking for is drug money?"

"Course it is you stupid dick head!" Shorty said. "What did you think? Did you imagine we had collected it to make a charitable donation? We were moving the money in the skip lorry. We knew the police were coming to search our yard so we had to move it."

"Shut up Shorty!" snapped Geordie. "That's enough!"

"Sorry." Shorty realized he'd said much more than he should have.

"You really are a stupid wee man sometimes!" Geordie scolded.

"I know nothing about any money." William was doing his level best to deflect his interrogators. It was all he could think of doing.

"Look." Geordie said, "You know all about it ballick brain. The skip lorry hit an Armco barrier and the bag of money fell out and down onto the cycle track. That's where you found it! We stopped to look for it and saw some guy wearing a reflective yellow cycle coat pedaling away like hell with a bag on his back!

"Exhibit 'A' ma Lud." Shorty held up the yellow coat and imitating a court barrister continued "Found in the bag on the cycle rack of the accused's bike."

We have your photograph." Geordie went on, "We set a trap, the bag of newspaper bundles mimicking the money. You looked inside the bin bag on the cycle track. You nearly shit yourself when you read my note. That's how we knew it was you. So don't try all this 'I know nothing about it' tripe because it won't wear.

Shorty tried his hand. "Where is it big man? You could save yourself a world of pain if you tell us now. I mean, once Big Bill gets here, you'll wish you had never been born!"

William said nothing. He withdrew into a world of complete silence.

"Frig this," said Geordie. "Leave him to Big Bill. I'm goin' outside for a smoke," he opened the door and went out. Shorty followed him out.

Geordie lit up. "We'd better take it in turns to watch yer man here until Bill gets here. I'll do the first shift." He consulted his watch. It's ten o'clock near enough now so you go home and sleep for a couple of hours. Be back here by four o'clock and you stay here then until Bill arrives. That should be between eight and nine.

Shorty also lit up a fag. "That sounds good to me."

After Shorty had driven off, Geordie went back inside to check on his prisoner.

"I'm really thirsty." Complained William. "How about a drink of something?"

"Too bad. I'm fresh out of champagne." Geordie retorted. Despite his reservations, he went outside and filled a mug with tap water.

"I'm not about to unstrap you, so you just sip the water and I'll hold the mug. Understood?"

William nodded and gratefully gulped at the water. "Thanks."

"Don't thank me, I don't even like you!" snapped Geordie. He knelt down and pulled off Williams training shoes. "I'll just take these with me as an extra precaution. Can't have you running away, can we?"

Geordie went out and locked the door of the shed. Bill kept an old caravan on the other side of the yard for kipping in on the odd occasion. Geordie decided he'd hole up in it for a while. He found the key hidden under a big planter pot and went inside. Lying down on the couch he was soon fast asleep.

59.

There was a knock at the door. Julia ran to answer it.

"I'm so glad to see you!" she said throwing her arms around Philip.

He was slightly stiff in his response and did not return the gesture. Alarmed, she released him from her embrace and looked into his eyes.

"What's wrong?"

"Everything!"

"What do you mean?" she looked puzzled.

"This is all too much. I just invited you for a drink that night because I thought you looked cute. I thought it would be fun!"

"Well it has been fun, hasn't it?" she smiled at him.

"Yeah. Well it was. Then you go saying you're leaving your husband! Then you want to move in with me. As if that's not a big enough shock for me, you then casually add that now you are pregnant!

"Sorry. I didn't mean to get pregnant."

"How the fuck did that happen anyhow? Did you forget to take your pill or something?"

I didn't take any pill. I've got so used to not taking them when I'm with William. It's because in five years of marriage, I never got pregnant. I didn't think I could!"

She began to sob gently and went to sit down on the settee.

"I don't make a habit of this Philip. Like I said, I've been married about five years or so and in that time, you are the only one I've slept with apart from William. The only one!" She emphasized, "I'm not a tramp."

The tears were coming more freely now. Philip sat down beside her and gently held her in his strong athletic arms.

"Believe it or not, I'm no great Don Juan myself. Everybody out there thinks I'm the playboy of the western world or something, all my friends."

"But you are, aren't you?" Julia teased.

"No!" He looked at her denying it.

His big brown eyes were so full of innocence. They were just so beautiful she thought. Her eyes moistened as her pupils dilated. He could not resist the force of nature and found himself drawn towards her. There was something just so sexy about her. The way she looked. The way she smelt, the way she felt in his hands. He gently took her head in his hands and kissed her.

They had a certain chemistry together. It was undeniable and somehow, totally irresistible. As he led her slowly upstairs, he was thinking. Was there anyway he could make this work with her in the longer term? In the short term, it all felt so good!

60.

A SMALL WINDOWLESS INTERVIEW ROOM AT POLICE HEADQUARTERS.

"You'd better tell me exactly what happened, and I do mean exactly. Nothing is being taped. This is still unofficial. But don't even think about being smart with me. This is your one and only chance."

Dobson was in no mood to mess about.

"I really don't know where to start." Henderson looked wretched.

"At the beginning."

"It all started when I was passed over for that promotion about a year ago. They decided to go with that upstart Sweeney instead of me. I couldn't take it. I knew it was my last chance at promotion as I'll be retiring next year."

"Or sooner!" Dobson commented.

"I was thinking about my pension. It is, as you know linked to my final wages. I was really counting on getting that promotion. When it didn't come through, I got worried. The wife and I took on a second mortgage a couple of years ago. We had some great holidays and bought a fabulous conservatory. Only thing is though, the monthly payments are crippling. I needed the extra wages the promotion would have brought with it. It was a disaster when I didn't get it"

"Go on." Urged Dobson.

"Well, I woke up in the middle of the night a few months ago. Couldn't sleep. It kept going around in my head. Where could I get the money to make ends meet? Then it all became clear. We'd just started to investigate Cartwright and his gang. I saw an opportunity to cash in. This was going to be the ticket!

"So you made contact with Cartwright?"

"Yes. I set up a meeting with him at an obscure location where I was pretty much certain no one would see us."

"What did you say to him?"

"I told him he was under investigation and that I would feed him information if he paid me."

"How did he pay you?"

"It was in cash, always in cash. Thought about a Swiss bank account but decided it was way too risky."

Dobson wanted to know more. "How much money did you receive?"

"They were usually payments of five thousand pounds at a go. I've got about twenty grand off him."

"I just don't believe it!" Dobson was incredulous now. "You've risked all this, including your pension for a measly twenty grand?"

Henderson hung his head in a downcast manner. He was desolate. Sometimes in life, you realize you've done something terribly wrong that alters the entire course of your life. This was just such a moment.

"What sort of information did you give Cartwright?" Dobson asked.

"I suppose really, all I agreed to do was to help him keep one jump ahead of the investigation. I promised him just enough to keep him out of jail."

"What about Rooney?"

"Well, I knew very little about him Ma'am. I mean, you didn't actually divulge his identity or tell us where he was. You only told us about him after his disappearance."

"But you knew of his existence, didn't you? Did you tell Cartwright about him?"

Henderson remained tight lipped. There was a palpable tension in the air.

"Well did you?" Dobson raised her voice and moved closer hovering over the slumped figure of Henderson threateningly.

"I can't lie about it. Yes, I did tell him. I informed him that one of his van men had delivered a starter motor full of cocaine to the wrong place. I told him the police knew about it."

"That's all it took. You stupid bastard! That was enough to allow Cartwright to piece it all together. All he had to do was ask his van drivers who had made the mistake and where they had delivered the part to in error."

"It never occurred to me . . . ." Henderson didn't get to finish his sentence.

"That's right. It didn't. That's why you never got that promotion Henderson. You never think things through far enough to see what might happen as a consequence"

"I'm sorry."

"It's a bit late for that now. Try telling Paddy Rooney's wife and children you're sorry! All the man wanted to do was help. He came to me in all innocence offering to help us catch these drug dealers, these thugs! All he wanted from us was to keep his anonymity.

"I take it he still hasn't been found?" Henderson said more out of hope than anything else.

"No. We haven't found him. I don't think we will either, at least not alive. I reckon they've pumped him for information. God alone knows what they put him through! Then they've very probably killed him. That's all thanks to you Henderson. Thanks to you and your mortgage, your holidays and your bloody conservatory!" Dobson shouted.

"I'm sorry. I'm sorry!" Henderson was starting to blub now as he realized the enormity of his indiscretions.

"I'm sorry too Henderson. I'm sorry that you have effectively jeopardized my entire investigation. I'm sorry that Rooney is probably lying in an unmarked grave somewhere. I'm sorry that his wife keeps ringing to ask if we've any news for her. I'm also sorry Henderson about you."

"Whats going to happen to me?"

"I had hoped that we might have found a way through this. I honestly wasn't holding out much hope, but now that we've talked, I can tell you that sadly there is no hope for you. I could possibly have forgiven your conversations with Cartwright. We might have found a way round that by saying that you were acting as a double agent and collecting information for us as part of the inquiry. What I can't forgive however is the fact that you gave up Rooney to them!

"So I'm finished then?" Henderson said resignedly.

"I'm afraid so. I've no alternative but to interview you formally, take a statement and forward it for prosecution. You'll be sacked, lose your pension and almost certainly go to jail."

With that, Dobson turned on her heel and left the interview room. She closed the door firmly behind her leaving Henderson in no doubt as to the symbolism of the gesture.

61.

At last the light was coming and with it the first glimmer of a watery dawn on the horizon. It had been a long drive through the darkness for Bill. He'd left Killarney about midnight after having dinner with his mates and restricting himself to just two pints of beer all evening. He'd been raging that he'd had to cut short his special fishing weekend just because they'd found this wee creep. All the same, if he got him to spill the beans and tell him where the money was hidden, then he'd be up twenty five grand!

It was the thought of the money that had driven Bill on through the night. He'd stopped just once, somewhere near Mullingar in central Ireland. He'd gone to sleep for about two hours and then his alarm watch woke him again. He'd cursed at it, remembered the money and got going again. Now he was almost home. He was tired, hungry and badly needed a pee!

Bill stretched his shoulders back and forth as he drove in an attempt to banish the stiffness from them. Just at that, his mobile phone rang.

"Who's this?" he answered gruffly.

"It's Shorty. How are you going, where are you at?"

"Going good. I'm nearly there. Just coming into Belfast on the motorway."

"That's great. So you'll be here soon?"

"Aye. Should be with you in about ten or fifteen minutes, pretty close to eight o'clock as agreed."

"See you then." Shorty replied, but Bill had already cut the phone off before he got finished his sentence.

Shorty had a quick smoke and then checked on William. Their captive was slumped over snoring softly but uneasily in his seat. Shorty wasn't entirely happy about all this. Through out his adult life he'd been a criminal. He'd stolen anything he could get his paws on. It never bothered him in the slightest. What he wasn't happy about though was Big Bill.

Oscar had once said that Bill was mad in the head. Shorty had no doubt about it. In the coldness of the dawn he shivered as he remembered what Bill had done to Paddy Rooney. The cruelty Bill had inflicted on that wee man had been horrific! Afterwards, Shorty had helped Bill dump the man's body into the pond at the nearby-disused quarry. Inwardly, Shorty had felt sad as he watched the lifeless Rooney sink slowly into the murky waters. Those eyes would never see daylight again he'd thought. By contrast, Bill had laughed and chuckled ghoulishly. He mockingly waved and said "Bye bye!" as the corpse disappeared from sight into the blackness of the freezing water. It hadn't cost the psychopathic Bill a second thought.

Shorty hadn't signed up with these guys to be involved as an accomplice to murder. All Shorty was after was ill-gotten financial gain. Killing people wasn't his thing. He drew the line at that. In his mind if it was necessary to persuade someone to talk, that was just fine, if it hurt, too bad. Shooting the man stone dead afterwards was going too far. He wasn't happy about it. Not at all!

As he pondered this, he heard stones crunching under tyres somewhere along the lane that led up into the disused farmyard. It was Bill. Moments later his pickup style jeep drove quietly into the yard.

"Hi Shorty." Bill said as he got out of the pickup. He stretched and yawned pulling a contorted ugly face as he did so.

"Fuck am I tired." he said. "I've driven all bloody night to get here!"

Bill wandered over to the side of Shorty's van, unzipped his fly and urinated profusely against the side of it.

"Jeez you are a dirty bastard aren't you?" Shorty protested.

"Sure the rain will soon wash it off." Bill laughed. "Oh! Thank goodness for that he said in relief. I've been holdin' that since Mullingar about three hours ago!"

"Congratulations." Shorty was unimpressed.

"Where is this wee Cunt then? Do you have him tied up in the chair?

"Aye, he is alright. He's ready for you."

Bill went over to the water tap on the outside wall and began filling a steel bucket. "Did you light the stove inside as I asked you?"

"Yes. It's burning away there, should be hot enough for your needs."

"Good." The bucket was full now. "Lets wake yer man up he giggled fiendishly."

Quietly, Bill opened the Judas door of the shed and carried in the bucket. Moments later, he lashed the whole lot round the slumbering incumbent of the high backed chair.

William awoke with a start, yelling a protest at the icy coldness of the water.

"Good morning sunshine!" said Bill grinning at him.

Shorty watched as Bill laughed. He remembered something someone had once told him about villains in movies. The really, really bad ones, the ones who were worst of all always smiled! It was certainly true when it came to Bill.

"Where is the money?" As usual, Bill came right to the point. In his mind, why beat about the bush?

"I don't know what you're talking about. I have no money!" William protested shaking his head vigorously in a largely futile attempt to dispel moisture from his hair and face.

"Oh you have it alright." Bill said glowering at him now in a sinister fashion. "You have it and very soon you'll tell me where it is, very soon. Very soon indeed."

His voice dwindled away into a mumble as he went over to the stove. He opened the doors and his face instantly dropped in disappointment.

"Aw for fuck sake Shorty! The bleedin' stove is nearly out!"

"It can't be! I put wood in it about an hour ago."

"Well it's nearly out now you clown you!" Bill was clearly irritated. "I didn't ask you to do too much. What sort of a twat are you anyway? Any idiot could keep a fire burning for dear's sake!"

"Sorry if I've been stupid and allowed it to burn out."

Bill glared at him. "Shorty, as usual you've gone way past stupid and into an entirely different category altogether!"

Bill started re-lighting the stove with some twigs and firelighters. Soon he had it burning again. After a few minutes he added some small split logs and eventually coal.

"That's better now." He said. "Only thing is it will take about half an hour for those coals to get hot enough for the poker."

Bill lifted a poker from the table, brought it over and gently shoved it into one of William's nostrils.

"What do you think of that?" he cackled. "Once its red hot, I'm going to shove it right up your arsehole!"

William could say nothing. He looked extremely concerned. He was terrified at the prospect. This wasn't very good.

"You'll tell me where the money is then O.K. I know you will. You'll reach a stage where you'll be happy to tell me."

"Actually," Bill continued. "I was watching a documentary last week about your woman Odette Sansom. She was a British spy in the last war you know. They often confused her with being related to Churchill but she wasn't. Important that."

Bill was being almost conversational with William now.

"They sent her over to France to do some sort of espionage lark, but unfortunately for Odette, the Germans caught her. They took her to Gestapo headquarters for interrogation. I really love watching all that sort of stuff! It's interesting. I find it very enjoyable!"

"What happened?" asked Shorty.

"Aw, It was bad." Bill pulled a long serious face. "Very bad. They branded her on the back with a white-hot iron, then pulled out her toe nails with pliers." Bill picked up a pair of pliers from his table of torture instruments. "Pliers just like these." He held them up for William to see.

"Bet that hurt a lot." Said Shorty.

"Hurt?" Big Bill giggled evilly. "Hurt! It was absolute fucking agony! The screeches and yells of her could be heard about half a mile away.

It was terrible, terrible! The pain was beyond human suffering. At least she had an excuse though. She was a brave war hero."

Bill turned around and looked William straight in the face.

"Were as you; you're just scum, pure scum. You're the scum that stole our money and boy are you going to pay for it!"

Bill looked round at Shorty and nodded towards the door.

"Let's go." He said.

"Where?" Shorty looked puzzled.

"Outside."

Shorty followed Bill out through the Judas door and into the yard.

"Right Shorty. I'm absolutely fully fuckin' famished. Lets go up to Margaret's café and get something to eat. I fancy a massive big egg bacon and sausage soda with chips and beans!"

"What about our friend inside here?"

"Stuff him. He can wait. Sure he's going nowhere. I need the fire to warm up to red-hot first before I can torture the bastard anyway. Like I said, that will take about half an hour or so. Lets go to the café and get some breakfast." Bill started towards his pick-up truck.

"What are you going to do with him afterwards?" Shorty asked somewhat anxiously.

"Once he's told us everything, I'll slit his throat and let him bleed to death. I may hang him upside down like veal to drain of blood. I was thinking about it coming up the road."

"That sounds terrible!" Shorty was disgusted at the prospect.

"Serve him right. He stole the money after all. The Fatman will want me to get rid of him and if it's a slow horrible death, sure that's all the better."

"You're very cruel aren't you?"

"Yes. Very!" laughed Bill insanely. "Then, once he's dead, We'll mix the cement and he'll go into the pond at the quarry with that other traitorous bastard the police informer. A fitting end for the pair of them if you ask me!"

Bill climbed into his pick up truck and cranked the diesel engine. It took rather a long time to fire up. The noise awoke Geordie who emerged sleepy eyed from the old caravan across the yard.

"What's happening?" He shouted.

"We're going for breakfast." Shorty replied. "Are you coming?"

"Sure, just give me a moment to get my boots on first."

Shorty was hovering outside the shed door. "I'll be with you in a minute Bill, I think I've set my fags down somewhere inside. I'm away to look for them."

"O.K. but hurry up! I'm hungry and I'm not waiting long."

Shorty disappeared back into the shed. He rushed over towards William.

"What now?" William looked alarmed.

"I haven't much time so listen carefully," said Shorty as he handed William a small penknife. "Use this to cut through the straps. There's a key for the lock hanging on a nail over beside the door. Go to the back of the shed and you'll find there's a loose panel high up on the left hand side. I reckon if you use a hammer or something lying around, you can probably bust out."

"Why are you helping me?" asked a puzzled William.

"I'm a drug dealer, not a bloody psychopathic murderer. We'll be back in about half an hour. For God's sake, don't be here! That big bastard that's with us is going to torture you. Then slowly and very painfully he's going to kill you! If you don't escape, you'll be dead within a couple of hours!"

Shorty ran towards the door. "Good luck!" he said quietly as he stepped through the Judas door and into the yard.

"Make sure the door is properly locked," yelled Bill from his pick-up. "We don't want ass hole there waddling off whilst we're away eating."

Shorty locked the door and jumped into the pick-up. He sat there totally quiet beside Geordie.

"Bugger me I am famished! I may eat two sodas!" Said Bill as he drove off down the gravel-covered laneway.

62.

The Fatman picked up his phone. It had just started to buzz on his desk. Looking at the diminutive screen, he saw that it was his sister in-law Aggie.

"Hello Aggie. What can I do for you?"

"Hi James." The voice was soft and polite. "I'm very sorry to bother you, but I just wanted a short chat."

"That's ok so long as it's short cause I am quite busy to-day."

"It's about Oscar."

"Oscar? What about Oscar?" Cartwright was surprised. What could Aggie possibly want to know about Oscar?

"It's actually about Oscar and Cecil. Oscar has been very good to Cecil recently. He bought him a lovely scooter for his seventeenth birthday you know."

"Is that right? I didn't know that. That was very good of him right enough. He must have taken a rush of blood to the head or something because he's not well noted for spending money on anybody other than himself."

"Well it was very generous of him. He's been exceptionally helpful with Cecil. The boy lost his father as you know and he's been a bit lost ever since. Oscar has been good enough to provide a father like figure for the boy. He's even advised Cecil to go back to school. Cecil was going to leave you know, but after Oscar talked to him he's probably going to go back to do his A levels."

"Is that a fact right enough?" said the Fatman a bit bewildered by all this.

"Yes." Aggie continued. "He takes Cecil down to his gym and does weight training with him. Cecil is very proud of the biceps he's starting to develop."

"Oh aye?" the Fatman was losing the will to live. Frankly he didn't give a damn about Oscar and Cecil. All he wanted was his money back!

"Cecil has really taken to Oscar. I thought it was all good James, really I did. Then earlier, I was talking to your Maureen and it got me to thinking about it all."

"Thinking about what?"

"Thinking about Oscar and Cecil. Maureen shocked me when she said that maybe, just maybe Oscar is being a wee bit too nice to Cecil!"

"What on earth are you raving about Aggie?"

"Well I didn't believe it myself. I figured Maureen was just saying it to be hurtful. I don't mean to annoy you James but she can be a bit nasty sometimes."

"Yeah," the Fatman replied, "that she can. I should know after all I have to live with her!"

"Anyway, I don't really know how to put this, but do you think there is even the slightest need for me to worry?"

"About what?" the Fatman was being his usual insensitive self.

"About Oscar! Is Cecil in any danger from him? You know Oscar very well, probably better than anyone else."

"Are you asking me if Oscar is fruit merchant?"

"Well yes, I suppose I am. I'm just a mother who's concerned about her son. Hope you understand."

The Fatman was chuckling fit to be tied by now. He started to roar with laughter. He thought about how many people he had watched Oscar beat the crap out of. The injuries he had caused, the broken bones and scars, the people he had put in hospital. There was even the time he'd had to shoot someone who point blank refused to pay up for a consignment of heroine. The very idea that Oscar was an uphill gardener!

"You are joking me aren't you? I mean you really can't be serious about all this?"

"I'm serious."

"Well in that case let me be serious too. You're talking complete and utter rubbish! Oscar is straight. He's been my friend for donkeys years and frankly the very suggestion you're making is completely ludicrous. It's not only ridiculous, but it's also an insult to me personally. How dare you!" the Fatman shouted.

"I'm so sorry James." Aggie was almost in tears by now. "I hate asking you but its only because I'm worried about Cecil. He's still only a wee boy really."

"Well don't worry about it any more! You're barking up the wrong friggin' tree! Only for the fact that you are Maureen's sister, I would tell you where to go at this stage. Now please go away and give my head peace!"

With that, the Fatman slammed his mobile phone shut disconnecting the call. He looked at it sitting on the desk. He sat stunned by what Aggie had said. What a bloody cheek he thought! The idea however was now seeded in his mind. He found to his astonishment that it had registered a slight doubt and he couldn't get it out of his head. The more he thought about it, the more plausible it seemed. Now he just wasn't quite so sure about Oscar after all.

63.

Cecil climbed aboard his scooter. At last it had stopped raining and he was going to take a run down to Oscar's apartment. There was supposed to a good football match on tonight. Cecil reckoned it would be loads more fun to watch it on Oscar's wide screen TV.

Once he was well away from the house and out of sight of his mum he stopped. Parking the scooter under some trees, he sat cross-legged on low wall and lit up a cigarette. As he drew gently on it and exhaled through his nose, he laughed to himself. He had everybody well fooled. They all thought he was an innocent little angel. He reckoned they didn't know him too well.

He looked at his well-polished D.M. boots. They were so comfortable to wear. He laughed as he admired his bright pink socks. That really was a masterstroke of genius. Even Oscar now thought he was probably gay! He chuckled to himself. They were all so totally gullible!

He sat there thinking about it all. From the time he was no age at all, he'd realized that he was very different from the other children in his class. He watched in astonishment as they all struggled with their lessons. He couldn't contain the fact that to him, it all seemed easy.

It had all come to a head one day in a third form math's class. The dotty old dear of a teacher had offered a prize to the first one to solve a complicated mathematical problem. The prize was a very attractive looking silvery coloured pen. Usually bored with it all, that day Cecil had something to shoot for. He couldn't resist the temptation! He got his head down and really worked hard at the problem. Within about five minutes he put his hand up to say he had the answer. The old dear of a teacher had got him to bring up his jotter complete with workings. She glanced briefly at it but said nothing.

She'd sent him back to his seat and waited to see if anyone else would come up with an answer. After ten minutes, three others had brought up their written workings. After twenty minutes she told everyone to put down their pens. That was long enough she'd said. She pronounced that there had been only one right answer. Cecil Brown was asked to come out to the front of the class to receive his prize. Proudly he had held his new silver pen aloft for admiration.

Cecil remembered how pleased he'd been with his triumph. It underlined in his own mind his undoubted superiority over his classmates. Inwardly, that day it really registered that intellectually he was a cut well above the rest of them. The dotty old teacher knew it too and thereafter, she treated Cecil differently. She suspected she had a young genius in her class. Cecil often was first to work out the problems she set on the board. He quickly became her star pupil and everyone knew it.

However, Cecil also discovered that he wasn't going to bask in the admiration of his peers. By and large, they hated him. They were very jealous of his apparent abilities. He soon discovered he was living in an environment of complete resentment.

He was horrified at the level of hostility his newfound fame had brought with it. He was being bullied and jeered at on a daily basis.

Someone bust into his locker and threw all his books into the toilet and then flushed it. Once or twice, he actually got into fights with other boys. They beat him up quite badly. He wasn't as proficient with his fists as he was with his brain. He soon figured out that the bullying was the result of him being different from the rest.

Shortly afterwards, there had been a school holiday. Cecil had thought long and hard about his predicament. Eventually, he worked out a new policy, which would help him to reintegrate with his peers. He called it 'operation chameleon.' The idea was to blend quietly into the background and disappear from view.

He executed his clever plan quite brilliantly. He kept a low profile and purposely handed in lots of poor homework. Teachers now berated him in front of the class for his shoddy work. Notably, in math's his marks took a complete nosedive. At the year-end, his overall exam marks put him just ahead of average in his class. His teachers were perplexed and greatly disappointed at his performance. On the way home from school, Cecil tore up his report card and threw it in a dustbin. His mum didn't need to know anything about all this.

His plan worked. Now showing no sign of any special talents, he had blended seamlessly into the background. He was the picture of acceptable mediocrity amongst his peers. He was as he called himself privately, 'the invisible man.' It was just as he wanted it.

Sitting cross-legged atop the low wall, Cecil grinned to himself. It was so wonderful to have everyone fooled. He knew he was pretty damn clever but virtually no one else even suspected his intellect. That he thought to himself gave him a distinct edge in many situations. An edge that, he would often use to his advantage!

He stubbed out his cigarette and pulled a mobile phone out of his pocket.

"Hi Oscar, it's Cecil. Can I come over to yours to watch the football please?"

"Of course you can. Have you eaten yet? How would you like me to order up a nice Chinese for us to have whilst the match is on?"

"Yes Uncle Oscar! That would be great!" he sounded as enthusiastic as possible.

"I've told you before Cecil. You don't need to call me Uncle!"

"Sorry Uncle Oscar . . . . I mean Oscar." He stuttered on purpose struggling to stop himself from laughing and giving the game away.

"That's alright Cecil. See you soon then?"

"Yes, see you soon."

Cecil rang off and started to laugh to himself. Its too easy he chuckled thinking to himself. 'Like taking candy from a baby!'

64.

William was desperately cutting at the leather strap that restrained his right hand. It was very awkward as the little penknife wasn't all that sharp. He had been cutting away at it for about ten minutes now and he still was only about half way through it. He sawed away at it as fast as he dared. It required him to double back his fingers against the palm of his hand. He could just about engage the blade of the knife with the strap at his wrist. He had to stop every now and again as the cramp in his wrist was too painful to continue. It was proving very difficult indeed and several times he had almost dropped the small knife. He knew if he did that, that it would be game over.

There was a clanging sound somewhere from the rear of the shed. Alarmed, William broke out in a sweat. Surely they couldn't be back again already? He listened carefully but could hear nothing more. Clang! There was the noise again. Then he twigged on. The wind was getting up and that must be the loose corrugated panel banging in the wind. He knew he just had to saw through the strap. He began again cutting like fury. Sweat was dripping off the end of his nose with the exertion of this desperate enterprise.

His fingers were sore now and even they were getting all sweaty. Suddenly, the knife took off out of his fingers and clattered onto the floor. "Oh no!" he shouted out dismayed. With that he gave a great yell of exasperation and pulled with all his might at the strap. Inside his head he could see light briefly flashing so great was his effort to break the strap. Then just when all seemed lost, the strap just gave way and pulled apart!

William looked down in disbelief. The strap had broken. Blood was seeping out of his forearm near the wrist where he had wrenched violently at the leather strap. He gave a great sigh of sheer relief and rapidly started undoing the other strap. He had it free in a trice. Next he had to rid himself of the chain around his ankles. Sitting on the floor, he dragged himself over towards the door. Sure enough, there was a bundle of keys hanging on a rusty nail just as the man who gave him the pen knife had said. The third key he tried opened the lock and he was able to unwind the chain and cast it off. Now he had another problem though. One of the thugs had taken his training shoes so he was in his sock soles. *Won't get far like that.* He thought.

He started hunting around the floor of the shed. Initially the search proved fruitless but then he found a very old pair of wellington boots. They were at least two sizes too big but he was glad to find anything at all. Next, he made for the rear of the old shed. He soon found an old wooden ladder that enabled him to climb up to where the metal panel was banging in the wind.

He put his full weight against the panel, but it barely moved at all. He was only able to open up a gap of about three inches. He descended the ladder and hunted around the shed. There was all sorts of old rubbish lying around everywhere. The place was a veritable dump and scrapyard all rolled into one. Eventually he found a four-foot length of iron bar. It was very rusty but that didn't matter. He climbed the ladder again and began to use it as a pry bar to lever the panel off the shed wall. Unfortunately, it wouldn't shift at all. He kept trying, still no dice. The stubborn panel wouldn't budge.

Breathing heavily, he stopped for a rest. He wiped away sweat from his brow and discovered his wrist was bleeding badly. He needed to do something about it. Back down the ladder again he saw a first aid box on the wall. *What luck!* he thought to himself. He ripped it open. The box was empty except for a few spider's webs. He felt inside his pocket and found a paper napkin. He put it on the wound to staunch the bleeding. Next he looked around and found some tank tape. Presumably the big guy used this to tie up his victims. William tore off a length of the tape and quickly wound it around his forearm. The worst of the bleeding stopped almost immediately.

William was aware that the thugs would soon be back again. Motivated by the thought of what would happen to him when they returned, he climbed back up the ladder and started levering the panel for all he was worth. His redoubled efforts soon paid off and the panel at last began to work loose. He gave it one last great heave and then something snapped. Suddenly it burst open leaving a gaping hole for him to crawl through.

Excited, William leapt out forgetting he was maybe twelve feet off the ground. He landed heavily in the midst of a thorn hedge. Apart from cuts and scratches though he was alright. Mildly dazed he got to his feet and started running from the shed. It was rather hard to make progress in the over size wellingtons, but soon he was two or three hundred yards away and climbing over a gate into an adjacent field. Just as he landed on the other side of the gate, he heard a van or something coming up the gravel path towards the shed. In the distance he could see a pick-up truck drive into the yard. He didn't hang around, but instead ran as fast as he could go.

He could soon hear a great deal of shouting and yelling in the distance. They'd obviously discovered he had absconded. He ran as hard as he could go. He decided to avoid the roads, as that would be an all to obvious way to get caught. He made for the next field and then the next after that. He climbed over another gate in an ungainly fashion and ended up falling awkwardly on to some boulders. Just as his foot touched the ground he knew he was done for. He went right over on his ankle and gave a sharp yelp of pain. Luckily he was now far enough away not to be heard by the rogues.

As he got to his feet he gingerly put weight on his right foot. The action confirmed his worst fears. He'd sprained his ankle really badly. He could now hardly walk. This was really bad. He could hear the thugs coming across the fields in his general direction.

In desperation he hobbled downhill towards a small copse of trees nestling in a dip between two drumlins. Just below him, he could see there was a whole thicket of nettles and brambles around it. It was a virtually impenetrable tangle of undergrowth.

"You go over towards that field and I'll look down here. Geordie, come you with me."

He recognized the voice. It was that big guy who had threatened to torture him! He was just out of sight somewhere not far away.

"Let's look over there where those trees are," added Geordie.

William realized they had nearly caught up with him. It was do or die now. He knew if they caught him he was finished. Despite his injured ankle, he leapt into the brambles. He landed like a crashing aircraft among the brambles and nettles. The plants stabbed him like a thousand small daggers as he clasped his hand over his mouth to stop himself from shouting out in pain.

Nearby he could hear Bill's voice. "What was that?"

"What?" Geordie looked over.

"I thought I heard something over there in those bushes. Lets take a look. I definitely heard a branch break!"

William very gently pulled some grass and undergrowth over him and lay face down hardly daring to breath. He had fallen into a dense nettle patch. As he lay, the nettles were right against his face and stinging him. Terrified, he lay as still as he possibly could.

"Do you see anything?" whispered Geordie.

Through the undergrowth, William could just about make out a figure walking towards where he was hidden. It was a large man so he deduced it must be Bill. He pressed his face down into the nettles and grimaced as they stung his face again. He didn't make a sound.

"No." came the gruff answer. "Not a bloody thing. Must have been a bird amongst the branches or something."

To William's vast relief, soon afterwards he heard the voices become progressively less distinct as they moved away from him. After ten minutes they were gone. He lifted his face from the nettles. It was throbbing with the pain of the stings. He cast about and sure enough, nearby he found some Docken leaves.

"Good old mother nature!" he said softly to himself as he rubbed them vigorously against his face and hands. After a few moments, the long time natural remedy began to afford at least some relief from the stings.

He elected to remain in the dense copse. He didn't dare make a break for it as he knew he wouldn't stand a chance if they saw him. His ankle was very sore now. On hands and knees he crawled painfully deeper into the undergrowth. He stopped. He imagined he could hear something. Something was trickling nearby. It was water.

Right in the heart of the thicket, he found a little stream running gently through what must have been an old drainage ditch. He stared at it and smiled. He stuck his hand in it and to his delight it was ice cold.

Carefully, he removed one of his filthy old wellington boots and gently plunged his injured ankle into the water. His medical knowledge had come flooding back to him now. He knew that the cold of the water would help the sprained ankle. The cold would cause the surface blood vessels to constrict and thus help prevent seepage of blood into the surrounding soft tissues. This would greatly reduce the extent of the bruising and ultimately the pain caused by the injury.

This was all good and well, but the cold water in itself was very painful. The treatment would only be of help if he could endure the freezing water for twenty or more minutes.

Every so often, he withdrew his foot from the water to recover a little from the discomfort. He then stuck it back in and tried to last out as long as he could. Timing it on his watch, he eventually managed the better part of a half hour in total. He removed his foot from the water and gently put on the boot again. Very carefully he stood up. His foot and ankle were stiff from the cold, but he felt he could now probably walk a short distance on it. He could hear rain falling heavily onto the leaves above. He'd wait a while and then make a run for it.

65.

The Fatman was growing ever more impatient. He hadn't heard from anyone and he didn't know what was going on. He'd just tried phoning Oscar but could get no reply. He scrolled through the menu on his mobile and Geordies number eventually appeared. He hit call.

"Geordie, what's going on? Did Bill arrive with you yet?"

"Yes. He's here alright, but we've had a problem. That cyclist guy who stole the money has escaped from Bill's shed. We're out in the surrounding fields searching for him as I speak."

The Fatman went silent. He just didn't quite know what to say. He frankly couldn't believe what he was hearing.

"I'm sorry, I didn't quite catch that. Did you say he's escaped?"

"Yeah, he's got away."

"How the hell did he escape? You guys were watching him weren't you?"

"We were with him all night. Bill arrived and then he decided he wanted to go for a fry up breakfast at Margaret's café. We had yer man all strapped to a chair and a chain round his ankles. The shed was locked up too. Thinking there was no way he could escape, we all went for breakfast. We were only away about twenty-five minutes. When we got back the bugger was gone! We can't understand how he got away. He must be friggin' Houdini or something!"

The Fatman was absolutely flabbergasted. "Geordie, you're telling me that it was all because that stupid shite Bill went for breakfast, that our guy got away? Is that what happened?"

"Essentially yes. Mind you, we did go with him."

"Geordie, you tell Bill he if doesn't find this guy I'm going to shoot him in the fucking stomach! He'll eat bugger all after that!"

"Are you serious? Do you really want me to tell him that?" Geordie was concerned at the likely reaction he'd get form Big Bill!

"Yes! You tell him. After all the efforts you and Shorty made to find the bastard and then he lets him get away!"

"OK boss." Geordie was thinking it would probably be very difficult to find a boss who would be more awkward to work for.

"I'm going to get Oscar and we'll come over there to help you search. That guy can't have got far. I'll see you soon."

"Alright. Hopefully we'll have found him before you get here."

As Geordie hung up, Bill came over.

"Was that the Fatman?"

"Yes it was."

"What did he say?" Bill wanted to know.

"Well let me put it this way. He's not best pleased and you're not too popular."

"Why just me for frig sake? You were all with me. One of you should have stayed behind and guarded him! Everyone always blames everything on me!"

Geordie had decided not to tell Bill exactly what the Fatman had said. He felt it would be counterproductive. Not only that, but he couldn't be bothered weathering the tirade of abuse that would likely result.

"Come on," said Geordie "there's no point in crying about spilt milk. Let's just find this guy before he gets away."

66.

The Fatman rang Oscar again. This was the third time in ten minutes. There was still no answer to his phone. 'The big bugger must have slept in or something.' He thought to himself.

Eventually he lost patience completely. He decided to drive over to Oscar's apartment and wake him up. He knew he needed everyone out there looking for the phantom cyclist! He opened his safe in the wood paneling and removed the Glock pistol and its magazine of bullets. He slipped them into his pocket.

He barked some instructions to the girls in the office and then climbed aboard his trusty Mercedes convertible. Inside, the mushroom leather squealed and creaked a little as he heaved his enormous bulk into the seat. The engine caught first time and he roared out of the yard and off in the direction of Oscar's flat.

Only a few minutes later, he arrived at the apartment building. He tried phoning Oscar once more, still no answer. He remembered he'd been to Oscar's apartment some months ago. Oscar had given him the code to the front door. He pulled out his mobile and opened the 'notes' section. Soon he found what he was looking for.

OSCAR 4718.

He parked the convertible on the footpath right at the front door of the building and waddled over and punched the code into the keypad. Electronically, the glass doors slid silently open to admit him. Soon he was in the lift and pressed the button, which would take him to the penthouse. Nothing happened. When he checked the console that controlled the lift, he saw a message prompting him to key in a code. He remembered that Oscar had lazily made it the same code as the front door. He keyed in 4718 and smoothly the lift began to rise towards the fourteenth floor penthouse.

He was laughing at Oscar's cavalier attitude towards security. "Just as well I'm not a hit man Oscar." He chuckled to himself.

The lift doors opened and he stepped out. He was in a softly lit small private marble floored lobby, which was dedicated solely to Oscar's penthouse apartment. He was just about to ring the bell when something stopped him. For the sheer hell of it he decided he'd burst in and surprise Oscar. If he could catch him still in bed or in the shower that would be really sweet he thought. It would serve him right for not coming into work on time. Especially on a day like this when he was really needed.

The Fatman lifted the base of a potted plant and looked under it. No key. He knew Oscar would keep one somewhere as he was forever misplacing his keys. He tried under the mat. Nothing. He was just about to give up and ring the bell when on a final hunch he reached up and ran his fingers along the top of the doorframe. "Ah ha! Got ya!" he whispered to himself.

He inserted the key in the lock and as quietly as possible opened the door. He was enjoying this now! He couldn't wait to see the look on Oscars face when he woke up to find him right beside his bed. That would give the big bugger a shock! Mischievously he chuckled very quietly to himself.

He entered the main living area of the apartment. It was very smart looking except for the sitting area in front of the widescreen television. The huge coffee table was covered in beer cans and empty pizza boxes and plates. "Jeez, Oscar must have had a party or something!" he whispered to himself.

The double doors that led to the master bedroom were closed. The Fatman gently opened them and peered inside. In the semi darkness of the room he could make out the indistinct figures of sleepers in the bed. *Oscar must have got lucky*! He thought to himself.

"Wakey wakey!" he yelled switching on the lights and laughing out loud. Oscar's stunned face appeared incredulous from beneath the covers. The blond haired figure beside him shot bolt upright in the bed also. The Fatman did a double take in utter astonishment for it was Cecil. It took a moment to register.

"Cecil!" he yelled out bewildered by this. "What in fuck's name are you doing here? Here in Oscar's bed!"

"I, ... I, can explain!" Oscar got up uneasily and lifted his trousers off the floor. He immediately started trying to pull them on.

"You can explain fuck all!" shouted the Fatman.

"Cecil came to see the football. He stayed over as he'd had a few beers. I couldn't let him ride the scooter like that."

"Aye. A likely bloody story." The Fatman wasn't buying it at all.

Cecil sprang out of bed. He was completely naked. He started pulling his underpants on.

"Cecil, get out of here now! I'll speak to you later. Get out and go home!"

The boy looked shit scared. He quickly gathered up his clothes and D.M. boots off the floor and scarpered out of the room.

"As for you, you fucking big fruit you!" The Fatman growled at Oscar, "You're fuckin' dead! Can't believe you'd try to shag that wee boy! You're a complete fucking bastard!"

Oscar had been using the time wisely. By now he'd pulled his trousers on. Quickly he also slipped on his shoes.

"Will you give me a chance to tell you what happened?" he said.

"No!" came the terse reply. "I can see with my own eyes. I'd never have believed it if I hadn't seen it. You fucking big pedophile!"

The Fatman was white in the face with sheer rage. He felt in his pocket and pulled out the Glock pointing it at Oscar.

"Wise up! Put that away you stupid fat bastard!" Oscar screamed clearly concerned now.

The Fatman pulled the trigger of the Glock. All it did was give a metallic click. He pulled it again. Again it only gave a click. He realized it wasn't loaded. He hadn't put the magazine of bullets into it. He started to fumble about in his jacket pocket for the magazine.

Oscar meanwhile grabbed his shirt and ran for the door. The Fatman shoved the magazine into the handle of the Glock and felt it click home. He pulled back the slide to load it and raised it to fire at Oscar who was by now half way out into the hall. Bang! Bang! The Fatman let off two rounds. Both bullets hammered into the woodwork of the doorframe splitting it in the process. Oscar was gone out into the hall.

The Fatman made after him as fast as his enormous bulk would permit. As he ran for the door he eyed Cecil sitting on the sofa pulling his DM boots on.

"Stop Oscar you big poof you!" he yelled.

In the hallway, Oscar knew he couldn't hang around waiting for the lift to arrive. He opened the fire escape door. The Fatman was in close pursuit behind him. Oscar got halfway down the first flight of steps as the Fatman shot at him again. This time the bullet shattered a glass ceiling light above Oscar's head. The Fatman was just about to fire again when suddenly the legs were taken from beneath him. Cecil running at full speed had hurled himself at the Fatman who unbalanced fell into the stairwell.

"Fuck!" he screamed enraged.

"Run Oscar. Run!" Cecil shouted.

Oscar rounded the turn at the bottom of the first flight of steps. Moments later the Fatman came to rest having tumbled down the stairs. Cecil had just landed still only half dressed on top of him.

"There! Serve you right for slapping me in the face you fat fucker you!" the boy shouted defiantly.

"Fuck you, you wee bastard you!" The Fatman kicked out savagely landing his boot in the boy's ribs. Cecil staggered to one side yelping in agony. "I'll deal with you later son!"

The Fatman struggled to his feet and scrambled painfully back up the stairs to the penthouse lobby. Puffing and wheezing out of breath, he pushed the call button for the lift. It seemed to take forever to arrive. Eventually after well over a minute there was a 'Ding' and the doors slid soundlessly open. The Fatman tumbled inside and pushed the button for the ground floor lobby.

Meanwhile, Oscar was descending the stairs in leaps and bounds. He was running for his life, literally! He knew that if the Fatman caught up with him again he would be lucky to survive. He was also aware that the Fatman was actually a good shot. It had been a miracle he hadn't been hit upstairs. He didn't want to push his luck. It was time to go!

At length, Oscar made it to the basement garage and ran towards his Mercedes Coupe. He reached beneath the rear of the car and eventually clutched hold of a small magnetic box he kept a spare set of keys in. Soon he was heading for the up ramp of the underground garage.

Above, the Fatman puffed his way out onto the street. He looked left and right and then heard the mechanical clanking of the roller shutter garage door opening a few yards away. He could see Oscar's car getting ready to make off.

As he got to his own car, he saw a traffic warden wearing a red coat. He was just about to stick a ticket on the windscreen. He could tell instantly that this was an officious wee git.

"You can't park here sir." Said the sanctimonious little Hitler obviously well pleased with his handiwork.

"Fuck off!" the Fatman lashed out viciously with his right fist. Instantly a gout of scarlet blood poured from the warden's nose. He fell to the ground groaning and clutching his face.

The Fatman stepped over him and quickly got into his car and set off after Oscar. The dark coloured Coupe was only about two hundred yards away. Oscar had had to slow down for a pedestrian. The Fatman gunned the throttle and caught up with him. Oscar stopped at a red light. Big mistake. The Fatman wound down the window of his car and started to shoot at him. People in the street were screaming in panic and running for cover. A shocked cyclist lost his balance. He struck a kerb and fell heavily from his bike. Other folks fell flat on the pavement hoping they wouldn't get shot.

Alarmed by the gunfire, Oscar stamped on the accelerator and roared off. Looking in his rear view mirror, he could see the Fatmans ruby red convertible was in hot pursuit as it screeched around a corner after him. Oscar could hardly believe how fast the Fatman was driving to keep up. Next time he looked, the Mercedes was in a complete four-wheel drift slide out of the corner behind him. He was really struggling to get away.

There was however hope, as a section of dual carriageway now lay ahead. Oscar knew his car was ultimately faster as it was more powerful than the Fatmans classic AMG car. He started to pull away now and before long was doing a good hundred miles and hour. In the distance ahead of him, he could clearly see a whole queue of traffic, which appeared to be stopped at a red light. This was bad. Oscar approached at high speed. He glanced in his mirror. To his vast dismay, he saw that the Fatman wasn't as far behind as he'd hoped.

Oscar rushed up towards the light and to his joy saw that there was actually a green arrow if you wanted to turn right. The long queue of cars were all waiting to turn left. There was no one in the right lane at all! The light was at a T-junction with the By-pass. He elected to make a right turn as it was clear to that side. A large double decker bus was waiting at the lights blocking his view of the lane he was turning into. Oscar braked as late as he dared his tyres chirping as the ABS cut in. He scrambled round the bus and drove off along the By-pass.

The Fatman came hurtling up behind him. The light was still green. He screeched towards the junction locking up his tyres. White smoke poured from them as the tortured rubber burnt.

The Fatman hurled his car to the right rounding the waiting bus. As he did so, to his horror a large red fire engine with blue lights flashing and sirens blaring was at point blank range in front of him. It was on the wrong side of the road and coming head on, straight at him, going at full speed!

He took in the terrifying sight in an instant. There was no time to think. He whirled the steering to the left in a desperate effort to miss the charging fire engine. But it was too late. He thundered into the front of the fire truck. There was a sickening dull thud as he hit it. He felt his body go numb with the shock of the impact. The Mercedes glanced off the front of the fire engine and took off into the air. It barrel rolled viciously away over the Armco barrier and down a grassy slope eventually coming to rest upside down in a field. Watching motorists who witnessed the accident would later report that it had been spectacular, like something out of a Formula One Grand Prix race!

Moments earlier, Oscar had had a very lucky escape narrowly missing a similar fate. He had just made it onto the hard shoulder in the nick of time. The Fire engine was obviously going to an emergency and had been travelling at very high speed on the wrong side of the road. Afterwards, the Fire Chief would remark that they thought all the traffic had heard their approach and had cleared a way for the speeding Fire engine. His assumption was very wrong.

Oscar stopped only briefly looking to see what had happened. Seeing the car on its roof alarmed him. He knew the Fatman could well be dead or at least seriously injured. He was powerless to intervene. If he stuck around, there would be a lot of very awkward questions to answer once the police arrived. Stealthily, hoping no one would notice him he drove smoothly away.

67.

William crawled out of the thicket of bushes. He'd been in there nearly all day. At last, it was just starting to get dark. Only now did he dare emerge from his hiding place. The rain had been on for hours. He was absolutely freezing by now. The rain had soaked through all his clothes. Only his upper body was still relatively dry as he'd found an old plastic fertilizer bag in the bushes. The bag was quite new so he cut holes in it for his head and arms and pulled it on like a coat. It might not have won many prizes as a fashion accessory, but it had helped keep him dry!

Keeping a wary eye out all around him, William made off over the field. He could only hobble slowly along as his ankle was giving him terrible jip. To his right he spotted a field with a high point. He decided to move towards it.

Several minutes later, he arrived at the top of the hill. Sure enough, despite the gathering gloom it gave him a view of the surrounding countryside. Away in the distance, he could just make out a silvery streak. The dying light of the sun had lit it up. It was a road. That had to be the way out of here. He'd have to chance it, as he couldn't walk too far with his injured ankle. He made a note of a high tree between himself and the road. This would serve as a landmark to head towards.

He hobbled back down the hill and wadded through a shuck of water and mud. He was glad of the wellington boots as at least they were useful at this stage. A good twenty minutes later he arrived at the tree. The road was only a short distance now. This was just as well as by now as it was really beginning to get dark.

The rain had abated somewhat turning instead into a fine mizzle. By the time he reached the road, it was shrouded in an eerie mist. The road was obviously a minor one as after a couple of minutes, not one car had appeared. William was very cold by now and shivering spasmodically. He sat on a rock near the roadside and waited. He was not just weary but very concerned. What if the next car that came along the road had the drug dealing thugs in it? If that happened, he was a dead man.

In the distance, he heard the muffled noise of a diesel engine. Whatever it was, it was struggling up some unseen hill as he could clearly hear the engine toiling heavily. The noise came gradually closer and closer. Eventually, two dimly lit headlights pierced the gloom. As it came closer, the vehicle at last took form.

William was amazed at the ghostly unreal image before him. Emerging spectre like out of the mist came an old red bus from the early nineteen seventies. The number on the front was 76 and the destination read 'Gilnahirk'. It was like something that had appeared out of a time warp! He ran on to the road and flailed his arms desperately for the bus to stop. It quickly came to a halt. Astonished, the driver climbed out and ran towards William.

"Are you alright?" he looked alarmed.

"Yes, just cold and wet. Can you give me a lift down into Belfast?"

"Have you been in an accident or something?" the bus driver was still very concerned. The man he'd found wandering about on the mountain road looked terrible. "Maybe I should take you to hospital. You look white with cold!"

"I'm OK. If you could just give me a lift I'd be very grateful."

"Of course I'll give you a lift. Climb aboard. You'll have to sit in the passenger compartment. There is no room in the drivers cab I'm afraid."

The driver helped him climb into the back of the bus explaining that he had been at a vintage transport rally. The bus had won a prize as it was in such pristine condition. Luckily, the driver was passing within a half-mile or so of where William lived and agreed to let him off there.

William sat in a nice burgundy leather upholstered seat in the back of the bus. He could remember going to school in one of these buses many years ago just before they went out of service. It all brought back old memories.

They were memories of days long gone past when life had been much simpler and without all the pressures of modern life. As he sat there, he was contemplating it all. With all the new technology mankind had invented and created, was life actually any better for it all? Somehow the old bus seemed comforting and peaceful as it chugged along into the night.

68.

Oscar was on the phone.

"Maureen, I'm so sorry to have to tell you this, but James has crashed his car up on the By Pass."

"Is he ok?" came the anxious reply.

"I don't know. It was a very bad crash indeed. He rolled the car over an Armco barrier and it ended up lying in a field upside down."

"Oh my Lord! What hospital is he in?"

"He's in the Royal."

"What condition is he in? Did they say?"

"They won't tell me as I'm not related to him. But I did get the impression that it was very serious. He's in Intensive care. I can meet you there or do you want me to come and collect you and give you a lift over?"

"No thanks. I'll make my own way over there. I'll see you at Intensive care."

"I may be a wee while as I need to urgently sort a problem with the boys first. I'll be there as quick as I can though." Oscar assured her.

"O.K. Thanks Oscar. I'll see you over there."

69.

Oscar had arrived up at Bills yard. By now it was after midnight. The whole place was in darkness except for a glimmer of light that came from a small bulkhead lamp above the shed door. Despite the gathering gloom he could just make out Bills pick up truck and further away across the yard under a tree, Shorty's van was parked.

There was no one around. He listened for a moment but could hear nothing. He entered the shed by the Judas door and switched on the lights. Above him, one fluorescent light lit up. The others all started to flicker on and off uncertain as to whether they should join in or not.

"Typical Bill!" Oscar said quietly to himself. "Probably hasn't changed the starters in those lights for years!"

He walked over towards the high backed chair that William had been strapped into. It was clear from what he saw that the leather straps had been cut through with a blade of some sort. He was about to walk away when he saw something glinting in the flickering light beneath the chair. He knelt down and retrieved a small penknife with blue plastic sides. Closing the blade, he pocketed it to examine later.

"Hmm. That's obviously how he cut himself free. Wonder where he got that?" he whispered to himself. Oscar had the vague feeling he'd seen the knife somewhere before, but he couldn't quite place it.

Just at that there was a noise behind him so he whirled round to see the Judas door opening. It was Geordie and Shorty.

"Did you find him?" even as he asked the question, he could see by their expressions that the answer would be negative.

"No." Geordies voice betrayed both weariness and exasperation.

Oscar could see that the pair of them were both totally soaked and pissed off.

"Suppose the Fatman will have our guts for garters over this" Shorty said resignedly.

Oscar gave a muffled ironic chuckle. "Maybe not actually."

Geordie looked at him in a puzzled manner. "What do you mean?"

"Mr. Cartwright has met with an unfortunate accident. He crashed his car this morning up on the By Pass."

"What happened?" Geordie enquired looking concerned.

"Don't really know." Oscar sounded strangely detached and uninterested" ⸺

"Is he ok?" Shorty asked.

"Not sure." Again it was as if Oscar couldn't care less. "He crashed into a fire engine or something and rolled into a field. He's in hospital in intensive care."

"Can we go up to see him?" Geordie asked anxiously.

"No." Oscar was now taking command of the situation. "Maureen's already up there. She'll phone me if anything happens. Right now we have a job to do. We need to find this guy and get the money back before he scarpers and disappears for good!"

"I just can't understand how the bugger got away!" Geordie was scratching his head and looked clearly perplexed as he looked at the cut straps on the chair. "Like I said on the phone to Mr. Cartwright earlier, we had him strapped and chained up. Its like as if he was friggin' Harry Houdini or something!"

"That's right Oscar." Shorty agreed. "Just like Houdini the famous escapist or whatever he was?"

"Escapologist" Oscar corrected. He stared at Shorty somehow feeling slightly suspicious that something here just didn't add up. At length he asked,

"What did this guy look like anyway?"

"He was just an ordinary looking bloke, nothing special about him. Actually, I've got a photo of him out in the van. It's the one I took of him on the cycle track." Said Geordie.

"Go and get it for me. I'd like to see it." Oscar ordered.

Whilst Geordie went for the photo, Oscar looked at Shorty. He was examining the cut ends of the straps.

"Shorty, how do you think this guy got out of here anyway? I mean, you had the shed all locked up when you went for breakfast didn't you?"

"Yes, it was all locked up alright. I checked the lock myself. It was still locked when we got back." Shorty walked towards the rear of the shed and soon called Oscar to see something.

"Look up there. Someone has forced the corrugated sheeting apart. That must have been where he got out."

Oscar looked up at it and nodded agreement.

Just then, Geordie reappeared. "I've got the photo Boss."

Oscar took a quick look at it and then did a double take.

"I don't believe it!" he looked amazed. "I know who this guy is! I bought a scooter from him. The one Cecil got for his birthday! I also know where he lives because I collected it from his house and paid him the money!"

"Are you serious? You are joking aren't you?" Geordie said.

"Absolutely serious!" Oscar was laughing now. "The bastard haggled like hell with me making me pay through the nose for the bloody thing! All the time he had over a million pound of our money hidden away somewhere!"

"Do you remember where he lives?" Shorty enquired.

"Too right I do. We're going over there now to get the bastard!"

Suddenly, there was a noise outside. It sounded like a door of a car slamming shut.

"What's that?" Shorty looked alarmed.

"Don't get all excited. It'll just be Bill arriving back," said Geordie

"Say nothing about the fact that we know where this guy lives!" Oscar whispered a warning to the others. "He's done little enough to help us find him and if we don't have to pay him its more money for the rest of us!"

Moments later, the Judas door burst open and sure enough, it was Bill.

"Any sign of yer man?" he shouted coarsely.

"No, not at all." replied Geordie." Did you find anything?"

"Not a bloody thing. I'm totally soaked through with all this rain. Not only that, but remember I got fuck all sleep last night as I was driving up from Killarney."

"That's too bad Bill." Oscar tried to sound at least slightly sincere.

Bill glared at him. "Anyway, I'm off home for a hot bath, something to eat and then I'm going to bed."

"Good idea. We're going now too. We'll look for bugger lugs again tomorrow," said Shorty.

"Pull the door of the shed closed when you leave." Instructed Bill yawning loudly as he went over to his pick up truck. Moments later they heard the engine chug into life and Bill drove off.

"Right!" Oscar was all business now. "We'll go to this guys house and pay him a wee visit." He glanced at his watch. "Its nearly one thirty. He's probably made it home by now and will be fast asleep by the time we get there."

"You've met him," said Shorty. "What's his name?"

"William something. William Foreman I think." Oscar paused thinking. "No! I remember now. It's William Forsythe! Aye, that's his name. William Forsythe."

"Where does he live?" enquired Geordie.

"East Belfast. Shorty we'll all go in your van. Don't want to arrive up there like a whole flippin' posse. Come on, let's go!"

70.

TEN MINUTES EARLIER . . . .

William was crouched down behind a hedge. He was in a neighbor's garden just across the road from his own house. The whole street was in darkness. Only the forlorn barking of a dog somewhere in the distance broke the silent still of the night. He checked his watch. It was twenty past one. Everyone in the street including Julia would be asleep by now. He sat completely still watching for a few minutes more. He wanted to be absolutely sure no one was watching the house or hanging around before he made a move across the road. Eventually, seeing no movement anywhere at all he decided to chance it.

He quickly scurried across the street and down the side of the house. Fumbling about under the bin, he found the spare key for the back door. He turned the key in the lock and gingerly opened the back door. Quiet as a mouse, William climbed the stairs being careful not to wake Julia up. The door of her bedroom was tight closed. He entered his own bedroom, which luckily was virtually right at the top of the stairs.

The two soft bags he had packed still lay on top of the bed exactly as he'd left them yesterday before he went out on his bike. He'd planned to take a few more small personal items with him, but under the current circumstances, he'd make do with what he'd already packed. He lifted the bags along with his coat and the keys of the Porsche. He cast a quick look around in the darkness and decided to get out as fast as possible just in case anyone turned up.

Soundlessly he descended the stairs. Then, in the graveyard still, one stair gave an enormous creak! William had forgotten that the extra weight of his luggage had made him heavier. He paused half expecting Julia to emerge from her lair. Nothing. She must be out for the count he thought. Gently he continued down the stairs and along the hall back to the kitchen. He found he was almost shaking now with excitement as he grabbed the key for the garage from a small hook near the back door. He had almost made it now. He felt like a tennis player serving for the match. The championship in his hand now, he just needed to serve out to win. That's when the real nerves set in.

Just as he opened the back door to go out, there was a terrific crashing sound! He could hear voices shouting as a shower of breaking glass flew into the hallway. The wood of the front door was splintering and cracking open under a vicious assault. William went outside and closed the door behind him. Momentarily, he was worried about what they might do to Julia. Instantly he made the decision that no matter what, he was in great peril and Julia knew nothing anyway.

In the darkness, as fast as he could, he stumbled desperately towards the garage. He very nearly went over on his sprained ankle as he stepped on the edging stone of the rear lawn. Wincing he kept going. The back garden at number 32 Kings Wood Park was quite big and moreover long. This meant that the garage was surprisingly about forty yards behind the house. William would have to hurry! Behind him, he could hear the muffled crashing sounds of something breaking inside the house.

The three men had the front door completely off its hinges by now. Geordie led the charge up the stairs. He burst into the first bedroom on the landing. He switched the lights on. A few items of men's clothing and a pair of shoes lay strewn on the floor. The bed hadn't been slept in, no one there. Shorty opened the next door. A small bedroom, probably a spare room with a desk and many cardboard boxes full of junk. Oscar opened the next door. It was the bathroom. He grimaced briefly at the horribly outdated green suite. There was a huge bath towel lying beside the shower. He picked it up and felt that it was still wet but not warm. Someone had used it and maybe quite recently.

The three men almost ran into each other on the landing as they all eyed the last bedroom door. Oscar lifted his boot and gave the door a massive kick with all the force he could muster. The door burst open.

Oscar ran into the darkened room. Behind him Shorty hit the light switch. The bed was empty. There was no one there.

"There's nobody here boss!" exclaimed Geordie somewhat out of breath with all the charging about.

"Aye. Tell me something I don't know!" Oscar said in disgust. "Looks like this William fella was too bloody clever for us. He obviously had enough wit not to come home after all. Lets have a hunt around for the money. He must have hidden it somewhere."

They all began pulling drawers out of dressers and upturning mattresses. Oscar opened up the wardrobe and threw everything out of it onto the floor.

"Better hurry up boss!" Shorty pointed out the window. "Lights are coming on in houses all up the street. They must have heard us busting the door down."

"Next thing the bloody police will be here and this is a cul-de-sac. We'll be trapped like rats in a barrel!" Geordie added.

"Fuck!" said Oscar exasperated looking out the window. The front door of the house across the street was opening. "You're right. We'd better get the hell out of here fast." He started running down the stairs.

He went into the kitchen and turned the light on. A note was sitting on the kitchen table. It was obviously intended for William who hadn't noticed it in the darkness.

"AS YOU DIDN'T BOTHER COMING HOME FOR DINNER AS ARRANGED, I'VE GONE TO A FRIENDS HOUSE. I'VE FINALLY HAD ENOUGH OF YOU. I'M NOT COMING BACK. GOODBYE!

The note had been signed love, Julia but she had obviously had after thoughts about it and the 'love' bit had been heavily scored out!

Somewhere outside, a car engine was starting up. Oscar was first out onto the driveway of the house. Suddenly a car emerged from the garage it's headlights blazing in the darkness. It spun its rear wheels as the driver accelerated savagely. It was coming straight at Oscar. For a second he considered standing his ground. The Porsche was rapidly gaining speed now. As Oscar jumped to one side, he caught sight of the driver. It was William. He was giving Oscar the fingers! Briefly, their eyes met. They recognized each other. William realized with surprise it was the chap he'd sold a scooter to a few weeks ago! The Porsche rushed past him and out onto the road. Its air-cooled engine whirred audibly as it accelerated rapidly away and was gone.

Oscar stared after it bemused. "The bird has flown!" he shook his head in resignation.

"Quick!" yelled Shorty. "After him." He jumped into the van, started it up. It was facing towards the blind end of the cul de sac. Shorty began turning it around in the street. The whole operation took about a minute and a half. "Come on hurry up!" yelled Shorty.

Oscar didn't make any effort to rush. He climbed in beside Geordie who was already on board and slowly closed the door of the van.

Shorty let the clutch out and the diesel van started to accelerate gradually away up the street.

"Never bother Shorty," Oscar said dryly.

"But he's getting away!" Shorty screamed excitedly.

"He's in a fucking Porsche Shorty you idiot. You're not going to catch him in this bloody van." Oscar was totally pissed off.

"The only thing you'll ever catch in this van is pneumonia as the heater doesn't work properly!" added Geordie.

"Lets try and catch him!" Shorty still wouldn't give it up. By now he'd reached the main road. They all looked in both directions. No sign of the Porsche. It was long gone.

"Did anyone even get the registration?" asked Geordie.

"No." Shorty was crestfallen.

"All I saw was HXI something," said Oscar. "I never saw the number. He did leave rather quickly after all. It was a white Porsche 911 though, an older model. There aren't that many of them about these days."

"What do we do now?" Shorty looked defeated.

"Firstly, lets get the hell away from here before the police show up. Some of the neighbors probably dialed 999. Keep her lit Shorty. Head back for Bills yard. I need my car back." Oscar demanded.

"What then" enquired Geordie.

"Then, I'll head for the International airport to keep an eye out for this guy William. He may just be stupid enough to try and hop a plane somewhere. If he shows up at the airport, I'll nab him. We'll leave Geordie off at the Geordie Best Airport in the city." Oscar laughed out slightly realizing it sounded almost funny.

"You Shorty will head for Larne harbor and keep and watch out for him in case he tries to get on a ferry over to Scotland."

"Ok. Sounds like a plan." said Shorty.

"I'll keep in touch with you at regular intervals so keep your phone with you at all times." Oscar instructed.

"What if he doesn't show up?" Geordie wanted to know.

"Then he's got away. At least for now anyway."

71.

William just kept driving and driving. He'd decided to go first to Dublin. He didn't fancy his chances going to catch a boat now at either Larne or Belfast. Soon, he was miles away heading south at high speed. He felt safe and cocooned inside the Porsche. The instruments were lit with a warm soft glow, the speedo reading ninety miles an hour.

It was the middle of the night by now and the motorway was all but deserted. A sign read Dublin 40. He then realized the sign was in kilometers as in the southern part of Ireland, the signs didn't read in miles per hour. A quick calculation told him he was only twenty-five miles away from Dublin. He glanced at his watch and reckoned he'd left his house escaping from the drug dealers only about an hour ago.

"I've made great time!" he said to himself.

He lifted his phone and rang a number on speed dial. It was a very long time before it was answered.

"What the hell do you want?" Julia was outraged. "Its nearly three o'clock in the morning!"

"Sorry Julia, but this is important. I'm away for a job interview. I'm currently in Edinburgh in Scotland." he lied. "I have an interview in the morning. It's a Company who need a medical representative."

"So what? Why do I need to know this at three o'clock in the morning?"

"Are you at home at the moment?"

There was a pause before the reply came.

"Actually no," she confessed. "I'm staying with a friend for a few days. I did leave you a note. Didn't you read it?"

"Never saw it. I had to leave in rather a hurry I'm afraid. Got wind of this job so I rushed off fairly quickly."

"But why call me in the middle of the night?"

"Its an emergency. I've had a call from one of the neighbors saying we've had a break in at the house. As I said, I'm in Scotland so would you mind dealing with the police?"

"Oh bloody hell, burglars!" she had jumped out of bed by now. "I'll go round immediately. When did this happen?"

"I believe it was about an hour ago. I'd suggest you phone the police first, just in case the burglars are still there. It's probably most unlikely though. Actually, under the circumstances, ring the police tell them you're away overnight and that you'll be home in the morning if they need a report on what's missing."

"Yes." She sounded relieved "That's probably much more sensible."

"Good. I'll check with you in the morning to make sure you're alright."

"Thanks." She said sounding stressed. "By the way, what happened? Why didn't you come home for dinner as we had arranged?

"I got knocked off my bike on the road. I was actually unconscious for a while. Spent the night in hospital actually." He lied through his teeth knowing full well Julia didn't need to know what had really happened.

"Oh my goodness! Why didn't you call me?"

"Well, as I said, I was unconscious for quite some time. Even when I came to I wasn't really able to speak. They had me on oxygen or something."

"How are you now? Are you alright?" Julia actually sounded concerned.

"I'm fine. I've twisted my ankle a wee bit, but apart from that I'm fine. I'm just sorry I can't be there to help you with the police. I hope the burglars haven't messed the place up too much."

"Aren't you worried about what they may have stolen from us?"

"Not really. I got the impression they weren't there long enough. Think someone must have phoned the police and they scarpered."

"Oh. Well that is a relief. Maybe they didn't take too much then."

"Perhaps not." He was thinking fast now. "Julia, what did you say in your note?"

There was a sigh. "I said I'd had enough of you as you hadn't shown up. I was really mad! I said I wasn't coming back again!" he could hear the anger in her voice still.

"Well, that makes this easier for me. I'm not coming home either. I'm going away for a while. Just going to take sometime to myself."

"Where are you going?" she enquired.

"Don't really know. Just away somewhere where I can chill out and find myself."

"What about our divorce?" Julia was being practical. "Will you send me a contact address?

"No. Not for a while. I want to be alone. My solicitor will be in touch with you. Send all future correspondence on to him."

"This is all a bit final isn't it?"

"Yes it is. I know about your boy friend. So yes it is a bit final. Good bye Julia."

William rang off. He imagined her being somewhat stunned. He chuckled to himself. She probably didn't know that he had figured out that she was having an affair. Well, she knew now!

The Porsche sped on into the darkness. He stopped once at services near Dublin airport to re-fuel before rounding the city via the ring road and heading south. The road had been greatly improved in recent years and it was now motorway nearly the whole way to Rosslaire. Once in Rosslaire, he would catch the morning ferry over to Wales. He would be there by dawn. The light would be coming up soon.

Eventually the stresses of recent days started to melt away. He felt safe. He'd done it! He had escaped, got away! At last, he felt happy and relaxed grinning widely as he drove. Over the last few months he'd been subjected to all sorts of problems, difficulties and challenges. He had managed to overcome the obstacles and now felt that in the big game of life at last he was a winner! He was on his way to Dorset and dreamt of finding a quiet little cottage there to live in.

The ferry over to Fishguard in Wales would provide his portal to freedom. Freedom to enjoy his wealth and a whole new life!

THE END.

EPILOGUE

1.

William was enjoying his lunch. It was an unexpectedly delicious meal comprising lightly scrambled eggs, mushrooms and prawns, laced liberally with garlic. He was sitting eating outside a little restaurant near Famara on the northern shore of Lanzarote. In the background, a ridge of ancient volcanic peaks rose majestically against a pale azure sky. Benign small fluffy clouds drifted cheerily across the peaceful vista. The temperature was in the mid twenties Celsius. It was perfect. He was wearing just shorts and T-shirt, basking in the warm and pleasant sunshine.

The little restaurant had initially promised little, judging by its rather ordinary nondescript appearance. The meal now being consumed with eager relish however had proved to be a culinary delight! William was reading a copy of the Daily Telegraph purchased in a large hotel in Costa Teguise near where he was staying. He was doing his best at the quick and therefore supposedly easy cross word on the back page. He wasn't that quick though!

He'd decided on a short holiday in Lanzarote when he'd spotted a special deal in a travel agent's window whilst shopping in Dorchester. Life in Dorset had turned out to be pleasant enough. He'd originally stayed in a nice bed and breakfast type establishment with a beautiful thatched roof. After about a week, as he became accustomed to the locality, he'd decided to stay on. After a further week of searching around the area, he'd discovered a small cottage that was up for rent. The cottage wasn't exactly ultra modern but it was in an excellent location midway between two small villages.

A little haggling with the agent had eventually yielded an agreement on a one-year lease. William had been delighted as the cottage was already comfortably furnished and all he had to do was move in. The cottage had its own garage, which gave him peace of mind at night as he could lock up the little Porsche inside it.

The two nearby villages were both within walking distance. One had a lovely pub whilst the other had a petrol station, shop and excellent pub-restaurant. The location of the cottage had turned out to be just perfect!

Despite the beauty and tranquility of the Dorset countryside though, there still wasn't any cure for the British winter, which had turned out to be quite cold and wet! It was thus that he'd decided on a whim to go on this cheap package type holiday. The marvellous thing about Lanzarote, and indeed the Canary Islands in general, was the predictability of the weather during the winter. You pretty much had guaranteed sunshine most days and this wonderful warm temperature. It was warm without being overbearingly so. You could walk around in a T-shirt and feel neither hot nor cold!

William was sitting finishing his meal in the sunshine and thinking that, all in all, he just couldn't be happier! As he sat, he looked across the road towards where the beautiful white Mercedes SLK sports car he'd hired out for a few days was parked. It was a super little car and great fun to drive! He'd been out exploring the island in it and he was having the time of his life! With the roof down and the perfect temperature he was picking up a great golden suntan!

As he sat there quite contentedly, he became aware of a creamy white coloured mini convertible parked about forty yards away. The roof had been folded down. The single occupant was a large dark haired man wearing heavily tinted sunglasses. William wasn't totally sure of it, but it appeared as if the man was staring straight at him. He found this mildly unnerving and tried to ignore the car by working on his crossword puzzle. After about two minutes, he looked up. The car was still there. The driver started the engine and gently drove towards William. He then pulled over to the opposite side of the road and parked alongside William's Mercedes in the little car park opposite him.

As William watched, the tall heavily built man got out of the Mini and closed the door with a slight clunk. He walked slowly away from the car in a cool, relaxed manner. The man was crossing the street and heading deliberately towards William's table!

"Hello William. How you doing?" The voice was deep, quiet and had a slight hint of menace to it. With horror, as the man removed his sunglasses for a few moments, he recognized that it was Oscar!

"Just fine thanks." He tried to look calm despite the fact that inwardly he was quaking with unease.

"Bet I'm the last person you ever expected to see here?" Oscar chuckled slightly, revelling in the shock he had caused. "I take it you don't mind if I join you?" He sat down in the chair opposite William setting down his car keys and sunglasses as though he was taking up permanent residence.

"What do you want?" William was fearful now. His voice had suddenly developed a minor quivering stutter.

"Relax my friend. Here we both are enjoying the beautiful sunshine on this fine Island, relax."

Just at that, a white shirted waiter approached. He had the well worn, dark tanned and lined face of a mafia hit man. He didn't smile but politely asked Oscar,

"Would you like something to drink sir?"

As he did so, he started preparing a place at the table in front of Oscar and then set down a menu. He looked expectantly at Oscar.

Oscar looked at William and said. "Why not? I'll have a large vodka and coke please."

The waiter nodded politely and wandered off into the innards of the restaurant.

Oscar continued to stare at William making him feel very uncomfortable. After an awkward silence, William had to ask the question.

"How the hell did you find me?"

"I won't say it was easy, but when you're looking for over a million quid that's gone missing and you have the time, its not impossible. We did a wee bit of investigating and here I am!"

"Still don't know how you did it?" William protested.

"You're never going to know either" Oscar replied casually. "Because I'm not going to tell you!"

Oscar put his dark glasses back on again which made him look even more menacing. He sat virtually motionless and looked at William smiling at him in a most sinister fashion.

The waiter returned and neatly set the glass of vodka and coke bottle in front of Oscar.

"Would you like to order something to eat sir?"

Without looking away from William he answered, "Yeah, I'll have whatever he had," he nodded slightly in the direction of William.

"Certainly sir." The waiter was off again and over to the next table where he started lifting plates and glasses onto his tray. Moments later he turned away towards the kitchen again.

"Where do we go from here?" William asked nervously.

Once again Oscar continued to stare. William found his overall demeanor to be deeply disturbing. Then he sat back in his chair and smiled at William. He seemed visibly to be changing tack.

"Like I said earlier, let's just relax. Let's be like two old friends chatting to each other whilst enjoying their lunch."

"O.K. Tell me something then, what happened to that big gorilla of a guy who was going to torture me?"

"Big Bill? He's out of the picture. The Fatman brought him in. That big guy as you call him is mad in the head. I had to get rid of him."

"Who's the Fatman?" William looked puzzled.

"The Fatman was my boss. He ran our operation for years and I was his number one so to speak. I took care of guys like you who owed the company money!"

"You're speaking about this Fatman in the past tense. What happened to him?"

The conversation was once more interrupted as the waiter returned with Oscar's meal. After he was gone, Oscar continued,

"The Fatman had a most unfortunate accident. He crashed his car and suffered multiple serious injuries. He's been in a coma for the last six months. The doctors don't really expect him ever to recover. They think he probably has brain damage. They'd have switched off the life support machines long ago if it hadn't been for that interfering bloody wife of his."

"Sorry to hear that." William said attempting to sound concerned.

"Don't be sorry! You don't need to. You've never even met him and know nothing about him. It doesn't concern you at all!" Oscar sounded angry. "Anyway, don't you worry about the Fatman, he's the least of your worries!"

William was on edge again. "So where does this leave us?"

"I want the money back. You got over one million pounds from us. I'm going to be very reasonable about this. I'm quite sure that by now you've spent some of it."

"Quite a lot of it actually." William agreed.

Oscar nodded reluctant agreement. "I just want a half a million of it back. You give me half a million pounds and we're all square."

"How come you're not after all of it?" William asked suspiciously.

"Look, the Fatman is out of the picture. He'll probably never wake up again. No one else knows I've found you. This is just between you and me. I've done my research. I know you've spent a brave bit of the money so all I want is a quick pay off of liquid cash and I'll leave you alone."

William was silent now for a while. Oscar started into the scrambled eggs, mushrooms and prawns. After a couple of mouthfuls he looked up and grinned.

"Hey this is pretty good! You've got a good taste in food Mr. Forsythe."

William laughed uneasily.

Oscar reached into his pocket and opened his wallet. He produced a small slip of paper.

"Take this."

"What is it?" William queried.

"The details of the Swiss bank account where you will deposit the money. It's a numbered account. No names and no way to trace anything. Make sure the money is in my account there in thirty days.

"That's not very long Oscar. Can you not give me a bit more time. The money isn't all that accessible just now. I've invested some of it."

"I don't care. That's why I'm letting you off with giving me just half a million. You should be able to lay hands on that amount fairly quickly without a whole lot of messing about."

"That won't be easy." William said his voice trembling slightly.

"Just do it!"

Again Oscar glared at him. Nothing was said for several minutes.

Oscar began eating again. He quickly wolfed down the remainder of his meal.

"What happens if I don't pay you?" William couldn't quite believe he'd just asked this question. But he had to know.

Oscar swallowed the last mouthful of his meal and carefully wiped his mouth with a napkin. All the time he was watching William.

"Just picture the scene. You're sitting somewhere. It could be here, it could be a tearoom in Dorset. It could be anywhere. It's a lovely sunny day and you're reading your newspaper. You're enjoying a nice coffee. You won't even hear the shot. You'll possibly just feel a sharp sting of absolute agony as the high velocity bullet rips through your skull tearing your brain apart. The pain won't last long though because you'll be dead instantly."

Oscar sat back in his chair and looked at William who had gone completely pale with fear.

"It's not very good that William, sure it's not?" Oscar added rubbing it all in. "If I were you, I'd quickly sell whatever you have to and get the money together. Let's face it, you'd be doing yourself a favour. No point in having the money if you're not around to spend it!"

At that, Oscar stood up to go. "Good bye William. You've got thirty days. Don't dare disappoint me. I take it you don't mind paying the bill for lunch?"

Without a backward glance he walked away and soon got into the mini convertible and drove off.

2.

William sat for a few moments and then left enough money to pay the bill and a generous tip. He ran across to the SLK and quickly left.

For a while he just drove. He drove aimlessly to nowhere in particular. The sun was still out and he had the roof open, but now he didn't notice it. It was as if he was numb from head to foot. His whole world had suddenly been shattered by the arrival of this thug.

After about half an hour he saw a fingerboard sign for Mirador del Rio. He drove there and parked up. He paid the entrance fee and walked inside the low interesting looking building. He discovered Cesar Manrique the celebrated Lanzarote architect had designed it largely as a viewing point.

He took a seat near the window and ordered a coffee. William was amazed at the wonderful view. The viewing gallery with a huge glass window was around fifteen hundred feet above sea level. As he sipped his cappuccino it was like looking out the window of an airplane at the island of La Graciosa far below.

It was such a wonderful vista that momentarily he forgot his plight. As he sat, unbelievably, a figure appeared drifting outside the window. It was a man in a hang glider! He wheeled round and did a close flyby of the window waving to the customers before sailing off on a thermal air current. What an amazing sight thought William standing up in sheer disbelief.

The hang glider disappeared beyond a rocky outcrop and was gone from sight. William sat down again. Sipping his coffee and looking out the window again down at La Graciosa. The island was shrouded in an ever so slight blue grey mist, which it wore about it like a mantle. The view was truly wonderful. He couldn't quite reconcile his feelings. What the hell was he going to do?

He was mulling over his problem. Images of Oscar wielding a fearsome looking gun kept drifting before him. He saw himself lying lifeless, a bullet wound on his forehead. Blood trickled out of his mouth. He must have sat there for about an hour, deep in thought, he'd clasped his hands in front of his face resting his nose on them. His eyes had assumed a hardened look now as he stared away into the distance.

Eventually, he started to relax just a little. He had formulated an idea. It would require much further thought and planning, but the gist of it was there now in his head. He grinned and chuckled quietly to himself. At last, he knew what he was going to do!

3.

The next day, William was up before the sun. For the first time in many weeks, he had a serious agenda. The night before, he'd returned the Mercedes SLK and hired a small dark coloured Fiat. It was nondescript and would blend seamlessly into any background.

William started his tour of the island's hotels. He was determined to track down Oscar. If he'd actually realized how many hotels there were on the island, he probably wouldn't have bothered. As it was however, he was motivated to find Oscar. They now had unfinished business to attend to.

One bonus was that he had noticed the name of the hire car company. When Oscar had thrown down his keys on the table top, somehow, on a subconscious level, he had memorised the car's registration number. He clearly remembered the digits '5665.' It was a cream coloured mini convertible with a brown hood owned by a firm called 'Canara Car.' That company was based in Costa Teguise so it was likely that Oscar would be holed up there somewhere.

The search proved much more arduous than William had ever anticipated. Even in Costa Teguise there were many hotels and apartments which could be rented for a holiday. It was after four in the afternoon by the time he spotted the cream coloured convertible, hiding in the shade, outside a small development of apartments. It had a brown roof and the numbers '5665' in the registration. A sticker on the rear read 'Canara Car.'

Ah ha, I've found the bugger! William thought to himself.

William parked up and walked into the reception area. The middle aged lady behind the desk spoke with a German accent to someone on the phone. Abruptly the conversation ended and she set down the receiver. She never looked up from her desk, completely ignoring William. It was as if whatever she was writing down on a notebook was of vast importance.

"Hola!" William broke the silence.

"Hola!" came the reply. The receptionist never looked up.

"I'm looking for an old friend of mine who's staying in one of your apartments. His name is Oscar. Could you please give me his room number?"

"No."

"Why not?"

"It's not our policy to give out room numbers," came the curt reply. The woman's tone was on the edge of rudeness.

"Well I'd like to speak to him!" William became more assertive.

At long last the receptionist lifted her head and glared at him. She pointed over to the far side of the lobby.

"Use the house phone. I'll connect you presently."

William wandered over to a phone, which sat near the entrance. After several minutes it began to ring. At first William ignored it. Then he noticed 'Grim Helga' at the desk staring at him.

"Pick it up you idiot!" she shouted.

William lifted the receiver.

"Who's this?" Oscar answered.

"William."

"What do you want William? The reply was gruff, unfriendly.

"I want to talk again."

"No point. I've made my position totally clear. Just put the money in the Swiss account within the next thirty days."

"I still want to talk and there is a point. I have some of the money here in Lanzorote. I could meet you tomorrow afternoon at three o'clock and give you, say, a hundred thousand pounds?"

"Hmm. Not sure I want to carry that amount home on the plane."

William decided to lay it on. "Look mate, I didn't exactly find it gift wrapped! You make up your bloody mind. Do you want it or not?"

Oscar thought about it. It didn't take long. He was every bit as big a crook as any. Greed was deeply ingrained within him.

"Yeah. Alright. Where are we meeting?"

"Somewhere public, Mirador del Rio."

"Where the fuck's that?"

"Mirador del Rio. A famous beauty spot here on the Island. Buy yourself a map Oscar."

"You'd do well not to be so cheeky to me." He paused, "I'll see you there tomorrow at three oclock. Make sure you have the money with you."

"Tomorrow then." William set down the phone and quickly left. Grim-Helga ignored him entirely and tapped away at her computer keyboard.

4.

That night William was off on a mission into Arrecife. Earlier during his holiday a man at a bar had approached him. The Nordic looking guy introduced himself as Sven and was encouraging William to come to a particular nightclub in Arrecife. He gave him a card with information on the club and also asked him to look him up. Sven was interested in selling drugs. William had politely repelled him but for some reason had stuck the card in his wallet.

Eventually he found 'The Dunes' nightclub. It was a really seedy looking dive in a rundown area of the city. Inside, the place was alive with young people, all dancing to some loud, monotonous beat. The lighting was mostly a dark blue and gave the joint an almost sinister atmosphere. It took a little while but, eventually, he spotted Sven at a table in a darkened niche at the back of the club.

"What can I do for you brother?" Sven smiled.

"Like to buy some stuff from you."

"Oh yeah? What?"

"Got any Rohypnol?"

Sven leaned back in his seat and grinned.

"Looks like you believe in tilting the odds of success in your direction!"

"Yeah, something like that."

"It's going to cost you though. It's real hard to lay hands on out here. You're in luck though, because I do have a small private stash exclusively for my best customers."

"How much?"

"One hundred Euros per tab."

William knew that this was probably extortionate but felt there wasn't much future in a failed negotiation. He just didn't have time to find some at a better price.

"That's a huge price Sven. Suppose I took three tablets?"

"You could knock out a fuckin' elephant with three tabs man!"

Sven fixed him with a mildly suspicious stare but then his business mind kicked back in.

"Give me two fifty Euro and you can have them."

"Done," nodded William.

Sven disappeared through a darkened doorway. Within five minutes he was back with a small cellophane pack containing the three tablets.

"These now only come with a blue dye in them. If you're going to slip them in a girl's drink make sure its some dark coloured cocktail or whisky. The blue colour shows up in a clear drink."

"Is it easy to taste it? Would someone know it was in their drink?"

"Not at all. It's totally tasteless man, undetectable"

"That's just what I need." William handed over the money.

"Just one more thing Sven, I didn't see you tonight and you didn't sell me anything. Is that clearly understood?"

"Totally. I have a very bad memory anyway." Sven took a draw from his joint. His eyes looked well glazed.

"Couldn't be anything to do with that shit you're smoking?"

Sven just shrugged in admission and William grinned to himself as he walked away.

5.

The next day.

William had arrived early at Mirador del Rio. He needed to prepare himself. Never in his life had he even contemplated doing something like this. He found he was shivering slightly with nerves. He selected a table near the viewing window and again marvelled at the incredible view. The Island of La Graciosa far below was again mantled in a blue mist. There was an air of tranquility about the scene.

In stark contrast, William felt awful. This was going to require every fibre of nerve within him. He was after all going to do something absolutely ruthless.

A short while later, William saw the powerfully built figure of Oscar walk into the restaurant. The big man was dressed in dark blue T-shirt and shorts. His expression was distinctly ominous. The dark glasses again added an air of menace. This was a dangerous man and not a person to be messed with lightly.

"Afternoon William," Oscar nodded sitting down at the table.

"Afternoon."

"I wasn't expecting to see you again so soon."

Oscar began looking about on the floor around the table.

"Where's the money William? Do you have it with you?"

"Cool yer jets big man. After all, here we are on this beautiful island. Two old friends enjoying a coffee together," he said sarcastically mimicking Oscar a few days earlier.

Oscar actually grinned very slightly seeing the funny side of it.

"O.K. For a hundred grand I'm prepared to put up with a small amount of your nonsense, but not too much."

A waiter arrived and the two ordered a drink each. Oscar ordered a large vodka and coke. It was just what William had hoped for. The blue dye in the tablets would be undetectable in the dark coloured drink. Now all he needed was a chance to slip the pills in the drink. William positioned his sunglasses case in the middle of the table and began absent-mindedly rotating it between his fingers.

The two men sat drinking and even Oscar seemed impressed by the view outside.

"It's amazing! Just like as if you were sitting in an airplane looking out!" Oscar took a large slug of his drink.

"You should go outside to the balcony and take a proper look," encouraged William. But it didn't work.

Oscar slowly removed his sunglasses and wiped them with a napkin. All the while, he stared at William. It was a long glassy stare. His eyes had a strange deadness to them. At the same time they were full of a malevolent evil. William had read once that psychopaths stare like this. As he looked at Oscar, he became convinced that that was exactly who he was dealing with, a psychopath.

"Stop fucking about William." The voice was a barely muted growl. Oscar drained his glass and set it down on the table with an emphatic bang. "Where is the money?"

"Just a few more minutes and we'll go and get it."

"What do you mean?"

"The money is in a safe deposit box in a nearby town. The bank closes for a while in the afternoon like many Spanish businesses. About half an hour from now they'll be open. We've just time for another drink!"

Oscar looked impatiently about him. He was obviously becoming irritated.

"Let's have a coffee and then we'll go," suggested William. "They do a really excellent apple tart and cream here too. Would you like some?"

"Why not, seeing as we have to wait for this bloody bank to open."

William ordered the apple tart and coffee and again waited for an opportunity to slip the tablets into Oscar's coffee. Oscar, however just sat there looking at him. He never looked to left or right. Again William tried to distract him.

"You should take a look up those stairs over there. They go up on to the roof. From up there you get a wonderful panoramic view all around. It's well worth going up to look!"

He might as well have been talking to a brick wall. Oscar showed absolutely no enthusiasm whatsoever. Inwardly, William was beginning to panic. A quick glance at his watch confirmed his fears. He was running out of time fast. If he couldn't carry out his plan soon he was going to be in big trouble.

"The apple tart is good right enough." At last Oscar had spoken.

"Told you so. Would you like another coffee before we go?" William noticed at least half of Oscar's coffee was now gone.

"Nah. That's enough coffee for me."

William felt a feeling of utter dismay begin to sweep through him. Time was up. He'd failed.

Suddenly Oscar swivelled around to look out the window.

"Holy shit!" he exclaimed jumping to his feet.

Outside, two men flying hang gliders were wheeling about right in front of the viewing area. Oscar ran over to the window to watch. He was utterly absorbed by the spectacle. One of the men waved towards the dozen or so tourists who had rushed to the window to watch.

William was quick as a flash. He opened his sunglasses case and removed a small container. He quickly poured the three powdered tablets straight into Oscar's coffee. As Oscar was totally entranced by the hang gliders, William lifted the coffee cup and swirled it gently to dissolve the powder.

Oscar was still enjoying the show and was now urging William to come take a look. William feigned interest for a moment or two until eventually the aviators disappeared from view.

"Frig me! That was amazing." Enthused Oscar. "Did you ever see anything like it in your life?"

"Incredible. They have a hell of a nerve to do that." William lifted his coffee cup up and made a great play of finishing it off. "Hmmm! Delicious!"

Without a moment's hesitation, Oscar lifted his cup and downed the rest of it in one. "Yeah. Nice coffee."

"I'd really like to have a go at that." Oscar pointed at the window enthusiastically. "Reckon it would be a terrific blast!"

"Yeah. Looks like fun." *I wouldn't risk my life flying one of those things for all the tea in China!* he thought to himself.

"I'm going to the toilet." William announced, throwing down a fifty-euro note in front of Oscar. "Would you mind paying the bill?"

Oscar nodded. "Don't be long. I'm keen to be off now."

William went to the restrooms and then wandered out onto the viewing area. He wanted to wait a good ten minutes after Oscar had taken his dose of Rohypnol. Eventually he went back inside. Oscar was sitting there looking distinctly impatient.

"What the hell kept you? I thought maybe you'd fallen down the bowl or something!"

"Sorry. Come on then, let's go."

6.

Out in the car park, William gave instructions to Oscar to follow him to the town where the bank was. As Oscar got into his Mini convertible he noted that he looked slightly off balance. That was exactly what he wanted. He watched as Oscar put the roof down opening the little car up to the elements. Oscar obviously enjoyed the sunshine and fresh air.

William got into the little Fiat and led the way out of the car park and on to the beginning of the treacherous cliff-side road that led away from the carpark. For the first five minutes or so, William drove very slowly. Oscar eventually tooted his horn to get him to speed up.

William was watching Oscar carefully in his rearview mirror. At last he noticed that the progress of the Mini was becoming erratic. Oscar was starting to weave about all over the road. This was just about perfect. William began to speed up and noticed that Oscar was really struggling to keep up. Next he accelerated as hard as he could going down a step hill. Oscar was rushing up behind him now in an ill-advised attempt to keep up.

William knew the hairpin bend was just ahead. He accelerated towards it. Oscar was large in his mirrors. William saw he was doing seventy miles an hour now. This was a ridiculous speed for a narrow mountain road. At the last possible minute, he braked really hard and turned into the tight bend. The little Fiat car barely made it around the corner. Behind him he heard a screeching of brakes as Oscar desperately tried to slow the Mini. There was no chance. Oscar was half unconscious by now as the drugs were truly kicking in.

The Mini slammed hard into the flimsy barrier and went straight through it. The car somersaulted over the edge and went careering down the mountainside. It tumbled over and over and over as it fell, clattering its way down the mountainside, smashing to pieces on the rocks below. William had estimated the fall off the road to the sea from this point to be at least five hundred feet and more; probably seven hundred plus. As he watched he also reckoned Oscar's chances of survival at pretty much nil. He felt a retch in his gut and then realized it was time to get out of there fast. As he drove away, he didn't see any other cars for about two minutes or so. That was good. No one would remember a grey Fiat.

7.

Four hours later the Holiday Tours flight 493 lifted off from Arrecife airport. William was on his way home. He had barely made it to the check-in on time.

Looking out the window of the jet he could make out the volcanoes of Lanzarote clearly in the distance. He wondered what had happened to Oscar. Was he definitely dead? He figured he must be. That was too big a fall for anyone to survive.

His eyes rested on the window. For a moment he could see his own reflection. Who was that? he wondered. Who was this person who had suddenly turned out to be a murderer? A premeditated murderer at that! He didn't even recognize himself. How could he have done such a terrible thing? He had changed, metamorphosed into someone else. It was chilling to come to this realization.

All at once he felt utterly exhausted. All the dashing about, and the tension of it all, had thoroughly worn him out. He felt vastly relieved as he started to doze off. After all as Oscar had said to him, he was the only one who knew he had the money. Now there was no one alive to tell the tale. No one would come chasing after him anymore. It was all his. Now it was just him and the money!

POSTSCRIPT

Oscar was starting to come round. He found himself lying only yards below the shattered Armco barrier. Some bushes had broken his fall. It appeared he must have been thrown clear out through the convertible roof. The car itself had then plunged hundreds of feet down the cliff side and now lay a tattered wreck on the rocks below.

He had no idea how long he'd been lying there. He felt terrible. It was getting dark and the colder air was making him shiver uncontrollably. He became aware of sirens above and soon two ambulance men, using ropes were on their way down the treacherous terrain with a stretcher to rescue him. One of them spoke English and kept telling him it was remarkable but he didn't seem to have broken anything. He kept telling Oscar it was a miracle he hadn't been killed.

Soon the ambulance was away towards the hospital in Arrecife. Oscar lay there semi-comatose. He had no recollection of what had happened. He was able to piece together that he must have been driving along the road but how had he crashed? He couldn't remember a thing. What had he been doing on this piece of road? He had no idea. His memory seemed to have been erased. As he felt himself losing consciousness, his last thought was that in time his memory would restore itself. Eventually he would remember.

TO BE CONTINUED....

COMING SOON!!!!!

THE SEQUEL!!!!

COUNTERFEIT!